AUTHOR'S NOTE

Navaratri is a Hindu festival that celebrates the victory of Goddess Durga over the demon king **Mahishasuran** (the Bull Demon). Nava-Ratri (meaning 'Nine Nights') spans nine nights and ten days, symbolising the epic battle between the goddess and the demon's vast army. On the ninth night, after a fierce and relentless fight, she defeats Mahishasuran. The tenth day is commemorated as **Vijayadashami**, the day of victory.

The legend says that Mahishasuran was a powerful demon king who ruled the Earth thousands of years ago. He had a special boon that made him nearly impossible to defeat — he could not be harmed by man, god, animal, illness, or old age. With this power, he became cruel and caused great suffering. When people could no longer bear it, they prayed to the gods for help. The gods created **Maa Durga**, a strong and fearless goddess, to stop him.

For eight days, she fought his huge army and destroyed it. On the ninth, she confronted Mahishasuran himself in a climactic duel. After the most intense battle of all, she finally vanquished him under the night sky.

Though Navaratri is less known outside India, it is a lively and colourful celebration. Different regions of India have their own ways of celebrating, but dolls and idols are always important. In the South, people display small dolls in decorated steps, while in the North, large statues of Maa Durga are worshipped. They play a vital role in telling the story of the brave goddess who fought selflessly to protect the world.

Navaratri is ultimately a celebration of feminine strength and the enduring truth that good shall always prevail over evil.

यदा यदा हि धर्मस्य ग्लानिर्भवति भारत ।
अभ्युत्थानमधर्मस्य तदाऽऽत्मानं सृजाम्यहम् ॥
परित्राणाय साधूनां विनाशाय च दुष्कृताम् ।
धर्मसंस्थापनार्थाय सम्भवामि युगे युगे ॥
(Bhagavad Gita 4.7, 4.8)

'Whenever there is a decline in righteousness and a rise in unrighteousness, O Arjuna, at that time I manifest Myself on Earth. To protect the righteous, destroy the wicked, and establish dharma (righteousness), I appear age after age.'

Nine Dolls

NINE DOLLS

RUPA MAHADEVAN

Winner of the Joffe Books Prize 2024

JOFFE BOOKS

Joffe Books, London
www.joffebooks.com

First published in Great Britain in 2025

Cover art by Nebojša Zorić

ISBN: 978-1-80573-232-7

MIX
Paper | Supporting
responsible forestry
FSC
www.fsc.org
FSC® C013604

PROLOGUE

The knife plunges into her in a single, smooth motion, and her insides part obediently. It's cold, oh so cold, she thinks rather bizarrely, her mouth forming a misshapen 'O'. Her blood rushes to her hands, warming them for a moment, only to dissolve into the chill damp of the storm. No, no, no. This is all wrong. This isn't how it's supposed to be. It should be the other way around — the knife should be in her hands.

The shock of the cold blade brings some sense to her addled brain. She tries to take stock. Here she is, hair pinned under the rock, hands tied in front, legs of jelly and heart fatally pierced. There's no hope. The slanting rain whips at her face while her guts spill their precious cargo. And she can't help but marvel at the irony of it all — dying here, of all places. On the tomb of Mhairi, the maiden wronged all those centuries ago.

With her last breath, she lifts her head to stare into the eyes of the one who, with a shaking hand, drove the knife into her. Something's not right. There's no rage in those eyes, no jealousy, no hatred — nothing that screams 'good riddance'. Instead, there's pain. Deep, agonising pain that turns the whites of those eyes a bruised purple. A single tear falls, a fat droplet, not for themselves but for the victim, for her wasted life, for what could have been.

Then she collapses, her forehead touching, barely registering the knife handle beneath it. The cold spreads from the blade to the rest of her body until it is as icy as the air. She no longer breathes.

CHAPTER ONE

Day Nine: Leela

The seconds ticked by while the flies' buzz intensified until it was a steady drone that echoed in my ears, rising above the raging storm outside. I turned my head, but the movement only made them angrier, the buzz louder. Whirr . . . buzz . . . and repeat. I told myself it must be the fruits; I could smell their earthy tang of rot and rust. It had to be the fruits. The alternative was too scary to contemplate.

The lights flickered twice and then died, and the night's blackness intensified. I didn't even hear the low hum of the generator; it must have been drowned out by the howling of the wind. In the two months and three days since I'd left the golden warmth of India for grey, wet England, one thing I hadn't missed was the power cuts. Today I realised how much I'd taken for granted.

I was engulfed in darkness. Squinting into the blackness, I was willing myself to see beyond the veil, to make out the shapes of the woods and the shed with the generator that I knew were right there. As I stared, two tiny, glowing eyes appeared, spitting light as a warning of an unknown creature lurking behind them. Transfixed, I could not tear my eyes away. Slowly, the eyes grew until they were two fiery orbs, their light rippling outward in bands, expanding into concentric circles that stretched wider and wider like the ripples in a pool . . . until they dissolved into the night.

The two points of light gave way to a stream of kaleidoscopic images, snapshots of the past nine days. Of the people I'd believed were my friends. The secrets they kept, the vengeance they'd nurtured secretly, their intentions for me and my dolls, all converging like ants swarming to a nest, leading to one terrible ending — tonight, and the terrible, terrible opportunity it presented. It was clear now, the evil. Pure and unmistakable. It palpitated through the dark, echoing in the screaming winds.

The points of light swam. The creature, whatever it was, shook its head, and as suddenly as it had begun, the hallucination came to an end. A sudden flash of lightning cracked across the sky, illuminating the figure behind those glowing eyes. It was a badger. For some reason, I thought of the bins by the main house, and the metal trap waiting for it there. I shuddered. I hoped it stayed safe, alive until tomorrow. One more night to get through, a night to survive. And then — everything would be fine.

Even from the safety of the cabin, with a glass door between me and the storm, just the thought of the icy wind was enough to make me shiver. I took the loose end of my saree and draped it across my shoulders. The wind rattled the window as if it intended to break in. The chill seeped into my bones.

Dhruv kept telling me the storms here were nothing compared to the Indian monsoon. That may be true, but Indian storms didn't howl like a birthing woman. Indian storms didn't threaten vengeance, just a few slaps with the flat of a palm, not a fist. The English were obsessed with the weather, as if endlessly talking about it somehow made it better, banished the never-ending grey. Now it seemed I'd caught the habit too. I shook my head. Now was not a time to deviate, to be distracted.

I clasped my hands. Just one more day. That was all I was asking for. One day, and then we could leave this wretched place. This was not how I envisioned our first holiday here. The honeymoon we'd been promising ourselves for three months, ever since we left Chennai for our new home in London, city of dreams and Bollywood movies.

Travelling far from the bustle of alien London, we'd arrived in what Dhruv called the 'rural roots' of Britain. He kept telling me that Oban is not in England. 'We're in Scotland now, Leela. It's a different country.'

So he said, but to my Indian eyes, the people all looked the same. They spoke the same language, had the same miserable weather. India is one country, yet we speak over seven hundred languages, they say (though I hadn't really counted). And we don't all look the same.

Our time in Oban should have been a happy one — tease-filled days and lust-filled nights. But there's nothing less romantic than having eight other people tagging along on what is supposed to be a honeymoon. And it was not just them. Things hadn't been normal since the first day, when the dolls were moved. It was as if the ten years of bad luck this portended started right then. I'd warned them. 'This is no game,' I'd said. 'The dolls must not be moved. Not until the tenth day. They are not toys. It brings bad luck.'

They'd laughed in my face. 'Oh, Leela, you're so traditional,' they'd said, rolling their eyes. 'Don't be so ridiculously outdated.' As if beliefs came with an expiry date.

Even Dhruv had joined in the laughter, his eyes reflecting a hint of disappointment. 'Don't be silly, Leela.' Then he'd leaned close to my ear and hissed, 'Stop all this nonsense.'

It was the first time he'd shown any real anger towards me. I could tell he meant it by the way his eyes glittered, his hands clenched. He'd leaned forward and pushed out his chest, as if to make himself look bigger. Like our first kiss and our first night together, this was another milestone. Our first fight — an intimate bubble where only the two of us existed. I'd pictured it in detail, even planned the perfect comeback — my eyes shining with unshed tears, I would face him in silence. Then, after a suitably lengthy pause, I would pull myself up to my full height and say quietly, 'Is that it? Is that all you've got?'

I would move closer, my nipples not quite touching his chest, a challenge, a tease to him not to give in, to stay angry. But he'd be unable to resist, and then we'd have the best sex of our lives — the wild, tearing-at-clothes make-up sex that everyone raved about. See, I wasn't so old-fashioned after all. But we weren't alone for our first fight, in our own romantic bubble. I'd been robbed of my precious moment. I'd wanted to scream. Instead, I'd laughed along with the others. Now see where it had led us to. The darkest day of our lives.

I squinted, straining to see into the darkness outside. But I couldn't even see the raindrops on the window. I knew it was still raining; I heard them pattering and spattering against the glass. We were in the middle of a forest, and the last of the candles went out an hour ago. Who said power cuts only happen in poor, third-world countries? The power had been out for over twenty hours. They called it the 'Beast from the East' but what did they know? It was the evil eye, let me tell you, the bad luck. They should never have moved the dolls.

I was so thirsty my throat hurt. I licked my lips, which felt like sandpaper against my tongue. I knew roughly where the sink was, and I could probably have found my way there, but I'd have bumped against the kitchen furniture and broken something. No, I'd better stay put. Like the British, I would keep my fingers crossed, keep a stiff upper lip. I let out a sigh.

Where was everyone? I'd told them to assemble by six thirty for the ninth-day festivities. Here was I, the welcoming host, alone at the cabin's sole window. I knew where Dhruv and Aswin were at least — they were trying to coax the generator into starting. It had run out of diesel. Aswin had just found a spare can in a cupboard. It wouldn't last long, but even a short respite would have been welcome. They'd taken the only torches with them, leaving me shrouded in darkness, a maiden of the night.

There was a draught coming in from the window, so I thought I'd better move further in. Arms outstretched, I flailed about, counting my steps — ten. I'd counted them before it went dark. One more step and I would crash into the dolls, which I had carefully placed nine days ago on fragile cardboard steps. The days were endless here, but in just one more day the dolls' ten-day vigil would be over, and I could finally breathe and, most importantly, leave.

What was that? A flicker of darkness, a blur of movement at the edge of my sight. Then I felt it — the subtle shift in the atmosphere that told me I was not alone. 'Shravan?' I called out. 'Is that you?' It had to be him. Who else could it be? 'Where did you go?' I gave a nervous giggle. He'd been here, just a moment ago, then gone. No sound, no word. Dhruv had been calling and calling, worry tightening his voice, before he left with Aswin to get the generator started. He didn't want to leave me alone, but I insisted that he needed the company more than me. Where was Shravan? And why wasn't he answering? 'Shravan?' I said again, my voice thinner this time. I heard a faint clatter coming from the steps where the dolls were. I flinched. Was it the draught from the window?

No. No, it couldn't be. Breathe, I told myself. The smell was even worse now, truly awful — earthy, rusty, and all-pervasive. I retched.

Flashes of lightning, their electric roots splintering the stormy sky, momentarily illuminated the corners of the room. Briefly, the silhouettes of the dolls were visible. A single flash revealed the body, the gaping hole in the chest, oozing blood. Then the darkness returned.

I realised I was screaming. The sharp whirr of the engine and the flickering lights did nothing to quell my terror. What I'd thought to be a trick of the light was now shockingly real. One thought pulsed through me — I had to go back. Back to the beginning. Back to the moment it all started. Before everything unravelled. If I could just turn back the clock, somehow undo it all, maybe, just maybe, it would all be fine.

The sound of urgent footsteps barely registered as everything turned black once more. This time, I welcomed the darkness.

CHAPTER TWO

Day Zero: Smitha

'Smitha! Where should I put these?' The 'These' were the nine empty cardboard boxes my husband's friend, Dhruv, had insisted on bringing, God knows why. Not ten, not eight, it had to be exactly nine. Nine identical boxes, custom-made to order. Jay must have gone to at least a dozen shops to find them. But when I asked him to pick up a new sippy cup for Veena, naturally, he was 'too tired'.

'I don't know, wherever you like,' I yelled back. For all I cared, he could toss them over the fence and go for a jog. It wasn't until I glanced out the window of our semi that I realised the next-door neighbour was outside, washing his car — his midweek ritual. Oops, he must've heard me. Who washes their car on a Wednesday afternoon? Apparently, Colin did — come rain, shine, or autumn wind. He took his time about it too, meticulously scrubbing every inch of his pathetic little car.

When he was finally done, he'd step back, admiring his handiwork like an artist before a freshly painted canvas. He'd then turn to any unfortunate passerby, obliging them to declare it the shiniest car in the neighbourhood. The funniest part? Far from being the Rolls-Royce you might imagine, it was a Ford saloon with a historic number plate.

Rubbing his hands together, he said, 'It's a nice crisp autumn day, innit?' To my mind 'crisp' and 'autumn' don't belong in the same sentence — at least not here in Edinburgh. It was the same when we lived in Stirling. There are many ways you can describe autumn — grey, wet, sodden — but none of them involve crispness. *That's an oxymoron, you moron!* I wanted to yell. Now *those* words belong together.

'It's lovely, isn't it?' Jay responded with a matching cheer. Right on cue, he added, 'And your car shines right back at the sun. Don't know how you do it, mate. Mine looks like it has a bad case of chicken pox.' He'd learned his lesson — Colin wouldn't stop until he'd wangled a compliment out of you.

He wasn't wrong about our car, though. Our poor Nissan Qashqai was a far cry from Colin's gleaming Ford. Still, when I'd asked him why he didn't take it to the car wash before the trip, he said, 'What's the point? We're taking it to the forest. I'll wash it when we get back, once and for all.' Yeah, right, another excuse for his laziness.

I was in a foul mood. Trying to get my Veena to eat always did that to me. At six years old, she still needed to be fed, and having to spoon her food in between her clenched teeth made me irritable. If that didn't, hearing 'Pep-ppp-pa Pig' for the thousandth time sure did. How I longed to grab that iPad and smash it to pieces. But if I did that, I would be sorry come next mealtime.

'Come on, eat up, yaar! We should be leaving. Everyone else will be there. Papa will say we're the only ones from Scotland and it's us who didn't get there on time.' Not that I cared. Almost as an afterthought, I added, 'Nany's getting old. She can't chase after you. Be good for her, and we'll get you that Nintendo Switch when we get back. Okay?'

I was resorting to bribery — not good, but what else could I do? I couldn't just give her a smack. Jay said it's illegal in

Scotland now. What kind of world are we living in when we can't even discipline our own child? Instead, we're supposed to say, 'Wow, well done! You didn't scream or pull my hair. How wonderful! Here's a sticker.' And it has to be the perfect sticker, apt for the occasion — in this case, a smiling mum with a star on her head. That worked when Veena was younger, but now she's older and wants a gadget as a reward for not pushing her nana down the stairs. At this rate, Jay will soon be posting bail for her. No wonder there's so many serial killers around.

Truth be told, I was in no hurry to leave. Jay's friends always treated me like the unpaid help. He knew it, but he let their flattering words influence him. When Dhruv had asked for those cardboard boxes, Jay could easily have told him to get them himself. But no. 'They've come all the way from London,' he'd said, as if the boxes were going to complain if they'd stayed locked in the boot for a few more hours.

When they were at university, I was designated the cook. They were studying during the day and working in the evenings. I hadn't had Veena yet, so I didn't mind helping out — at least, not at first. But over time, they began to take me for granted. What started as, 'Smitha, can you make Szechuan noodles for dinner, please?' quickly became, 'Make sure the noodles are hot.' It's been years, but some things never change. I just wish I'd known that back then.

'Smitha! Smitha!' Jay called out. That man can't go five minutes without misplacing something. What has he lost now? The only thing he hasn't lost yet is me, and that's no thanks to him.

'Where are my coolers?' he asked.

'Are you kidding? We're going to O*ban*, not O*man*. The only coolers you'll need are for the beer,' I said, and slapped my forehead. It hurt. Next time I should slap *his* forehead instead.

'Smart, huh? I might need them for the road. It could get hot in the car if the sun comes out,' he said, rummaging through the backpack I had packed so carefully, and scattering its contents all over the hallway.

I looked at the sky. 'Sun? What sun? Soon you'll need to report it missing.' Jay continued to pull items from the bag, sending his toothbrush flying so that it ended up face down on the soles of his trainers. I hoped the shoes had something unpleasant on them.

Having emptied the bag, he muttered, 'Must have left the coolers in the car.' Stepping over the scattered items, he added, 'Are you ready? We should have left by now.'

My nails dug crescents into my palms, but I held my tongue. It wasn't fear of him that kept me silent, but my mother-in-law, her ample frame a looming presence regarding us from the kitchen doorway. Normally, the sight of her wouldn't have deterred me. I'm not one to shy away from a verbal war, or a physical one for that matter. But she was set to take care of Veena for the ten days we were away. What if she changed her mind? Or, worse, what if Jay decided to cancel? He was already irritated. For the first time since Veena was born, we were planning to leave her. We were meant to be taking a much-needed break, just the two of us. It had taken him forever to convince his mum to look after the child.

She was here for a visit — six whole months, the full length of her visitor visa. 'What kind of mother leaves her poor baby alone?' she'd asked, as if I'd suggested we abandon Veena at a recycling centre or charity shop. Pre-loved children, anyone? Sometimes I wish I'd just let Veena push her down the stairs as she was always threatening to do. Maybe then she'd get it.

'When I come back,' Jay had promised, 'we can go shopping and buy your favourite grandson an iPhone.' His sister's son. Just another bribe for this trip, this time on his quota.

But that was before I invited my cousin, Aswin, to join us. It's not as you might think. Of course, I'd love to spend some alone time with my husband. Just picture it: a cosy cabin, a beautiful setting, ten days with my hubby and his endearing habit of drumming his bald spot and sucking his teeth every ten minutes. What's not to like, right? But who will keep me from pushing him off a cliff? Who will say, *Didi, take a deep breath*? And it's not like he would be staying with us; Maya mentioned an extra room. At least with Aswin in it, I won't be tempted to lock Jay in and escape his snores.

Moreover, this could be a perfect chance to introduce Aswin to Nancy. How long will that poor girl be alone? She and John split before Veena was born — don't ask, it was messy, like most divorces. No one wants a happy single woman around their husbands. I get sleepless nights whenever her name pops up on Jay's phone — those hushed conversations and the excuses he makes when I catch him, hidden away in the conservatory, grinning at his screen.

'Hurry up, we need to collect the keys, remember?' he called out. I was still busy putting away the items he had scattered. Yes, of course, we need to collect the keys. Has to be us since we're from Scotland. Apparently, keys won't work for those English folks.

There was a spot of mud on one of his trainers, and before I realised what I was doing, I found myself cleaning it with his toothbrush. 'Now I'm ready,' I said, putting the toothbrush back in the zip-lock bag and stowing it carefully in a separate compartment, trying hard not to smile.

CHAPTER THREE

Day Zero: Nancy

The early autumn air was so nippy it made the hairs on my arms stand on end, and I wished I hadn't packed my jacket in the case. It had been fine during the six-hour drive from Liverpool, cocooned in my Mini Cooper with the heater on. But now, standing in the chill Scottish air, my shoulder pressed against the locked front door of what was to be home for the next ten days, the evening breeze bit through my flimsy clothes. From where I stood, all I could see were rows of trees in a swirl of yellowing leaves. We hadn't really had a summer this year, and it seemed autumn was in a hurry to arrive.

Standing there, with my back to the Victorian manor house, I wondered — not for the first time — if it had been a mistake coming here. After what happened. After everything. Let's be honest, none of them wanted me here. In fact, when the normally dormant Desi Dorks WhatsApp group lit up with a message, my first instinct was to check if I'd missed a few months and it was already New Year. But no, it was only September — barely. Imagine my surprise when I opened it to find Shravan's suggestion of a reunion.

Initially, the reception was lukewarm. As in no more messages. A polite silence, the kind that says, lovely idea, but not really. Except, of course, for Maya's enthusiastic: *We should totally go. Amalfi Coast, here we come!* Complete with a link to a five-star cliffside hotel none of us could afford — not even with our collective life savings. Dhruv was tentative. His new wife was big on traditions, and it was Navaratri, he'd said. Jay replied with a two-word disclaimer: *Childcare issues*. Bhoo didn't even bother to respond.

It was only after Shravan's: *All expenses paid. Ten days. Scottish manor. Just bring yourselves.*

Ah, now that changed things.

Travel expenses are ours, I take it? (Bhoo, no doubt nudged by her penny-pinching husband.)

We're in, said Dhruv, suddenly unbothered by Navaratri.

Miraculously, Jay's childcare sorted itself. He even volunteered to pick up the keys and open up for the rest of us.

Speaking of Jay, where the hell was he, and where was Smitha? According to Smitha, they were ten minutes away, but that was at least an hour ago. If I'd known, I would have set off later, although I wasn't keen on navigating the Scottish Highlands in the dark. I could wait in the car, but the parking was a trek from the house, and I had barely managed to drag my massive case up the narrow steps the first time. At least it wasn't raining.

The sound of twigs snapping made me prick up my ears. Out here in the woods, with the encroaching darkness, every little noise made me jump. I wasn't the only one on edge. The birds suddenly flew up from the trees, calling out a warning. I held my breath, scanning the surroundings for escape routes.

The imposing three-storey manor house where we were to stay loomed above me, silhouetted in the fading light. I dared not venture into the woods, I'd end up getting lost, my body lying undiscovered for years. The only way out was back to the car. I would just have to abandon the suitcase.

I was about to put my plan into action when the sound of someone dragging what was presumably a suitcase reached my ears, along with laboured breaths.

'Jay? Smitha?' I called out.

'Nancy,' Jay gasped. 'Mind giving us a hand?'

With a sigh, I made for the stone steps leading down to the car park, and only just stopped myself from bursting into laughter at the sight of Jay. He staggered up the steps, all five-foot-something of him almost hidden by the cardboard boxes balanced precariously on his head, a backpack weighing down his torso. He had one hand on the boxes, which the wind kept threatening to snatch from his grip, while in the other was a case.

A visibly annoyed Smitha stood behind him, loaded with a number of bags — likely stuffed with enough curry paste and masalas to last for at least a month. Most South Asians can manage ten days without a curry, but Jay was not one of them. His very existence seemed to depend on dhal, home-cooked by Smitha. I often wondered why she indulged him so much. Perhaps she had pampered him in the early years of their marriage and now was stuck with it.

Behind her, a tiny backpack slung over his shoulders, was a man I didn't recognise. I hadn't realised they were bringing a guest. And not a nice one from the looks of it. The least he could have done was offer to share the load.

Thankfully, Jay was only a few steps away. After a bit of fumbling, Jay gratefully passed me the cardboard boxes. To my surprise, they weren't just awkwardly shaped but heavy as well.

'Are you moving in?' I asked.

Standing below me, still panting, I noticed that he'd acquired a slight paunch and a bald patch since the last time I saw him. Seven years had clearly taken their toll.

Once we reached the top and Jay had caught his breath, he said, 'They're for Dhruv's wife. She needs them to make steps.'

'Steps? Where to?'

'To heaven, probably, given how many there are of them,' Smitha interjected bitterly.

Shooting her a glance, Jay said, 'They're for Navaratri. They use these steps to display dolls.' With a sidelong glance at Smitha, he added pointedly, 'At least she's still following the traditions. Unlike some.'

Ignoring him completely, Smitha introduced me to their guest, with a bright smile. 'Aswin, this is Nancy. Remember, I told you about her?' To me, she said, 'Aswin is my cousin. He works for Apple and earns over ten grand a month. And that's after tax.'

As if I'd be impressed. Smitha was always like that, fluffing things up as if they were pillows, dressing them up, preferring drama to any semblance of truth.

'Hey,' Aswin said, blushing slightly. I wondered just what Smitha had said about me — probably that I was single and open to new possibilities, like they say on *Single, and ready to mingle* back home.

'Hey,' I said. He seemed like a decent enough guy — the type who did as he was told by his mother, sister, or now, his cousin. One of those geeky, sensitive, and somewhat bland types who lack any real edge. I have nothing against them personally, but they've never really piqued my interest. Nice, and no more.

'Let's head inside,' Jay said.

We had barely dragged our cumbersome luggage into the hallway when Jay asked, 'Smitha, where's the floor plan?'

Smitha rolled her eyes, and for once I agreed with her — this wasn't exactly Buckingham Palace, was it? Nevertheless, she opened the case and pulled out a stack of light-blue drawings — the blueprints of the house.

Jay snatched the papers from her hands and unfurled the first one. 'This is where we are,' he said with a self-important air. 'The ground floor.'

'You don't say,' Smitha said. Even as I smiled at her, I wondered at the new dynamics at play here. The Smitha I knew worshipped the ground Jay walked on. She didn't argue but adored his every word. Jay had always been a little dismissive, but at heart, he was proud of her. This was a new development. The air between them was so thick you could cut it with a knife.

'Since you know so much, why don't you tell us what's on this floor, then?' Jay said.

Attempting to defuse the situation, I said quickly, 'Jay, I'm exhausted. Just tell me where the rooms are, and I'll choose one.'

Jay shook his head. 'Uh-uh. They're all assigned. Look,' he said, pointing to a small room at the back next to the kitchen, marked with an 'S'. 'That's the spare room. It's the reason why Smitha had the idea of bringing her cousin along.'

Beside the spare room was a spacious kitchen/dining area, offering a view of the garden through large French windows. At the far end of the house was a cosy conservatory. Sandwiched between where we stood, the staircase and hallway, and the kitchen/conservatory, was a large rectangular living room.

Apparently unfazed, Aswin merely smiled more broadly. 'Gosh, it's beautiful. Can I go check out my room?'

Smitha seemed a bit let down. Maybe she had expected a biting response. Jay, however, looked pleased and waved Aswin off, whispering, 'At least he's not on the same floor as us. You know what I mean.'

He unfurled the first-floor plan and showed it to me. 'Now to the important stuff.' All the rooms bore an initial — the left corner room was marked 'N', for me. The middle room, 'J + S', was for Jay and Smitha. At the right corner was a room labelled 'B + 1' for Bhoo and her husband, Laxman. We'd all gone our separate ways after the wedding, so Laxman hadn't seen much of us. The '+ 1' did seem a bit dismissive, though.

Typical Maya. In control of every last detail — every step we took, every word we said, so it wasn't much of a surprise that she should decide who would stay where.

'What about Maya and Dhruv?' I asked. I didn't mention Shravan. Really, I didn't care where any of them stayed, I was just relieved not to be on the same floor as Maya. It seemed like she had strategically placed Bhoo on the first floor to serve as her informal deputy, keeping us in check. I had hoped Shravan would be placed close to me, and that this trip would bring us together again, like the old times. Before everything fell apart.

'Maya and Bala? Second floor,' Jay said, unfolding another sheet.

I peered over his shoulder. The right-hand corner room, directly above Bhoo's, was marked 'M + 1'. Typical Maya again, consigning Bala to the position of insignificant other, not worthy of a name.

The middle room was labelled 'D + L'. I raised an eyebrow. 'Dhruv?'

Jay nodded, with a hint of amusement. 'And Leela. The newlyweds are taking centre stage.'

'Wouldn't they prefer a corner room?' I asked. 'Somewhere private, away from the rest of us?' My gaze drifted to the only remaining room on the far left — directly above mine. Only Shravan was left. If everything went as planned, we might not need two separate rooms for long.

Jay shrugged. He looked embarrassed. 'That's reserved for the host.'

I knew the house belonged to a friend of Shravan's, which was why we were getting it for free. But why would this friend want to join a bunch of strangers? Unless . . . There it was, the reason for Jay's averted gaze. In bold letters: 'L + S'.

My heart sank. Suddenly, it all fell into place. The hushed whispers whenever I asked about this generous friend. The uneasy tone, the shifting glances. They all made sense now. All my carefully laid plans had come to nothing. Shravan had a plus one. A significant plus one. Dread spread through me as I imagined it — the nights filled with creaking bed, the days stuffed with sweet talk and stolen smiles, all of which I'd have to endure for ten whole days.

CHAPTER FOUR

Day Zero: Leela

We left London at six in the morning. Dhruv had warned me it would be a long drive, so I packed some chilli *idlis* (I'm supposed to call them rice cakes) for breakfast, and lemon rice for lunch. Dhruv liked me to feed him as he drove. His only complaint was my insistence on using cutlery. 'Who eats *idlis* with a fork? Not even three months, and look at you, all westernised,' he teased. My dear husband, who'd long ago swapped *idlis* for burgers, now wanted me to hand-feed him.

'So you can bite my fingers? No chance,' I retorted.

'Come on. I don't bite,' he said with a wink. I blushed even more.

'Here,' I said, spraying him with water, 'you're looking a bit hot.'

'Hey, careful. I'm driving,' he protested, his eyes sparkling in amusement.

At first, he had wanted to fly or take the train to Edinburgh. 'We can join Jay and Smitha. They won't mind giving us a lift.'

But I was intent on bringing the dolls. They were heavy, but this was our first festive season together, and I wasn't ready to give up on tradition. 'It's Navaratri. Can we just not go?'

For a moment, his eyes had flashed in anger. He barely spoke to me for two days, but afterwards, unprovoked he'd said, 'Okay, I'll drive. You can bring your dolls. What's Navaratri without friends, huh?' I didn't understand it then, the reason for his change of heart.

So, we drove the eight hundred kilometres in one day, only stopping to use the toilets or to grab a coffee. It still took us over twelve hours to reach Oban. And they say England is a small country. Oh right, Oban isn't in England, is it? It's in Scotland, as Dhruv keeps reminding me. It annoys him when I mix up the two. 'How would you feel if someone told you Punjab was in Pakistan?' I didn't tell him there actually is a Punjab in Pakistan. He knows best, right?

By the time we crossed into Scotland, the sun was dying fast, bleeding into the horizon. The eastward wind had picked up, slamming against the car in unpredictable bursts. In the distance, a hanging bridge appeared — its red metal frame burning in the light of the setting sun. Dhruv pointed. 'That's the Queensferry Crossing. The late Queen herself was there to open the modern part.' The sun's rays pierced through the bars, bathing them in a crimson glow. 'It almost looks like blood,' he said.

The sight made my stomach clench. It reminded me of an old memory, a voice I had tried for years to forget — the voice that taught me to look for signs everywhere I went. *And the sky bleeds* . . . I looked away, but it was too late. Now, I would never be able to relax.

We were cruising along just fine until we turned into a narrow, muddy lane reminiscent of those in India. It was pitch dark by then, and there wasn't a soul in sight. Dhruv said, 'Did you know, Scotland has more cattle than people.'

As the car jolted over the bumps, I worried about the dolls. Some were made of mud or papier mâché — fragile things that needed careful handling. If treated well, they were said to bring good luck. Otherwise, well, you can guess the consequences.

'Shit!' Dhruv slammed on the brakes, and the car skidded to a halt. Ahead, I could just make out the silhouette of a white farmhouse in the gathering dark. It was still a few hundred metres away.

'What happened?' I asked.

Dhruv bowed his head and took a deep breath. His hands on the steering wheel were trembling. 'I think I hit something. Look, you stay here.' Before I could protest, he was out of the car and limping into the darkness.

The drive had taken its toll. I could see that Dhruv was exhausted. All for me, and my dolls. With a pang of guilt, I promised myself I would make it up to him tonight. After that, he'd have to wait ten days. The dolls would be watching. Even to me, it seemed weird, but it was part of the tradition. For the ten days, while the goddess battles with the demon, we mortals must abstain, our sacrifice giving her the power to sustain the fight. You forego the injunction at your peril. Dhruv got back in the car, still visibly shaken.

'All okay?' I asked.

He shrugged. 'I think so. I couldn't see anything. Must have been a cat. Look, there it is, sitting on that mound like royalty.'

Two glowing eyes pierced the darkness, and then it rent the silence with an unearthly meow. A black cat. An omen. I shivered.

* * *

It was late, and I ought to have finished setting them up long ago. The dolls should have been arranged in position, their vibrant colours vivid against the white carpet of the steps. But it took me a while to calm down, and then there were the introductions. My cheeks ached from the effort of smiling.

'Only half the gang are here,' Dhruv announced as he introduced me to his friends. I repeated their names twice, hoping I wouldn't forget them. They were all strangers to me, apart from Shravan and his friend, who had not yet arrived. I guessed this was her place, the friend's — at least that's the impression Dhruv gave. I thought she must be nice to let us stay in this lovely house. Apparently, she was fascinated by Navaratri and the doll set-up, which was why Dhruv finally agreed to bring them along. It made me angry when he dropped it, almost casually, in the conversation later, as if it didn't matter. Somehow, the words of a nameless woman whom he'd never even met held more power than his wife's. And I was supposed to be okay with that? She'd asked me a lot of questions, and even brought me a gift to complement the set-up — a shopper Barbie complete with mini supermarket. It was in the bags, with all the other dolls.

By the time we had finished dinner and began stacking up the boxes, it was past nine, and still there was no sign of Shravan or his friend. I had wanted to set up the dolls in the conservatory, which had plenty of space for the three tiers of steps, but Jay was adamant. 'The host has specifically allocated the cabin for them,' he'd said, as if that settled the matter. The cabin was some distance away, and we'd have to trek along a forest path to reach them.

As we laid out the bottom row of boxes, I couldn't shake a strange feeling. The back of my neck prickled — the unmistakable sensation of being watched. Smitha remarked, 'Isn't it typical of Indian men? At home, they'll roll up their sleeves and do the dishes, but whenever there's company, they scatter to the couch.' I had asked her to help me assemble the steps. The broadest three boxes go on the bottom, I said, followed by three medium-sized ones in the second step, and finally, the smallest three at the top. That way they form steps and each doll is visible.

There was something undeniably cheery about the yearly ritual of unwrapping the dolls. I couldn't quite pin down why freeing them from the cocoon of old clothes and bubble wrap that kept them safe should feel so exciting. Perhaps it was the lingering scent of last year's incense, mingled with the faint fragrance of dried flowers — one or two petals still stubbornly clinging to the past, refusing to let go. It could even be the thin layer of dust tickling my nose and setting off a sneezing fit.

Or maybe it was the first glimpse of the dolls — their pale faces and rosy cheeks, their coiffed curls and eyes rimmed with kohl. Their colourful clothes and their cheerful smiles. It could also be the relief of seeing them whole and unbroken, frozen in time, poised and ready to grace the steps for yet another year. I suppose it was a blend of all these things, so small and insignificant separately, but when combined, creating something heady and special.

Nancy, towering at nearly six feet tall, took charge of the decorating. She had no trouble reaching the walls above the steps. For someone so tall, she moved with surprising grace. Handing her the string of plastic marigold flowers, I told her to alternate between orange and yellow, draping them along the walls so that they hung in the shape of an inverted 'U'. These she bordered with two long strings, framing the steps in a bright, floral embrace.

Pulling sticky tape from her mouth, she said with a sigh, 'Oh, it's all men, Indian or not. They don't see chores the way we do.' It wasn't a sad sigh, more like a resigned, 'been there' one. I recalled Dhruv mentioning that Nancy had once been married to an Englishman. The marriage hadn't lasted, apparently, and I hadn't pressed him for details.

'More tape, Smitha!' Nancy called out.

This wasn't how I imagined our first Navaratri. I wished it were just me and Dhruv in our tiny London apartment. He would've set up the boxes, and when I asked for the stool to hang the decorations, he'd have said, *What do you need the stool for?* and would have lifted me up, the plastic flowers still in my hand. Then, when I placed the flowers around his neck, he would've laughed that sweet, lingering laugh of his.

Instead, Smitha was laying the white cloth over the steps, carefully tucking it in and pinning it in place. She had obviously done this before, and needed no instruction.

'To be fair,' Nancy said, 'it's been a while since they all got together. Women bond over activities, but men seem to need a drink for some reason.'

'A little to your left,' I called out. The arch was a bit wonky.

24

Nancy moved the flowers an inch or two higher. 'This better?'

'I said left, not up. Down a bit, and to your left,' I directed. Unwrapping the dolls would have to wait. I couldn't let anyone else handle the fragile figures. Had they survived the journey? I was worried about the jolt when Dhruv braked for the cat.

'Is it okay now?' Nancy asked.

It was still a little off, the layers overlapped slightly, but it would have to do for now. I could always come back later to adjust it. Thanking her, I turned my attention to the five shopping bags containing my precious cargo.

And there it was again, the silent burn of unseen eyes. I turned slowly, expecting nothing and yet . . . there he was. A stag's head, mounted high on the wall. Majestic, still. His eyes — glass, yet startlingly alive — met mine. Deep, brown, and thoughtful, like he had a question to ask. Or a warning to give. The antlers rose like a crown, regal and terrible, a monument to some long-forgotten victory. He was beautiful, in a haunting kind of way.

'Creepy, isn't it?' Smitha's voice broke the moment. I hadn't noticed her come up beside me.

Creepy. That wasn't the word I would've chosen. Reverent, maybe. Sad. But I nodded anyway, returning my attention to my dolls. On top was the Barbie. Shravan's gift was encased in pink plastic.

'Barbie? That's a bit out of place, isn't it? I thought they were supposed to be gods.'

'Not really,' I said. 'Some are, but mostly they're just depictions of everyday life.' I tried to prise open the Barbie's casing, but all I managed to do was hurt my fingers.

'Here,' Smitha said, 'try the scissors.' She waved them, still eyeing the Barbie. 'I still don't get it. Why Barbie?'

Why not? I thought. Why the fixation with Barbie, anyway? 'It was a gift from Shravan's girlfriend,' I said, hoping that was enough of an explanation.

A sharp clang echoed through the room — the bell Nancy had been holding ready to hang under the arch bounced down the steps and landed near Smitha's feet, intensifying the throbbing in my head. It had been a long day.

'Are you okay?' Smitha asked, looking concerned.

'I'm fine,' Nancy snapped.

Smitha picked up the fallen bell and handed it to her. 'So, you've met her, then?'

'No. Shravan said he'd told her about the doll set-up and that she was really interested. She's a writer, I believe.'

'A writer?' Smitha asked. 'Interesting. What's her name?'

'He didn't say,' I said, suddenly uncomfortable with all their questions. They were his friends, I was the outsider. Surely they'd know more about it than me?

'Didn't you ask?' Smitha said.

'Dhruv did, but he said I'd meet her soon enough,' I replied, snipping at the plastic. Finally, I managed to peel it away and held up the Barbie. 'This could go on the bottom step — a shopping scene,' I said to myself.

Immediately, Nancy began arranging the tiny supermarket shelves with their contents on the bottom step.

My thoughts drifting to Dhruv, I began absently unwrapping the first of the dolls.

'A wedding? How lovely,' Smitha exclaimed. I looked down at the dolls in my hands — a smiling young bride and groom, all garlanded and joyful. 'You and Dhruv, eh?'

I hadn't thought of it that way, but, well, why not? The groom did look a bit like Dhruv, and the bride's rosy cheeks and black curls could easily be mine. A smile, my first since the black cat incident, spread across my face. 'This goes on the middle step, the right-hand corner,' I said, handing the precious couple to Smitha.

'You must add a little one soon. Don't wait too long.' God, this woman was nosy. 'Sometimes, if you wait too long, it doesn't happen. You know what I mean? We didn't have Veena until the third year, but that was because Jay was still a student.'

When I started unwrapping the school set-up, it turned into a game. 'Oh, this must be Jay. He wears square glasses like those,' Smitha said, pointing at the teacher doll, which had a perfectly round, balding head and middle-aged spread.

Realising that I knew almost nothing about them, I asked, 'Is Jay a teacher?'

'Chemistry professor,' Smitha said with a hint of pride. 'Teacher, professor — they're all the same really.' The resemblance was uncanny. She went on, 'Before Jay got into Stirling University, his mum offered his hair up to God. He had to shave it all off. You should've seen his head then — I was tempted to crack it open just to see if a yolk would ooze out. The whole semester, he had to wear a cap inside the classroom. Even then, it never really grew back.'

Nancy, who'd been mostly quiet so far — apart from the occasional clarification of instructions — joined in. 'And the Barbie?' She was smiling like she already knew the answer.

'Duh, Maya, of course,' Smitha said, flipping her hair. 'Louis Vuitton bag, Ted Baker shoes — who else could it be? And that shopping set-up? Perfect,' she said, and her face fell almost immediately, as if she regretted it. An uncomfortable silence fell after that. No more guess-who game.

I stepped back, admiring the display with the pride of an artist who'd just added the final brushstroke to a masterpiece. It was perfect. The slightly wonky marigolds glowed golden under the room's lights. Adorned with bells and lotus stickers, they created a stunning backdrop. No one would guess that the steps the dolls stood posed on were made from humble cardboard boxes.

My gaze wandered over the dolls. Their charming little faces seemed to beam back at me. I'd always had more of a soft spot for the human figurines than the deities. The deities were so stiff, conforming to strict rules that left little room for creativity: four arms, an elephant's face, palms sprouting coins. Each deity had its specific garments to wear, each must hold a certain item. They all seemed to have the same serene, knowing smile. There were exceptions, of course, such as the formidable Maa Kaali, the Goddess of Death. With her severed arm, skirt, and garland of skulls, she was always given pride of place on the top step.

The 'human' dolls, on the other hand, were freer and more expressive. Each one told a story. Some wore frowns, others had a hint of mystery in their eyes, but each was stunning in its own individual way — Maa's army of soldiers in her never-ending celestial wars.

CHAPTER FIVE

Day One: Smitha

Cold milk in coffee? Definitely not my cup of tea. Where did they put the coffee anyway? The kitchen cabinets were well-stocked, with more than enough food for twelve people. I mean, we were only going to be here ten days, not weeks.

I was already in a foul mood. The ancient cast-iron range was so outdated I couldn't figure out how to operate it. Eventually, I opened one of the doors and fiddled about until one of the plates lit up. Now I didn't know how to turn it off.

Standing on tiptoe, I struggled to get a better view, but at four foot ten I couldn't stretch high enough. Where was Jay when I needed him? Probably still snoring away, dreaming of naked women. I'd heard him muttering in his sleep. He wasn't much taller than me. No problem, I'd use that egghead of his as a stool. 'For God's sake!'

'Did someone wake up on the wrong side of the bed, Smitha?' Nancy asked, and I jumped. I hated when she did that. Sneaking up on people.

'Good morning to you too,' I snapped.

But she was staring at the cooker. 'Oh, wow, an Aga!'

'Looks like a roti maker,' I said. 'And the controls are hidden out of sight. Why did they have to make it so complicated?'

'Cool, isn't it?' Nancy said, gazing at it with fascination. 'I've never used one before.'

'Be my guest,' I said. 'And while you're at it, make me a coffee, will you?'

To my chagrin, it took Nancy all of five seconds to locate the coffee, which was right where it should be, in the cabinet above the cooker, hidden behind a big jar of pickles. As she made a fuss over the drinks, I settled onto one of the velvet-cushioned chairs at the kitchen island that doubled as a dining table. There were exactly twelve, one for each of us. A glass vase on the island held fresh white anemones that I was sure hadn't been there yesterday.

'There you go,' Nancy said, setting the coffee down on a coaster. Being posh, were we? Glad I got the memo. You'd have to be, I suppose, in a kitchen with velvet chairs and a porcelain sink — and a blasted Aga.

'How's Veena?' she asked, busy whisking eggs with her back turned to me.

'Fine, I guess. I didn't call, she's probably still asleep. It's half-term,' I said. The British schools were constantly on holiday, some of them seemed to go on for months. If that wasn't enough, they even threw in some random days and called them 'bank holidays'. Christmas, I understand. Do banks have birthdays too? I took a slurp of my coffee. Divine. I used to be a chai person until I married Jay, a South Indian with a taste for filter coffee. Now, I was hooked. Instant coffee isn't the same, but with the right kind of blend, it could come close. I was fine with close.

'It's good that Veena was okay with staying—'

'I had to bribe her. She's a true Indian, you see. Strikes a hard bargain. The iPad and as many episodes of *Peppa Pig* as she wants did the trick. Jay's mum is hard of hearing, so she won't mind.' I chuckled. I'd told Veena to turn up the volume if granny got on her nerves.

Eggs bubbled and spluttered in the pan, filling the kitchen with an inviting aroma and my mouth with water. We hadn't had much for dinner last night — some of Leela's leftovers with toast. They probably expected me to whip up a gourmet meal, like I used to. It wasn't just them either. Jay kept asking me pointedly what was for dinner. I had to pinch him under the table to make him stop. Funny how, even after all these years, we fall into our usual roles.

Nancy flipped the eggs, and my stomach rumbled. I heard the clatter of feet on the parquet, hoping it wasn't Jay. The way he slurped his coffee always annoyed me. Besides, I hadn't yet forgiven him for going on about having toast for dinner last night. 'Really, Smitha. Who has toast for dinner?' he'd asked, as if it was my duty to magic up a hot dinner for six. When I looked up, my jaw almost hit the table.

Not Jay. A blonde, her hair loose, the striped pyjamas sliding from her skin like satin on silk. 'Hi, what a lovely morning!' she said, and extended her hand. 'I'm Livi. You must be Smitha.'

Both hands cradling my cup, I said, 'The flowers . . .'

She dropped her hand. Then her gaze landed on the vase, and her face brightened. 'Oh, the anemones? Yes. That was me. We got here late — me and Shravan. We had some, er, work. Do you like them?'

Before I could respond, Nancy stepped forward and held out her hand. 'A bit pale for my liking.'

'Shravan likes them pale,' Livi said. I had an idea Nancy wasn't talking about the flowers, but neither was Livi. I decided I liked her.

'His taste has changed, then,' Nancy said tightly.

John used to call her his 'chocolate doll'. He adored Nancy, or at least that's what he'd led us to believe. I liked him and thought he was a calming influence on her. He fitted easily into our desi gang — even Jay had nothing but praise for him. John even got Jay into table tennis and crisp suits. 'You've got a smart one there,' John used to tell me. 'Don't be fooled by the nerdy look.' And I almost believed him.

Look where it got us in the end. I shuddered at the thought. None of us suspected John when things started going missing.

'Coffee?' I asked. The next ten days promised to be interesting. A *ghoree*, no less, and one who spoke with the tip of her tongue. I couldn't wait to see Jay's reaction.

It turned out Livi drank chamomile tea. 'How do you like it here?' she asked, spreading her arms. 'Beautiful, isn't it?'

'It is,' I said. 'This massive kitchen, and look at the view.' Through the wide French doors, you could see the woods, a tiny path weaving through them. I wondered where they led. The car park, maybe? Stupid Jay made me trek up the narrow staircase with all the bags when we could have come that way.

'That path leads to the log cabin,' she said, as though she could read my mind. She was referring to the place where we had set the dolls up last night. 'That's where we used to stay, our wee family. This place was always let out. Anyway, it was too big for the three of us — Mum, me, and my brother.'

'That's where we've set up the dolls,' Nancy said, cracking more eggs into the pan.

'Oh, the dolls, I almost forgot,' Livi said. 'I'm really looking forward to seeing them. Shravan told me a lot about them, and I've seen pictures on the internet. They're so fab! So colourful. Priceless. I think the cabin's a good place for them, nestled among the trees.'

Nancy grunted.

'Leela wanted to set them up in the conservatory,' I said. 'Then Jay suggested the cabin. She loved it. You should see them — and your Barbie. It was simply perfect.'

Nancy continued to beat the eggs viciously.

As if on cue, the newlyweds entered, laughing, Shravan trailing in their wake. He glanced at me, his eyebrows raised, and mouthed, 'Awkward.'

Calling out, 'Good morning,' they took their seats, Shravan and Dhruv next to me and Livi. Leela began fussing with the flowers.

'Eggs?' Dhruv said hopefully.

Leela wrinkled her nose. 'It's Navaratri. We don't cook non-veg.'

'Oh, eggs aren't non-veg?' Nancy asked.

'Of course they're not,' Leela said sarcastically.

'Nancy wouldn't know,' Dhruv said.

'Well, why didn't someone tell her?' Leela said, glaring at me. Great. So now it was my fault. I stared into my coffee. Her and her musts and must-nots. Now I can't eat those eggs. Who does she think she is, God's secretary?

'What does non-veg mean?' Livi asked Shravan.

'It's "Indian",' he air-quoted, 'for anything that's not from plants,' Shravan said, looking embarrassed. 'It's like veg or meat, but veg or non-veg.'

'But eggs are not meat.'

'Hmm . . . not technically, I suppose.'

'Interesting. So, milk and cheese are non-veg too?' she asked.

'Well . . . not quite.'

'They are veg?'

I chuckled. 'Oh, you'll be surprised by the number of dietary combinations we have. Vegetarians, non-vegetarians, and then there are eggetarians, who are essentially vegetarians who also eat eggs. If you're a vegetarian from Bengal, you can eat fish. I think they're called pescatarians. And then we have Jains who don't eat onions, garlic, or anything that grows underground. But veganism isn't traditional, that's a more modern concept.'

Shravan looked grateful.

'Wow,' she said.

I liked her more and more. For a start, she was the only one here who paid me any attention. She was practically lapping up my words.

Leela was scrubbing the Aga as though having had eggs cooked on it had somehow tainted it. Clicking her tongue, Nancy sat down opposite us with her eggs and toast. Dhruv mouthed a silent apology to her.

'You want some?' she asked me.

I shook my head, too scared to open my mouth in case the 'yes please' slipped out before I could stop myself.

'Suit yourself.'

'Chai anyone?' Leela asked.

Shravan scrambled to his feet. 'Livi drinks chamomile tea. I'll make her one.' Dhruv and Nancy exchanged smirks that said, *Look at him, serving his girlfriend.*

Oblivious, Livi smiled. 'Thanks, darling.' More smirks.

Nancy continued chomping her eggs. My stomach protested loudly, but I wasn't going near that fancy cooker. I knew what would happen if I did — the men would start placing their orders for breakfast. I planned to spend the next ten days pretending not to know how to use it. Then they couldn't order me around.

'Where did you get the flowers?' Leela asked. 'I need some for the dolls tonight.'

Livi flushed. 'Well, actually we got them on the way, from Aldi. But there's a flower bed in the woods. Not much, just a wee patch of dahlias and roses. It's coming to the end of the season, but there should be some left. You can also find some wild orchids. If you want, I can take you. I just need a shower first.'

'Is that the patch we saw yesterday?' Shravan said. 'Don't worry, I can take Leela. You go shower. We'll see you in the cabin after.' He leaned in and gave her a long kiss. My tummy clenched. The next ten days were going to be hard to get through.

CHAPTER SIX

Day One: Nancy

It was early October, yet the autumn leaves had already laid a wind-woven carpet on the barely trodden path. At least there was no wind which made my eyes water. I wasn't made for this weather. With every step, I shivered a little.

We were heading the same way we had gone last night — towards the cabin. The path was soft and squidgy with lingering mist, and old tyre tracks brimmed with water, glinting in the morning light.

It was at least two years since I'd last seen Shravan, and the shock of it hadn't yet subsided. He'd changed a lot. His hair was longer, tied back into a loose ponytail, he'd grown a beard, and he wore a silver ring in one ear. As an all-weather runner, he'd always been toned, but now he looked like a biker.

In the ways that mattered — not the superficial ones — he hadn't changed at all. That easy smile. The way he tilted his head when he spoke, as if you were the only person in the world. The slight squint he gave the sun, like it annoyed him, but he forgave it. I sighed. I couldn't let myself go there — lose myself in comparing then and now. It was too painful.

I didn't have much time. I had to leave before nine to pick up Maya and company from Fort William railway station. 'Be there at ten sharp,' she'd told me during our video call. 'The Caledonian Sleeper is always on time, and I don't like to be kept waiting.'

Maya had claimed she wanted to experience the sleeper train and somehow managed to convince Bhoo to join her. I didn't buy it for a second. I knew her too well. Where we come from in India, sleeper trains aren't a novelty, they're the norm, something to avoid if you possibly can. I suspected Maya had orchestrated it all just so they'd arrive last, and she could make one of her grand entrances. She'd even arranged for a chauffeur — me — to pick her up from the station.

I, however, had come a day early mainly to reconnect with Shravan. That was before I found out he was bringing a plus one. So much for that. When Shravan suggested taking Leela to the flower bed, I said I'd go along too. It was my one chance to catch him alone, away from his girlfriend, who clung to him like a creeper. Besides, being in nature is supposed to be good for the soul, or something. Leela and Shravan were walking ahead, while Smitha, who always had to be part of the action, had joined me. I didn't mind too much. She would be useful, keeping Leela occupied while I snatched a word with Shravan.

As soon as they were out of earshot, Smitha gave me a nudge. 'Fancy Shravan falling for a *ghoree*. Huh?'

'Don't be mean, Smitha. She seems nice,' I lied.

'*Ghoree* isn't mean. It just means blonde. Last I checked, saying someone's blonde isn't racist. It's not the same as calling someone brown!'

'Why not?' I knew what she was doing. She wanted to see me react, cry on her shoulder. But I wasn't about to give her the satisfaction. 'The most important thing is that they look happy together,' I said.

She gripped my wrist. 'Remember what happened the last time there was a white person in our gang.'

I didn't reply. John was the last person I wanted to think about right now.

'We'd better hurry, or we'll lose them,' I said. There was little chance of that; the path ahead was perfectly clear. I looked up. The trees formed an arch above the path. They looked even more ominous in the daylight.

Just as we drew near Leela and Shravan, a chill wind had us both hugging ourselves.

'Isn't it too cold for flowers?' Leela asked.

'Oh no,' Shravan said. 'Dahlias usually bloom right up to late October. We saw orchids too, last night.'

We came to the end of the path and turned west, along the side of the building. I gasped. Rising up in front of us was a monster, its giant metal jaws wide open. Another step and Leela would have put her foot in its mouth. She screamed.

'Oh, I'm sorry. I should have warned you,' Shravan said. 'It's a trap, for the badgers. Livi mentioned it last night.' He waved at the huddle of bins beyond it. 'Badgers vandalise the bins, you see.'

A shudder ran through me. One of us could easily have strayed off the path last night in the dark. One wrong step and we could have walked straight into the trap. The bone-crushing crunch, the blood-curdling scream. I could almost feel the metal teeth tearing through my skin, ripping it apart.

Leela broke the silence. 'What time did you get here? It must have been late. It was already ten thirty when we went to bed.'

'Well past eleven,' Shravan said. He began idly kicking the small stones on the path. One struck my foot. If he saw me flinch, he didn't apologise. But then he was trying his best not to meet my eyes.

'What, you were out looking at flowers at that time of night?' I asked. It must have been pitch dark, the lights outside the cabin were off and there was no moon.

I had directed the question at Shravan, but that didn't stop Leela from butting in. 'Navaratri always starts on the day of the new moon.' Of course. Leave it to Leela to stick her nose in. She irked me with her know-it-all attitude and her constant lectures. God, she was exhausting to be around.

Shravan glanced in my direction as if noticing me for the first time. Ignoring me so pointedly wasn't going to make me go away. Besides, where was the fun in it, eh?. But of course, Shravan knew it. The best psychiatrist in town.

Not willing to give me the satisfaction of a complete victory, he looked away, in the general direction of the woods. 'Livi wanted to see the dolls. She was so excited.' His face lit up with that special smile he used to reserve for me. A jealous knot formed in my stomach. I knew I was being unfair — after all, I was the one who left him, went and married John out of spite. Served me right, and look how it ended. Shravan should have learned from it. Learned that we were meant to be together. Why didn't he get it?

'Oh, I didn't realise she'd seen them already.' Leela sounded offended, as though Livi needed her permission to visit the dolls.

'She didn't. The cabin was locked,' Shravan said. 'She hadn't expected it to be, they always left the door open. We tried looking in through the window, but it was too dark.' He ran his hand through his hair, and the familiar gesture made me want to weep. All the times we had walked together, my hand in his. That special smile meant just for me. Now, it felt like those walks belonged in a dream, a fantasy of mine.

'Sorry, that was me,' Leela said. 'I have the key. In India we always lock up, you never know who might be snooping around. I learned that the hard way. The dolls are too precious.'

Glancing at me, Smitha said, 'We had things going missing too. Remember?'

All right. You don't have to spell it out. Maya thought John got away to easily. I remember her saying, 'He should be in prison!' Maya always did get off on righteous indignation. A bit rich, coming from her!

The path forked. Last night we took the right fork to the cabin, but now Shravan steered us to the left. 'There it is,' he said.

Thank goodness, we had arrived at the flower patch. I tried to catch up with Shravan, but he kept his gaze firmly on the flowers.

Now we were here, I saw that the flower patch wasn't far from the log cabin. The flowers were off to the left, on a patch of uneven ground, and not secluded at all. A row of trees formed a natural fence behind them, but through the gaps in their leaves and branches, you could still catch clear glimpses of the cabin.

My foot slipped on the soggy leaves, and Shravan instinctively reached out to help me, but at the last moment his arm fell to his side. I wished I'd fallen, then he'd have had no choice but to offer his hand and pull me up. I wondered if his girlfriend, with her golden hair and slender figure — and probably loaded bank account — had resorted to a similar trick to grab his attention. Then I remembered her open smile, and I was no longer so sure. Maybe she was as nice as she seemed. Then I hated her even more.

From where the rest of us were standing, the flowers formed a burst of colour, a mix of yellows, purples, the warm orange of the dahlias, and bordering them, the fragile pink orchids. Up close, the picture wasn't so bright. The dahlias had begun to wilt, while the orchids were little more than spindly sticks, struggling to rise through the fallen leaves.

'The orchids are a little thin,' I said.

'Oh, this is perfect!' Leela exclaimed, bending down to examine the flowers.

Leela seemed oblivious to the flowers' decay. In my head this flower patch, past its prime, mirrored my own situation. Once full of life, it was now, bit by bit, withering away.

From here, the cabin was hidden from view by the trees, birch and oak that sheltered the flower bed. Leela was busy cutting the flowers with a pair of tiny scissors. Smitha, ever the eager helper, held a plastic bag open for her to drop them into.

'Do you want to collect the orchids?' Leela asked me without looking up.

I didn't. But Shravan had moved away, and was inspecting something on one of the hazelnut trees — a strange, finger-like mass of fungus weighing down a sagging branch. I longed to be beside him, the two of us alone, the rest of the world fading into a blur. My sigh felt hot as my gaze followed his. Then I saw it, the opportunity. There were orchids growing near the hazel tree, giving me an excuse to be close to him.

I strolled across and cleared my throat. 'How are you, Shravan?'

His back was towards me. He froze, his hand on the branch. A long moment passed before he finally croaked, 'I'm fine, Nance. How are you?'

Nance — he was the only person who ever called me that. Well, him and my mother.

'You really want to know?' I hadn't meant it to come out so sharp. I sounded like my mother — someone I had always fought desperately not to become. I softened my tone. 'I've been worse. Apparently, I'm on the mend — at least that's what Diane says.'

'Are you still seeing the therapist?' he asked quietly.

It had been Shravan who insisted I go for therapy. His concern had touched me. Now it felt like an indictment — a reminder of the wreckage I'd left behind.

'Yeah. Diane's great. She thinks I'm getting there.' Whatever that was supposed to mean. The only therapist I ever wanted was him, and not in that capacity. His colleague, Diane, really was good, but she wasn't Shravan. Still, Diane's sessions weren't a waste. When everything fell apart, I blamed myself. First my mother, then John . . . I had convinced myself that I was the common denominator, that I somehow

40

brought out the worst in them. Diane helped me see the truth: it wasn't me, it was *they* who were the problem. But what did she know? After all, she only heard the things I wanted her to hear.

Shravan nodded slightly, but he didn't turn around. It didn't help that I could feel Smitha's and Leela's eyes burning into my back. Flower picking forgotten, they were eagerly drinking in every word.

'Good. Diane is brilliant,' he said.

A silence. 'Are you happy?' I asked.

'Very,' he said. 'Work is great. I've gone into private practice now — fully booked for the next six months. It was difficult getting these ten days off.'

'I didn't mean work. Are you happy with *her*?' The last word came out more sharply than I had intended.

Shravan flinched. 'Livi is great,' he said. 'She's the kindest person I've ever met. She loves deeply, cares like there's no tomorrow. I'm really lucky.'

'Deeply? Deeper than me?'

'Don't do this, Nancy. Not now.'

Oh, I was back to Nancy now, was I? I stepped closer. 'There's always a way. We just need to find it. Together. Give me a chance. Us, a chance.'

Shravan made a gesture of impatience. 'We,' he said slowly, 'were never going to work.'

'Why? Because I'm damaged goods?' I shot back. Typical Indian, I thought. Men want their brides pure, but they're free to do whatever they like.

'Yes,' he snapped. 'And not because of your marriage. You know why.' With that, he turned and marched back to the others.

Smitha and Leela weren't even pretending not to eavesdrop. They stared at us. Part of me didn't care. Maybe one of them would tell Livi about us. That part made me grab Shravan's arm. 'Shravan, please.'

He jerked away, shrugging me off as if my touch had burned him. 'I've had enough of your drama.'

'I'm no longer like that. I'm better now.'

Ignoring me, Shravan strode across to the flower bed. 'Are you done?'

CHAPTER SEVEN

Day One: Leela

His face set, Shravan marched off towards the wood cabin. We trailed after him, relieved that Nancy had left us, marching off towards the car park, muttering that she was late and Maya would kill her. None of us were fooled. I couldn't hear what they said, but it sounded like she and Shravan were arguing. Livi was waiting on the veranda. 'There you are. Did you find any flowers?'

'Yeah, plenty. I left some of them for tomorrow,' I said, hoping they wouldn't be ruined by then. 'Oh, and sorry I locked up. Force of habit, I guess.' I held up the key like it was some kind of prize.

Livi smiled. 'Nah, you did the right thing. The dolls are precious. I can't wait to see them.'

The cabin wasn't much — just a space, really, all open-plan. But compared to our cramped London flat, it felt like a palace. Dhruv had said the rent was still a fortune. 'London's a place for the rich — and the richer,' he'd joked. We were neither. Sometimes, I wondered if we even belonged in a city like that, so chic, so relentlessly bustling. But then I'd think of the blur of unfamiliar faces, our neighbours who were practically strangers, and I'd crave that anonymity only a city could offer. Here, among friends, we were too exposed.

'This used to be a hunting cabin,' Livi said, nodding at the stag's head. 'Before.'

That's when I noticed it, a wooden box beneath the mount. Positioned right under the stag, almost nestled into the fold of its preserved neck. It looked like it was guarding it.

'Do you hunt?' I asked, my gaze still on the deer.

Hearing a sharp intake of breath, I turned to look at Livi. Her face had gone red, as if I'd slapped her.

'Me? Oh God, no. I don't hunt.' Then, after an awkward pause, 'I don't understand it — killing an innocent animal. For what? Sport?'

I didn't tell her that innocence was a myth, a hoax. A comforting lie at best. People look at their babies — at their almond eyes, their chubby cheeks, the toothless grin. Hear their soft gurgles, breathe in that sweet, sweet scent. Their insides go *aww* . . . and they forget. Forget what they could grow up into. Forget that even the worst amongst us, started as an innocent baby once. 'Me neither,' I said.

Sunlight streamed in through the large windows draped in sheer white curtains tied back with ropes of silk. The place seemed larger than it had last night. There wasn't much in the way of furniture apart from chests of drawers, which were everywhere. And the drawers weren't empty. We'd tried moving a couple last night, to prop up the cardboard boxes, but they refused to budge. The sink was dirty from lack of use, but the rest of the place wasn't too bad, nothing a good dusting couldn't fix.

I glanced at Livi. Her mouth was slightly open in child-like curiosity, her eyes round. I smiled. Her enthusiasm was infectious.

'Livi's dying to hear what this is all about,' Shravan said.

'Dying' wasn't a word I'd use for a celebration, but I let it slide. 'What do you want to know? Shall we start with Navaratri itself?'

Livi's eyes were alight with curiosity. 'Let's grab a seat — oh.' There weren't any to grab. In India, the women sat on the floor beneath the dolls, but those floors weren't cold and hard like these Scottish ones. 'Hang on a minute,' she said, and went over to one of the chests of drawers and pulled out some throws. As she did so, her Nirvana T-shirt rode up, revealing half of a circular tattoo on her back in the form of a knotted ring.

Seeing me staring, Livi hastily pulled down her T-shirt.

Having arranged the throws and some pillows she'd found, so as to make a makeshift floor couch, she sat down, all attention. 'So, tell me about it.'

'Nava-ratri literally translates as "Nine Nights",' I began. 'It represents the nine nights of a battle in which the Goddess Durga fights a powerful army of demons.'

'I thought you said ten,' Livi said.

'Yeah, nine nights and ten days. On the tenth day we celebrate her victory.'

'Wow. I love it — woman power. So, why the dolls?'

I tucked a loose strand of hair behind my ear and smiled. 'In South India, we put up dolls to honour the great battle and the countless lives the goddess saved. It's like they're telling a story, not just of the battle, but of the lives that followed, lives that might never have been without her.' I stopped, remembering the Barbie doll. 'Thanks for the gift. It fits the theme perfectly.'

I watched her gaze move over the dolls. From the Barbie, it travelled to the football set, the scene at the school gate, the village with its lush green hut, the wedding scene, the boat, and finally the doctors. 'Aren't they supposed to represent gods?'

'There she is,' I said, pointing to the top shelf where Maa Durga stood in pride of place, her feet on a lion. Her ten arms each brandished a different weapon — a sword, a shield, a bow, arrows, an axe, and a hammer. Most striking of all was the three-pronged spear thrust into the torso of a demon lying beneath her. 'That's Maa Durga. She's the goddess of the festival, the one who defeated the demon king.' I gestured towards Maa Kaali standing next to her. 'And this one is Maa Kaali, the Goddess of Death.'

I pointed to the dark, fearsome warrior adorned with a garland of skulls hanging from bracelets made of intestines. Her bulging eyes blazing with fury, her legs anchored over a sea of demons. Her mouth was open, revealing pointed teeth and a viper's tongue.

Livi's eyes widened. Maa Kaali always has that effect. Then she said something unexpected. 'She's beautiful.'

I'd never heard anyone call Ma Kaali beautiful before. Not knowing how to respond, I pointed to the wedding scene. It featured a band with tiny ornate instruments, and a group of women dancing, all draped in colourful sarees, their long hair adorned with little knitted flowers. Other women carried large plates heaped with fruits and sweets, while the men danced at the rear.

I moved on. 'This one shows a school,' I said, pointing to the left-hand corner of the same step. A teacher was seated at his desk, facing a row of miniature students, all staring at the blackboard behind him. A woman, evidently late, judging by her harassed appearance, was dropping her daughter off at the school gate.

'And this,' I said, indicating the scene between the two tableaux, 'depicts a village.' A bare-chested farmer and his wife were walking towards their hut — him carrying a sickle, the wife with a bundle of reeds on her shoulders. Nearby, a couple of boys were leading cows towards a barn, while more women gathered around a well.

Livi pointed to the scene on the top step. 'Don't tell me,' she said. A doctor in a white coat and stethoscope was attending to a patient lying flat on a bed and clutching his stomach in evident distress. 'This is a hospital.'

'And the very top step is reserved for the gods.'

'Oh, look at these cuties!' Before I could stop her, Livi had reached forward and grabbed the bride and groom.

I could feel the blood drain from my face and my head begin to spin. 'No, don't! You mustn't.' But it was too late. Livi was already hugging the miniature dolls to her chest. My voice shook. 'The dolls mustn't be moved, not until the tenth day. They represent the goddess's soldiers in the battle against evil. They shouldn't be disturbed.'

'And if they are moved?' Livi asked anxiously.

'The evil will escape. It could bring us ten years of bad luck — and worse.'

Livi looked alarmed. 'I'm sorry,' she said, gently placing the dolls back. But the damage had been done. I struggled to hold back my tears.

'Don't be so superstitious, Leela,' Shravan said, putting his arm around Livi's shoulders. 'Besides, she didn't know, so it doesn't count.'

I wanted to say that it always counted, but I had lost the ability to speak. I fell to my knees, praying frantically, hoping and begging the goddess to forgive this unintentional sin.

Smitha giggled and put her hand to her mouth.

'Hey, listen, it was a genuine mistake,' Shravan said. 'Livi doesn't know our customs. She didn't mean any harm. I'm sure the goddess will forgive her. Let's just move on and start over. You're scaring her.' As if Livi was a small child, and he, her mother.

'You're right,' I said, still kneeling. 'She doesn't know. Unlike some,' I added, glaring pointedly at Smitha.

CHAPTER EIGHT

Day One: Nancy

A distant squeal heralded the approach of the Caledonian Sleeper. The long, square face appeared along the track, and soon, its four short carriages swaying loosely, it groaned to a halt at the platform.

The train was half an hour late, but I wasn't complaining. The station wasn't much — just two platforms, thank God. Trains didn't come through often. I'd only just made it to the station when its sleek blue body pulled up, though I wasn't going to tell Maya that, just in case should she say she was sorry I'd been kept waiting. Unlikely, but still. Knowing her, she wouldn't care if I'd been standing there for three hours, so long as I was there the moment she stepped out on the platform.

The train had hardly rolled to a stop when a door — first class, of course — swung open and Maya stepped out. She looked, well, 'in the pink'. The furry shawl around her neck, the fluffy jacket and the halter top — all pink. Even her balayage hair had pink highlights amid the golden blonde. The only thing that wasn't pink were her tights, but on closer inspection, they too bore pink speckles.

Behind her, Bala was struggling to pull out two large suitcases. Without a single backward glance at her poor husband, Maya strode forward.

'Hey, Nancy!' she said, extending one manicured hand. More pink. 'You're here, then.' She clapped the back of my hand. I felt like some five-year-old who'd made it to school on time. Where did she think I'd be?

'Where's Bhoo?' I asked, watching Bala haul the suitcases across the platform. If I'd known she was bringing so much stuff I'd have asked Dhruv to bring his car along. How were these massive cases going to fit in the boot of my little Mini?

Maya waved a hand dismissively. 'Oh, Laxman. You know how he is, he insisted on travelling in the cattle coach, even though I offered to pay for the upgrade.'

Maya tossed back her glossy hair, obviously expecting a compliment.

'Your hair looks lovely,' I said obligingly.

'Doesn't it? It suits me,' she said. I'd hoped my praise would distract her, but she continued with the subject of Bhoo and her husband's left-wing principles. 'Anyway, where was I? Oh, right. The first-class fare. Well, Laxman took the money, but he still booked second class. The cheapskate claimed first class was full.' She rolled her eyes. 'Turned out it was practically empty.'

Poor Bhoo. I bet he hadn't even mentioned it to her. Laxman fed off money in a way Bhoo never did, and the more he had, the more greedy he became. He was in finance, after all, and Bhoo was a consultant doctor. Between them, they had to be making a mint. Yet here he was, freeloading off Maya. I was sorry for Bhoo.

'What an awful experience,' Maya said, inspecting her nails. 'I'm going to sue the railway company. They charge such a premium for basic service. And it's so slow.' She flapped her arms like a butterfly. 'Look at my nails. What a mess.' I looked. They were perfect. 'No, this one.' She pointed to her pinkie, where a tiny chip was barely visible.

A panting Bala had finally reached us. I eyed the cases. 'One each?'

'Nah,' Maya said. 'Bala doesn't need much. They're both mine. She tapped a pink nail on the black floral Ted Baker case. 'This one's for everyday wear, and the other is my "ethnic" outfits.'

'My stuff's in here,' Bala said brightly, patting his backpack. 'I've br—'

Maya waved a dismissive hand. 'Tell me about the accommodation. Is there a pool?'

'If there was, it wouldn't be much use in autumn,' I said, glancing at the lowering rain clouds. 'We're in Scotland, not the Canaries.'

'Well, there could be a heated pool. No? There must be a hot tub, surely?'

I shook my head. I wasn't about to tell her that mine was one of the only two rooms that had a jacuzzi. She would find out in time, and would no doubt have something to say about the room she'd been allocated.

'No pool, no hot tub, I knew this was going to be a disaster,' Maya said. 'We should've gone to the Amalfi Coast like I wanted.'

I knew where she meant. The price of ten days in the Italian place amounted to a staggering five-figure sum, a little over the average national annual income.

By the time Bhoo and Laxman emerged from the second-class carriage, the train was already making departure noises. I noticed that Bhoo had gained a fair bit of weight — stress from long hours on the emergency ward, I assumed, and that worried me. Bhoo didn't do stress. It had happened before, and it had taken an anonymous email and a photo to make her see the effect it was having.

Bhoo was dressed in clothes that had obviously been thrown on carelessly — a frumpy grey jumper that had seen better days, and jeans at least two sizes too small. In her university days, she'd briefly tried to emulate Maya's style by shopping for high street lookalikes, until they proved too expensive both in terms of the cost and the effort required.

When she'd stopped, Maya had been disappointed. I suppose it made Maya feel like a celebrity, having someone emulating her style. But after a while of trying to tempt Bhoo and even buying her a cheaper version of her own clothes (because God forbid Bhoo wore the designers better) only for Bhoo to promptly ditching them for yet another full sleeved shirt, she'd given up.

Dragging her feet, Bhoo made her way across to us. 'Sorry. We overslept.'

I laughed. 'I was about to send reinforcements.' Bhoo looked away. Even after all these years, she still hadn't forgiven me.

'Come on, then,' Maya declared. 'Bala will drive.' And she snatched the keys from my hand before I could protest. A little issue like insurance wasn't going to stand in the way of what Maya wanted, nor would the fact that the car belonged to me.

* * *

'Ooh, this is lovely,' sang Bhoo from the back seat. The front passenger seat, which Maya had graciously given over to me, was pushed all the way forward to make room for Maya's luggage, allowing little space for my legs. By now, they were sorely in need of a stretch, and the rest of me desperately needed caffeine.

'The highlands are beautiful, aren't they?' Bala said, keeping his eyes on the mirror.

It was rather cosy in here, and smelled of cheese and crisps. Maya had taken up most of the space in the back, with Bhoo and her husband pressed closely together. Even though Bhoo had been married to Laxman for five years, he was still just 'Bhoo's husband' to us, an outsider.

'Oh, I didn't mean the view,' Bhoo said. 'It's been ages since we had a holiday together. What, seven years now?'

'Easily. The last time was before Nancy . . .' Bala's voice trailed off.

'Yeah, before my divorce. So, yes, it's seven years, easily.' No one said anything for a few seconds. 'You don't have to tiptoe around it, you know. It's been a long time and don't worry, I won't burst into tears.' Bala glanced at me, and we shared a smile. He let his shoulders relax; after all, he might get away with it this time.

'It's my first,' said Laxman through a mouthful of crisps. His tone was rueful as if we had purposely excluded him the last time. He and Bhoo had married two years after our last holiday together, but he didn't let that get in the way of his hard-done-by attitude.

'We have Shravan to thank for this one,' Bala said.

'And his plus one,' Bhoo added. 'I wonder what she's like.'

'I still think you could have found a better place for a holiday,' Laxman said. 'I mean, a forest? Who knows what kind of wild creatures are out there—'

'Oh, don't be such a killjoy, Lax. It will be a new experience. We've never been camping before, have we?' Bhoo said.

'Indians don't do camping. Or skiing for that matter. It's not in our DNA,' Laxman said. He and Bhoo were complete opposites: Bhoo, the ever-optimistic 'I fly when I jump' type, while Laxman was a staunch adherent of Murphy's Law, his first disciple. If something could possibly go wrong, it inevitably would. It's a miracle they'd lasted five years.

I wriggled uncomfortably in my seat. 'Can we take a break? My legs are cramped.'

'Okay. Five minutes,' Bala said.

We were nearing Oban, its emerald hills dotted with white peppercorn cattle. Beyond lay the glacial waters of Gleann Dubh. Beside the road stood a sign reading *ARDTORNA & ARDCRERAN*, along with five stars.

Laxman pointed at the sign. 'See, there are plenty of good hotels in the area. We needn't have chosen a place way out in the middle of nowhere.'

Maya said reasonably, 'But hotels like this cost a fortune. We're staying for free, remember? All we're paying for is the food.'

Laxman grunted. 'Why else would I have agreed to go there?'

I wondered, and not for the first time, where Bhoo had found him. I knew the answer, though — IndianMatrimony. com. And she didn't even find him, her parents had. I begged her not to let them do it to her, but did she listen?

'Do what, Nancy?' she'd said. 'You had a love marriage, and look what happened to you.' We didn't speak for two years after that. I didn't even attend her wedding. We've made up now, but it's not the same.

'You and Shravan, Nancy, you were so close,' Maya said. 'I can't believe you didn't know about this woman. I mean, he never even pees without telling you.'

'Oh, that's ancient history,' I snapped. Bhoo, for one, believed I started seeing John as a way of getting Shravan to propose. Clearly, that didn't work.

An uneasy silence ensued. I stared resolutely out of the window. The weather wasn't too bad, the sky was clear — for Britain — and the air had a hint of warmth. And for once it wasn't raining.

'Music, anyone?' Bala asked.

CHAPTER NINE

Day One: Livi

Oban. The closest thing I'd ever had to a home. I never knew who my father was, or where my mother came from. Home was just wherever she decided to go next. But Oban was always there, a constant in a life full of questions. It wasn't a permanent home — we lived in London or Paris, or some other big city — but spent every holiday here. Oban was where I had all my firsts: wild swimming, fishing, white-water rafting. My first boyfriend. Oban, with its sea-stained fishermen and weary fishing boats, under one of which I lost my virginity. Oban was where I belonged.

It was at its best in autumn. With its golden trees, pink-streaked skies and the emerald churn of the sea, there was no other place like it. How fitting that the signature colour of the first day of Navaratri was orange. According to Leela, each of the ten days had a designated colour in honour of one of Maa Durga's avatars. Shravan wasn't convinced. 'That's just a ploy by a clever textile marketing company. There was no mention of colours when we were growing up.'

'Just because you didn't know doesn't mean there weren't any,' Leela had said. 'Besides, it looks great in the photos.'

I didn't have that many Indian outfits, and I'd asked Shravan if I should go out and buy sarees in the appropriate colours. It seemed a bit excessive, but I wasn't about to be left out. And first impressions matter.

Shravan had suggested we skip the whole thing. 'We could just stay home.' He put his hand on my thigh. 'We've plenty to keep us occupied.'

I'd told him that wasn't happening. He wasn't going to keep me hidden from his friends any longer. I wanted to meet them. It had been long enough.

He'd laughed. 'Why would I want to hide such a gorgeous girlfriend?' He was a bad liar. He'd had plenty of opportunities to introduce me to them in the nine months we'd been dating, but somehow it never seemed to happen. They were always too busy, or he was. And when it wasn't either, he just couldn't agree on a place. It wasn't right, they were his best friends, his 'tribe' from his student days in Stirling. That's when I suggested the holiday — a way to eliminate every excuse. That way, the place and time couldn't be avoided. He couldn't keep me away from them forever.

And there was no way I was going to miss the dolls festival. The writer in me was itching to be part of such a visual form of storytelling. Shravan couldn't wriggle out of this one. Fortunately, Leela didn't expect everyone to have sarees in all the colours of the rainbow, especially not in Britain. Apparently, she was bringing sarees for everyone to wear on the ninth day — in peacock green, the colour of day nine. On the other days we could wear whatever we liked, as long as it was respectable — a dress or a kurta.

I'd learned that a kurta was a long, tailored tunic with elaborate designs and bright colours. Another thing I didn't have, but at least I could afford to buy a few before we left. With the kurtas and a few dresses, I was all set.

Now I was dressed in an orange kurta from Etsy, with embroidered floral motifs that resembled stars. I'd paired it with silver earrings and blue jeggings, just like the model on the site. My blonde hair fell loose over my shoulders. I would do.

'What do you think?' I asked Shravan, twirling in front of him.

'One final touch,' he said, and picking up my eyeliner he made a small dot between my eyebrows. He stepped back. 'Perfect. My gorgeous golden girl.'

'Shouldn't we be leaving to the cabin?' I asked, before he could kiss me and smudge my lipstick. Leela had asked us to be there by half past six, and it was already a quarter past. The cabin was a few hundred metres from the house and I didn't want to be late for our first official visit.

'What's the rush?' he said, and pulled me close. 'You know about Indian time by now. Six thirty really means seven, at the earliest.'

I gave him a playful push. 'Now, Mr Dan-Dha-Pan-Ey, don't get cheeky with me. It took me ages to put myself together, and I'm not having you mess me all up.'

He laughed — that full-throttle, throw-your-head-back laugh that always followed when I butchered his surname. No matter how hard I tried, I always sounded like a stuck-up steam train. 'Okay, I give in. But don't be surprised if we're the only ones there.'

Every time I looked at Shravan I couldn't help wondering how I got this lucky. My mother, bless her, was never good at picking boyfriends, or partners, or even husbands. She always went for the smart, shiny ones, like she'd been a magpie in a past life. My father and stepfather had been shiny too, though Dexter's dad was marginally better. At least he left us the house, not with loads of debt like mine. Dexter was no better. When it came to relationships, my poor brother inherited our mother's bullshit meter — that enduring lack of taste. Sometimes I wondered if I had too. My boyfriends never lasted either. All that changed when I met Shravan. Maybe — just maybe — a childless cat lady wasn't to be my destiny after all. It was a wonder, given the state he found me in, the terrible, terrible circumstances.

* * *

Outside, the cherry trees glittered with golden leaves. Spring blooms were always spectacular, but there was something regal about the hues of autumn. We'd spent many a spring here — Mum, Dex, and I. We'd wait for the full bloom, and when it came, I'd stand beneath the tree, arms outstretched, and Dex would grab the thick stem and shake it with all his might until I was covered in a blanket of petals.

How I laughed back then — the gentle tickle of blossoms against my skin, the air a perfumed mist.

Dhruv broke into my thoughts. 'Did you see the dolls?' he asked, looking at me like an eager child showing off their artwork on parents' night.

I nodded. 'The dolls are just gorgeous.' I'd seen pictures of them on the net. But the real thing was something else — so colourful, so vibrant. 'Do you think I could put them in one of my stories?' Our feet crunched on the gravel as we stepped onto the path.

Shravan merely laughed. He could be a bit more supportive. *Why won't he take me seriously? As if writing isn't a real job.* Daylight was fading fast. Soon it would be pitch dark, and the path between the house and the cabin was unlit. The torches on our phones weren't going to be enough. Leela had gone ahead with Maya and Bhoo.

'You should,' Dhruv said. 'Write about the dolls, I mean. Leela would be pleased, she's always telling me about the stories behind the different scenes. What kind of books do you write?'

'Psychological thrillers. Dark tales with a background in folklore. The dolls would be perfect for one of them.'

'Wow. Is that how you met Shravan?' Dhruv asked. 'A writer of psychological thrillers and a psychiatrist — a match made in mind-heaven.'

'No, that's not how we met,' Shravan said.

Dhruv looked from one to the other of us. 'Where, then?'

'We've another interest in common,' Shravan said.

It's true that we both have a deep interest in the way the human brain ticks, but that's not the only thing we have in common. From Dhruv's expression, it looked like he couldn't imagine us having anything at all in common. Just because our skin tones didn't match. As if people had to be the same colour to understand one another. In fact, we'd met on a hiking trip to Snowdon. Four days in the unpredictable Welsh weather, navigating boggy trails. Shared dinners by firelight. They were some of the best days of my life, though I didn't know it then. I was suffering, you see.

'We both love hiking,' I said. 'That's where we met, on a trip to Wales.'

'Oh, of course,' Dhruv said, 'I remember now. You were always going off on some walk or other, weren't you, Shravan?'

'A hike, Dhruv,' Shravan said.

'Hike?' Dhruv snorted. 'That's what you call it?'

I was relieved to see that we were almost at the cabin. Shravan had warned me that his friends might close ranks against me. He'd said they'd 'been there before', by which I suppose he meant Nancy's ex. They would see it as nothing but lust, and it would run its course before long. They couldn't have been further from the truth.

Tealights lined the foyer, their little flames flickering in the breeze. Lit candles among all this wood wasn't safe. I picked one up and blew it out.

'Must have been Leela,' Dhruv said, snuffing out another one. 'It's the tradition to light a lamp, I suppose she didn't think—' He yelped mid-sentence, jerking his hand back. Hot wax had splattered over his fingers.

Shravan followed behind us, picking up the candles as he went.

Bhoo appeared in the doorway.

'Don't you know not to put candles in a wood cabin?' Dhruv said.

'Hello to you too,' Bhoo retorted. 'Of course I do, but try telling your wife that.'

Inside, Leela was kneeling on the floor, holding a packet containing a white powder which she spilled in a pattern across the floor. Her welcoming smile faltered when she saw the tealights in Shravan's hands. 'What did you do that for?'

'Candles in a wood cabin are dangerous, you know,' he said.

Leela looked a little sheepish. 'That's what Bhoo said, but I so wanted everyone to see them as they arrived.'

Fascinated, I watched her design take shape, an elaborate pattern of loops and swirls. 'Gosh, that's beautiful.'

'Thanks,' Leela said, brushing a stray lock of hair from her eyes with the back of her hand. 'This one's quite simple. We usually do this outside, and then the designs are more elaborate. We use different colours then, too.'

'*Rangoli*, right?' I asked, eager to show off my knowledge.

'We call it *kolam*, but, yes, it's the same sort of thing,' Leela said. Her smile was dazzling. 'This is how we learn maths. Counting,' she added, placing a neat dot in the centre, 'and symmetry,' as her fingers moved deftly, looping around the dot into a swirl. When she finished, the design was perfectly balanced, its geometry so precise, it looked almost printed.

The dolls, now draped in fairy lights, looked almost magical. The dimples on their cheeks twinkled with every blink of the lights, and their smiles dazzled. There was a poise to them — a stillness that wasn't quite still. The longer I looked, the more it felt like they had something to say — like they were holding a secret they wanted to share.

'Sit,' she said, gesturing to the mats laid out around the edge of the room.

Shravan had shown me the correct way to sit — cross-legged, with the feet tucked under the body. 'The gods aren't supposed to see our feet, especially the soles.'

I'd been practising in secret, but it was still agony; after a few minutes my ankles started to hurt, and my legs went numb. To get out of it, I asked Leela if there was anything I could do.

'Um, you could lay out the flowers if you like, just two or three on each step. Start with the gods, up at the top.'

Gratefully, I reached for the bag containing the flowers Leela had collected. I began with Maa Kaali, the Goddess of Death. The dahlias were past their best, but they would do. I placed one of these between two of Kaali's four arms, the one holding up a severed head, and the one whose hand held a pot to catch the blood.

From the way her head tilted to the side when I picked them, I gathered that Leela wasn't keen on yellow flowers, not for Kaali — too cheerful or something — so I picked out white ones to match Kaali's garland of skulls. Her red-rimmed eyes leered at me when I drew close, and her protruding tongue was mocking, as if she could sense how nervous she made me. I averted my eyes from the skirt made of severed limbs. As beautiful as she was, I was glad to move away from the Goddess of Death and on to the next deity.

'Leela, did you move the dolls?' Bhoo asked suddenly. 'The Barbie looks different.'

Guiltily, I dropped the flower I'd been holding, before I realised I hadn't yet reached the Barbie. Not me, then.

'No, of course not,' Leela said. 'We're not supposed to touch the dolls once they've been set up. I told you that yesterday.'

My gaze shifted to the Barbie. At first, I couldn't see anything wrong with the miniature shopping scene — the shelves with their tiny packets of breakfast cereals, the cartons of milk and juice. The figure of Barbie pushing a shopping trolley and holding a tote bag looked just the same. But wait. The tote was wide open, and her other arm . . . Surely not? Little Barbie had her other hand at the shelf, and from the way it was positioned, it looked just like she was swiping items from it into the bag.

Her head had definitely been turned back, looking behind her as if on the lookout.

Leela hurried across. The rest of us gathered around her. 'It looks like . . . like she is *stealing*.' Someone gasped from behind. Tea candles clattered and rolled on the floor.

CHAPTER TEN

Day Two: Smitha

'Who's for a picnic?' Livi said brightly, like we were in an Enid Blyton novel and the Barbie business was just a prank. Poor girl, she was trying her best to cheer everyone up, as if slapping on a smiley face would cover the gaping cracks.

We were all sitting around in the living room, trying to get our heads around the mystery of who had tampered with the Barbie doll scene. We tried to laugh it off, pretend it never happened. All except Leela, who was still muttering darkly about ill omens and bad luck.

Jay clapped his hands. 'Great idea!'

I glared at him. If I'd made the suggestion, he'd have told me not to be so stupid. *A picnic in Scotland? In autumn? Do you want me to catch a cold and die of pneumonia?* Now that a shiny new girl had suggested it, he was all teeth and thrill.

Livi, who'd been sitting in Shravan's lap, sprang to her feet. 'Come on, then! We'll pack some sandwiches — and wine, of course. I know just the spot. Oh, and tomorrow, we're going white-water rafting. They only offer it on Saturdays and

Wednesdays, and since we weren't here on Wednesday, I've booked us in for tomorrow.'

I was the only one who didn't show any enthusiasm. She was practically a stranger, yet all she needed to do was cock her head and flash a smile and they all followed her like a flock of sheep. 'I don't swim. Neither do they,' I said, pointing at Jay and Dhruv, who were sprawled on the couch, hands behind their heads and their legs stretched out.

Livi laughed. 'You don't have to go in. And they'll give you a life jacket.'

That cut on my arm hasn't healed yet, and I don't want to be shark food. I had seen it in documentaries — they can smell blood from miles away. 'The sea is too cold to go out on a boat.'

'Oh come on, Smitha, don't be a spoilsport,' Jay said. 'Anyway, the rafting isn't in the sea. It's in the River Awe,' he said, as if he'd suddenly become an expert in all things rafting. My dear husband, who couldn't tell between a catamaran and a boat! 'Why don't you go and help Livi get everything ready for the picnic?'

He always did that. Pushed me around like I was some kind of unpaid intern in the business of making his life easier. 'Oh, don't worry, Smitha will clean that up, won't you, Smitha?' Or, 'Smitha cooks a mean fish curry, she won't mind making a batch for you. Right, Smitha?' Actually, I did mind. I minded very much. But I was just a housewife, what else would I be doing?

Scowling, I pushed myself off the sofa and trudged towards the kitchen.

'Oh, and make some of your chilli dip,' my dear husband called out after me. 'It'll go well with the sandwiches.' I've heard some chillies are poisonous. Who knew? I might just get lucky.

* * *

'I think we'll need two loaves,' I said, trimming the crust off a slice of bread. Jay was like a small child: his sandwiches had to be soft and made with plenty of butter. Not forgetting the chilli dip.

Livi was slicing cucumbers. 'Twelve is a lot of mouths to feed. I'm so glad you're here to help.' She flashed that dazzling smile of hers, the one that made you feel seen, important.

Maya and Bhoo hadn't offered to help, I noticed. Shravan had, but he was the boyfriend, and that didn't count. Just wait until they were married. *If* they married, I corrected myself. 'No problem,' I said. 'I'm happy to help.' I meant it this time, but somehow it didn't seem to come out right.

I cleared my throat. 'It's a beautiful house.'

She beamed. 'Isn't it?'

'I wish I had a house like this.'

She laughed. 'What? Out in the middle of nowhere?'

I shrugged. 'Jay says you own a whole island not far from here.'

'More like a rock in the ocean,' she said with a laugh. 'And it's not mine, it's my stepdad's.' For a moment she looked as if she were about to cry. 'How old did you say your daughter was?'

'I didn't,' I said drily. 'Veena's six.' Honestly, what was with everyone? The moment they hear you're a mother, it's like a switch flips — suddenly they assume that you must be bursting to talk about your baby. Like our vocabulary starts and ends with nappy changes and school lunches. As if without them, we're just . . . empty.

'Aww. Six is such a nice age.'

No, it's not. There's nothing good about six. That's when they go to school and start comparing notes with their friends. You have an iPad, I must have one, *check*. You have an Xbox, and I have a Nintendo. *Good*. Oh, you have a puppy, aww. *I need a pet*. Veena wanted a bloody mini pig, no less. As if the house didn't smell bad enough already. But I couldn't tell this woman any of that, she wouldn't have had the faintest idea about what being six involves. Instead, I said, 'Yes, she is cute.' That much was true, anyway — Veena could be very cute when it suited her. And when she slept.

'Do you miss her?' Livi asked.

'No!' Whoops. I didn't mean to sound so emphatic. Livi laughed, but she nodded as if she understood. I found myself warming to her more and more.

'Who do you think might have moved the Barbie?' I asked, keen to change the subject. 'I mean, it couldn't have been an accident, could it?'

Livi shrugged. 'Maybe Leela nudged it when she was drawing that beautiful pattern on the floor.' Livi was now busy packing the mini snacks — cheeses, nuts, crackers and slices of ham — and wrapping them in cling film.

We Indians don't eat ham.

My eyes on the ham, I said, 'But Barbie's hand had definitely been moved. It was deliberately positioned as though it was swiping things off the shelf. That couldn't have been accidental, surely?'

Livi turned to face me. 'You're right. It did look staged. So, do you think someone did it, like, deliberately?'

'I don't *think* so. I *know* they did.' My eyes met hers, which were an unusual colour, not blue as you might expect, but a deep peacock green.

She swallowed. 'You know?'

'Yes. Something like this has happened before. But it was a good few years ago now,' I said. 'It was Nancy's ex, John, who did it. A real cunning fox that John was. He even had me fooled, and let me tell you, I don't fool easily.'

Livi looked confused. 'You mean with dolls?'

I shook my head. 'No. No. Not dolls,' I said. 'It was anonymous emails. Videos and photos. This time, it's the dolls. But it's the same sort of thing.' Livi stared at me as though she didn't understand. 'What I meant was, the purpose of both is the same. The photos and videos were sent to reveal secrets about us. Same with the dolls now. Dirty and weird secrets among us friends. John is Nancy's ex. Nancy married him in too much of a hurry, after a whirlwind three-month romance. She didn't even meet the family until the wedding, and even then, it was only his mother. His father had left them, and his sister was overseas. That's what he said, anyway, and we had no reason not to believe him. He was charming. He knew just how to manipulate us. You know what I mean?'

'Where's John now? What happened to him?'

'We don't know where he is,' I said. 'They divorced after six months, and we never saw him again. It wasn't even a proper divorce, more like an annulment, as if the marriage never happened. I heard he left Stirling and went back to London. The anonymous emails started around the time he came into our lives. Maya was the second victim.' I stopped speaking, suddenly wondering if it was wise to share this so soon. After all, I barely knew this woman. What if she asked about the first victim? What would I tell her then?

'Maya?' she asked. 'Sorry. Perhaps you'd rather not say.'

I didn't mind. I had never liked Maya anyway, and Livi was, well, nice. And she was rich, and generous. 'No, you're part of the group now. You ought to know.'

'Well, if you're sure,' Livi said.

'She used to shoplift,' I said, lowering my voice though there was nobody else in the kitchen. 'We had no idea. I mean, it's not like she was short of money. Her parents are wealthy businesspeople, and I mean *rich* — Swiss bank account and private jet kind of rich. They regularly send her money from India so she doesn't have to work like the rest of us.' Even after all these years, I found it hard to believe. Back then, it was she who funded us all, throwing money around like spare change. If I hadn't seen it for myself, I would never have believed it.

'You mean like Kleptomania?'

'Is that what it is called?'

She nods, 'It's like a compulsion. People with the condition can't help it. An itch that just needs to be scratched.'

'Umm . . . that was her excuse at least.'

'What happened then?' Snacks forgotten, Livi gazed at me avidly.

'Like I said, Maya had this habit of shoplifting. The rest of us knew nothing about it — at least Jay and I didn't. Then the videos started coming, showing her in action. Taking small things like cosmetics, groceries, and even a cigarette lighter. She didn't even smoke.'

When the Barbie was moved, I'd thought Maya would lose it and scream the house down. But she hadn't. Instead, she'd laughed — this high-pitched, almost rehearsed laugh, like she was in on some elaborate joke I hadn't been briefed about. She didn't even demand to know who'd done it. No accusations, no drama, just a casual, 'Oh, that's funny.' For a moment I wondered if it was she who'd moved the doll. Was this one of her twisted attention-grabbing dramas? But what could I say when everyone was like, *Haha, what a joke. No one's hurt. No one's killed. How funny.* I didn't find it funny. Not in the slightest.

'Do you think that's what the Barbie was meant to show? Maya, shoplifting?'

As my gaze met Livi's, a silent understanding transpired. 'I'm certain of it.'

CHAPTER ELEVEN

Day Two: Nancy

We'd been walking for a good twenty minutes. We'd passed the flower patch ages ago, and the picnic bags were beginning to get heavy. But Livi had insisted we go on foot. 'It's a picnic,' she'd said, as if that meant tramping for miles loaded down with half the contents of the house.

So, we pushed on, through brambles and ferns, wading through knee-deep grass. The trees were taller here, crowded together, and little light penetrated the dense canopy of the evergreens. We trudged on in silence, amid the musty smell of rotting leaves and dead insects.

The handles of the bag I was carrying dug into my hands and it banged annoyingly against my legs. I wished I had accepted Aswin's offer to carry mine. I had refused after hearing Smitha prompting him. 'Go help her. This is your chance to impress.' Her matchmaking skills sucked.

He was probably keeping close to me so as to avoid her disdainful scowl. The way she was forcing it, it was a wonder she hadn't put Aswin off me altogether.

Poor Aswin had to keep breaking into a jog to keep up with me. His repeated offers of help irritated me so much that I finally snapped, 'Look, I'm fine. All right?'

To my relief, he fell back. Then I regretted being so sharp with him when I saw him carrying Smitha's bag. Smitha, with that whiny, needy demeanour that always seemed to get her what she wanted. She must have said something like, *If you can't charm a lonely single woman, at least make yourself useful.* And naturally, he obliged. Anything to avoid that lashing tongue of hers.

Listen to me, I thought. *I'm turning into my mother, nose always in other people's business — and then telling everyone about it.* Yet somehow it never spoiled her relationships. One day, it would be her sister she insulted, the next day Aunty Radha. But by day three, they'd all be best of friends again. I'd never understood how she managed it.

Relationships aren't like that nowadays. Now you have to handle people like fragile paper dolls. The smallest of comments, like, 'Oh, I don't think that's a good idea,' can be the death of a relationship. I can't afford that. I came too close to being an outcast after John, and the mess that followed. They blamed me. I blamed myself. None of them wanted me here. Another tear in the tattered fabric of our friendship and I'd be alone for the rest of my days.

Smitha's voice broke into my thoughts.

'Livi owns an island, you know. She's practically a princess! Do you think that castle could be theirs?'

'What?' I hadn't even noticed the castle rising ahead of us on the horizon. It was probably just an old ruin. Typical Smitha, always in the know, making up some story to impress.

'Yes! And I bet you don't know her last name, do you? It's MacDougall, and the castle belonged to them. I googled it.'

It wasn't, as a matter of fact. The name was on the post-box outside the house. Clear as day.

'Johnstone. Her full name is Olivia Johnstone,' I said smugly.

Smitha, being Smitha, wasn't abashed. 'Well, maybe they're distant cousins.' Oh, please. How distant? Fourth cousin, twice removed, via a sheep farmer and a shared fondness for tartan? Since when was Smitha an expert on Livi's family tree? If she traced it back far enough, I'm sure we'd all be cousins. After all, we're all descended from Adam and Eve. The Bible says so!

My gaze drifted to the lovebirds, walking side by side with the picnic bag swinging between them. They were laughing, carefree, as though they were the only two people in the world. And as if they knew I was watching, their lips brushed — a quick peck. Sickening.

I turned my attention to the ruins up ahead. It was hardly a castle, just a crumbling heap of rocks, perched on a cliff and smothered in ivy.

I laughed. 'Call that a castle?'

'Of course,' Smitha said importantly. 'Dunollie Castle. It's twelfth century, you know.' Her face lit up, like she'd mentally whisked herself away to medieval Scotland — strolling among clans, rubbing shoulders and sharing laughs, as though she belonged there.

I was about to retort and break the reverie when Livi called out, 'Here we are! The perfect spot for a picnic.' The 'perfect spot' turned out to be a clearing amid the trees, on a mound adjacent to the ruins with a few scattered rocks lying about that I supposed were intended for seats. From the trees the cawing of rooks — or were they crows? — only added to the crowding of the surroundings.

The men began moving rocks around, while the women busied themselves with the food.

Nauseated by this scene of domestic bliss, I wandered off to sit beneath a giant sequoia tree. Suddenly weary, I leaned back against the trunk and closed my eyes.

'Are you okay?'

Shravan sounded concerned. His fresh, clean scent filled my nose, his voice warm and close to my ear. I wanted to reach out, to touch him — just lightly, just to be sure he was really there. But I kept my eyes closed. 'What do you care?'

'I do care, Nancy,' he said quietly.

I opened my eyes.

'I'm sorry I was rude yesterday,' he said miserably. 'I don't want us to fight.'

I picked up a fallen twig and began tracing patterns in the dirt. 'I shouldn't have come. It was too soon, and I didn't expect—'

'It was just . . . Livi was so keen to meet everyone. She kept asking if I was hiding her from you all. I didn't have much choice.'

'Well, it's nice for us all to be together again after so long,' I said.

I didn't tell him that I almost didn't come. For weeks, I didn't reply. Watched the messages scroll past like trains I had no intention of boarding. I wondered if Shravan knew I was even in the WhatsApp group. He most likely thought I'd done the 'quiet quitting' thing. But leaving felt so final, like slamming a door on the past. On us. So I stayed, lurking. And when the invite came, I viewed the plans, saw the tickets being booked.

In the end, I posted my acceptance, part of me wanting to believe that the door wasn't locked. That something could be salvaged. Or perhaps it was just curiosity. Boredom. Stubbornness. Take your pick.

'It is, isn't it? Anyway, I'm glad you decided to come. I was afraid Maya or Bhoo would have had to drag you here.'

'No, I wanted to come,' I said. Actually, one of the reasons I came was to spite Maya and Bhoo. *You don't have to come if you're not up to it,* Maya had said, Bhoo adding, *We'll understand.* They were hoping I'd bow out. Well, I wasn't going to give them the satisfaction.

'Well, that's great.' But Shravan was already looking distracted. So much for my chance to reconnect. So much for my real reason for coming.

To my horror, I saw Livi running towards us. 'Sorted?' she said, flinging herself into his arms. It hurt to watch them together — her fitting herself to him like a lid on a jar.

Shravan whispered something into Livi's ear. So that was it. The apology, the concern. It was all down to her. My jaw ached from the fake smile I had somehow managed to summon. I couldn't let her see me bleed, how deeply her presence wounded me.

Be strong, Nance. Be strong.

'Not quite sorted,' I said. They shared a glance. 'The picnic, I mean.'

She coughed. 'You guys must be hungry,' she said innocently.

'Ravenous,' I said drily. 'I am *so* looking forward to it.'

It was going to be a delicious meal.

* * *

'This is so good,' Laxman said, devouring a chicken wrap dipped in sweet chilli sauce. 'Bhoo could never cook like this.'

What was it with these men? Smitha could cook up a storm, but according to Jay, she'd never be as good as Bhoo. And Lax always insisted that Bhoo couldn't cook. Why did they always point to a talent their women lacked, never what they had? Why did love, for them, always come with a balancing scale?

'Do you cook, Laxman?' Livi asked.

'What, me? No.' Laxman looked quite shocked at the thought.

A group of gulls had flown in from somewhere and were eyeing our food. One of them, bolder than the rest, had landed on the tablecloth. Bala tried to shoo it away, but it hopped to one side and attempted to grab a piece of bread. An open bottle of Stella Artois sat in front of Bala — his third already. Bala had a complicated relationship with alcohol. He'd told us all he was taking it easy, but it didn't look like that to me; he was downing it like a teenager. Every swipe of his arm threatened to send the bottle toppling over.

Maya shot him a disapproving glance, grabbed a piece of bread, and tossed it onto the ground. The bird hopped over and snatched it up with a triumphant air.

'I haven't told you what's so special about this place, have I?' Livi said.

'It certainly has a stunning view,' Shravan said, as if he were a schoolkid answering a difficult question. It might have been stunning without the trees in front of it.

She pointed to a far-off speck in the distant ocean. 'See that island?' We all squinted dutifully.

The 'island' was really just two mounds of rock — one smaller, like a head, the other larger and rounded with a narrow isthmus connecting them. Together, it looked like a turtle. 'Is that yours?' I asked.

'I wish.' With a pointed look at Shravan, she added, 'Someone's given you a wrong impression about me. I drive a Passat.'

'You own that castle, though, don't you?' I asked.

'And you definitely own the manor house,' Smitha said, 'and it's as big as a castle.'

'That's my stepdad's,' Livi said. 'No, what we own is much more precious than a piece of land. It's our memories. My brother and I spent every summer on that island, among the puffins and the seabirds.'

'Aren't there any buildings on it?' Laxman asked. 'No houses or anything? If this were India, that rock would have been turned into plots and sold at a premium. An island with ocean views and seals? A veritable treasure trove. What a waste.'

'Not everything is about money,' Livi said gently. 'Besides, it's really small. *And* it's haunted.'

Leela, who had been sitting with her back to the island, turned round. 'Haunted?'

'I was only joking,' Livi said with a laugh. 'There are all sorts of tales about it, but no one really believes them.'

73

'Oh, I love stories like that. Do tell,' Leela cooed. She dropped the fork she had been using to feed Dhruv with pieces of food. He looked relieved.

'Well,' Livi began, 'once, there was a Celtic warrior called Murdoch who fell in love with a poor girl from the local village named Mhairi. Since Murdoch came from the warrior class and Mhairi was poor, everyone was against their liaison. She was even accused of being a whore. Those were different times, of course.'

'And?' Smitha said. 'What happened? Did they elope?'

'If they had, they might have lived happily ever after, and the island wouldn't be haunted.'

'No one lives happily ever after,' Smitha said. 'Give them two years and they'll be totally fed up with each other. Their love would no longer be worthy of poems. They'd probably end up depressed. Or worse, killing each other and becoming a historic crime.' Everyone chuckled.

'So, what did happen?' Leela said, with an impatient glance at Smitha.

'The village folks proposed a test,' Livi continued, 'to prove Mhairi's virginity. She had very long hair. They decided to tie her by her hair to a rock on the island. If it held firm, it showed that she was indeed a virgin, but she would be drowned in the rising tide. If the hair came loose, she could get away and save herself—'

'But she would be proven guilty,' Leela said.

'Yes. And the mob would set her on fire,' Livi said.

'And either way, she'd die. Clever,' Leela added. 'So, what happened?'

'Murdoch made a brave attempt to save her, but he was swept away by the current. Mhairi drowned, thereby revealing herself to be chaste. They died for love.'

'Like Romeo and Juliet,' Smitha said.

'Like Ambika Pati and Amaravati,' Leela said nostalgically, gazing out towards the island. Then, she suddenly gasped. 'That's not a turtle.'

'What?' Smitha asked.

Leela's voice grew frantic, the words tumbling out in a rush. 'The shape of the island. That's not a turtle. It's Mhairi, face down in the ocean, her feet bound where they were tied. I can see her. It's a woman.'

'Oh, shut up, Leela,' Dhruv said.

But Livi hadn't finished. 'According to legend, she howls with the wind every night. They say that's the reason why the storms around here are so fierce. Some even say she haunts the island, seeking revenge on the people who condemned her to death.'

The moment she stopped speaking, a wind sprang up, catching up the debris from our picnic and sending it blowing into the trees. It whistled and shrieked just like a woman. Was it a cry of love for her lost lover, or was she howling for justice? A chill ran through me that had nothing to do with the wind. With a deafening screech, the seagulls rose as one.

Amid the noise, I heard a thud and the faint sound of hurried footsteps behind me. Leela was a fallen log on the ground, her pupils stirring under her closed eyelids.

Dhruv cried out, 'Leela!'

CHAPTER TWELVE

Day Two: Livi

White. The colour of purity, often associated with the virgin deity. It was today's Navaratri colour. In fact, my wardrobe consisted of little but white, apart from a few black dresses. There was nothing wrong with colour, but too much choice could be overwhelming. In the end, I settled on a white kaftan embroidered with lace. According to Etsy, the kaftan originated in Asia, so it seemed fitting. With dangling earrings made of feathers in my ears, I was ready.

When we arrived at the cabin, Leela and the others were already there. I'd been worried about her after the fainting fit, but Dhruv said that wasn't unusual. 'She's soft-hearted,' he'd said, like it was a compliment. 'And a little superstitious. She can't bear to hear horror stories.' He'd looked at me then, accusation in his eyes, as if this was all my fault, as if Leela hadn't asked about the myth, almost pleaded. But with some help and a slap of water, she'd woken up fine — no lasting damage, only embarrassment. After resting the afternoon, she was now renewed.

They were gathered around Maya, who was sobbing violently, her face in her hands. I glanced at Shravan, but he was staring at Nancy. And she did look amazing. The skin of her midriff was bare beneath her red blouse, and her stomach was flat. With her graceful movements, and the dahlia tucked in her black curls, along with the three strands of pearls around her long neck, Nancy looked like a goddess. The kaftan I'd been so proud of suddenly looked rather pathetic.

'Oh, is Maya upset?' Shravan asked.

'That's rather obvious,' I replied, and hated the way I sounded. Like a jealous girlfriend.

'Sorry, I was distracted,' Shravan said. Again, that was obvious, but this time I kept it to myself.

'So what's upset her?' Shravan asked.

No one answered. As soon as we walked in, the little party broke up. Bhoo hurried to fetch some water, while Maya proceeded to blow her nose loudly.

'What happened?' I whispered to Leela.

In reply, she gestured towards the dolls.

The Barbie seemed to be back in place, no longer shoplifting. That was a good sign, right? Leela pointed to the second step. 'In the middle,' she hissed.

I saw a small glass, filled with a honey-coloured liquid. Inside was the tiny figure of a man. I looked closer. It appeared to be a football player, taken away from the rest of his team. I leaned forward for a closer look, and a distinct smell of alcohol wafted up from the glass. I nudged Shravan. 'What's it supposed to mean?'

'It's Maya's husband, Bala,' Shravan replied. 'He used to play football until he got injured. I think it's him.'

I saw that the village scene had been cleared away, pushed unceremoniously to one side to make room for the glass and its contents. The wedding group and the school gate scene on either side were untouched, as were the rest of the figures.

'Bala drinks too much,' Smitha explained. 'He's even been in rehab. He sobers up for a while and then slips. Didn't you notice the way he was necking it at the picnic?'

So that was why Maya was in tears. This evening's scene, and the one with the kleptomaniac Barbie, were obviously aimed at her. Someone must hate her. I wondered what she'd done to offend someone like that.

After a while, we all dispersed, leaving Leela putting her dolls in order and muttering darkly about disrespecting tradition. She warned us, again, about how using the dolls as if they were toys would bring bad luck on us all. Something terrible was bound to happen.

As night began to fall, the autumn wind gathered strength, hurling leaves and other pieces of debris in its wake. The distant cry of a gull was like a memory of better times. Mum had always called this place our sanctuary. Now, the forces of darkness had entered, and it was all my fault. Oh, why had I invited these people here?

Lost in thought, I almost walked into Maya and Nancy. Half hidden under a tree, they were standing together, their backs turned to me. As I drew nearer, I heard Nancy mention Shravan's name, so I hid behind a tree to listen.

Maya had Nancy by the shoulders and was shaking her. 'What is it you want, exactly?'

Nancy answered in a low voice. 'You know what I want.'

'Shravan?' Maya's voice was edged with pain.

I moved slightly, in order to hear better, and stepped on a twig.

Hearing it snap, Maya called out, 'Hello?'

Cursing myself for my clumsiness, I stepped forward and greeted them with a cheery, 'Hi! Are you lost?'

CHAPTER THIRTEEN

Day Two: Nancy

The rays from the slowly sinking sun cast purple and orange streaks across the sky like the brushstrokes of a painter gone mad. The sun's departure brought a distinct chill. In my haste to follow Maya, I had forgotten my jacket, and now I regretted it.

Maya was only just ahead of me — I could see her silhouette as she weaved through the dark — and I slowed down to give her time to compose herself. I knew what would happen if I crowded her. The last time I did that, she'd slapped me across the face.

'What?' she snapped when I caught up with her.

'I'm sorry about what happened,' I said. 'It must be awful for you.'

'Yeah,' she said. 'It is. What did I ever do? Why target me like this? And poor Bala. It's not his fault. He's been through so much. First his football career. That stupid injury put paid to that. Then all the drama around my . . . my issue. He lost his mother last month. Can't we cut him some slack?' I didn't know what to say. This was cruel.

'And me. It's ages since I nicked anything. It took years of therapy, but I'm better now. It's not fair,' she sobbed. 'I can't even defend myself. My memory . . .' She was close to tears. 'My memory is not good. Not what it used to be. There are gaps.'

'What do you mean?'

'It's odd.' Now tears were properly streaming down her face. 'Sometimes I forget dates — Bala's birthday, our wedding anniversary. I lose chunks of time. I don't remember what I did the previous night. I'll walk into a room and forget why I'm there. It's . . .' She whimpered. 'It's like I have dementia or something.'

Could this be a side effect? My mind raced, trying to remember the fine print. Shravan had said it was safe, and I had no reason not to believe him. After everything he'd done. Everything we'd done. But what if . . . what if he was wrong?

A dead leaf drifted down from the tree above and landed in Maya's hair. Without thinking, I reached out to pick it off.

She stepped back. 'Don't touch me.'

'You have something . . .' I pointed at her hair.

She patted her head. 'Is it gone?'

'Let me.'

I reached out again, slower this time, and plucked the leaf from her matted hair. 'Listen, whoever it is—'

'Yes, who? Who do *you* think it is?'

I had my suspicions, but I didn't want to voice them until I was certain.

I stood looking at Maya, not knowing what to say. She was a sorry sight. Her fluffy hair was now matted, and hung in damp strands over her face. Her nose was red, her cheeks smeared with mascara and dirt. She was nothing like the stylish — if pink — woman who'd stepped off the train yesterday. And the worst part? She didn't even seem to care. Maya always cared about how she looked, how she walked, how she presented herself. She always put on a performance. All that was gone.

'You really don't know?' She gave a hollow laugh.

A chill ran through me. That laugh. So shrill it still echoed in my mind. The angry shouts, the harsh accusations, the glint of the knife . . . Yes, the knife. I rubbed the scar on my wrist.

'I think you do know,' she said, regarding me steadily. 'Who else would want to destroy me?'

'Maya—'

'It's John, isn't it? He's back,' she said, glancing around involuntarily.

'No, Maya. Not John.'

'Why not?' Suddenly, Maya turned on me. 'Why are you here anyway, Nancy? None of us wanted you to come.'

This was unexpected. 'What do you mean?'

'You heard me. The invite. It wasn't meant for you at all. Shravan didn't realise you were still in the group. We all thought you'd left.' There it was. 'And when you said count me in, he panicked. Why did you turn up like this, like nothing happened? Like your husband didn't destroy our lives—'

'Ex-husband,' I corrected.

She ignored me. 'I called you. I texted you. Bhoo did too.'

I'd been at my swimming lesson when the urge to go hit me. The thought of all of them all together, laughing and joking without me — probably about me — made me grind my teeth in rage. Before I could talk myself out of it, I'd sent the message: *Count me in.* Then I tossed my phone in the locker and dived into the pool. When I came back, there were eleven missed calls — eight from Maya, three from Bhoo. Messages too: *Hey, call me. Please don't feel you have to come,* which only served to strengthen my resolve. I was going. *I wouldn't miss it for the world,* I'd replied.

'What do you want?' she said.

Beneath her grasp, my shoulders slumped. 'You know what I want.'

'It's Shravan, isn't it?'

We heard a twig snap.

CHAPTER FOURTEEN

Day Three: Smitha

The lights in the open-plan kitchen were all controlled by a single switch —either all on or all off. Now, they were on. The harsh glare brought out everyone's defects pitilessly — lines on their faces a little deeper, their bald patches that much brighter, the shadows under their eyes darker.

Not much had changed in the last seven years. There was a bit of silver in the hair and some added weight, but otherwise, things were much the same. The men were still clustered like overgrown schoolboys, indulging in their bro talk and swapping stupid jokes. Maya, goddess forbid she touch a spatula, continued to treat the kitchen like it carried a contagion. No change there. And Bhoo — well, doctors don't eat, apparently. So there I was, slaving away at the stove, cooking for twelve.

My 'I don't know how the Aga works' lasted about half a day, until Jay called me out. 'It's not rocket science — just open YouTube and you'll find a dozen videos.' Then he added, 'What's for lunch?'

'Why don't you order something?' I said, glaring at him. 'How about a tasty pizza?' But after so many years of marriage,

Jay had become glare-proof. It just bounced off him like he was Teflon-coated or something.

'We can't order all our meals. Not for ten days. It's far too expensive,' Laxman said. So, why didn't he cook? Maybe he could ask his dear wife. She'd probably poison him, and he wouldn't have to count the pennies anymore. 'We've got plenty of stuff — rice, lentils, flour.' He counted them off on his fingers.

'Dhal and rice should be easy enough,' Jay said. Easy for him to say. My fingers itched to grab him by the throat and throttle him.

'But what about Livi?' Leela asked. 'What does she eat?'

'Oh, she loves Indian food. Lentils are her favourite,' Shravan said.

Here I was, standing at the stove in front of a pot taller than me. So tall that I had to get onto a bathroom stool just to stir it. The pot was bubbling away, as I skimmed off the scum that always appeared at the top when you cooked lentils, and poured it into the sink.

Secrets were like scum — no matter how much you stirred, they always found their way to the surface. My thoughts drifted to Maya, and the secrets she'd worked so hard to hide. Well, they had resurfaced, and how. Poor thing, her air of superiority had been badly dented. I was half expecting her to vanish in shame, but no. There she was, strutting back in like nothing had happened, chin raised, eyes daring any one of us to say a word. If it had been me, I'd have hidden under a rock or at least booked the next train out. But not Maya. She never did believe in guilt or consequences — only in appearances and survival.

'Pass me the tomatoes,' I said to Leela, holding out my hand for them. No way was I going to get off my stool and go to fetch them.

Leela brought them over in a bowl. 'Here. Anything else?'

I shook my head. 'Livi's cutting the onions. I'll sauté them separately.' I peered into the bowl — inside was a red mush that had once been firm, ripe tomatoes. Now, they were beaten to a pulp.

Leela was still hovering. 'What?' I asked, busy adding salt and more spice. There was no way I was cooking tomorrow. Let them starve.

'Can I ask you something?' she said.

I glanced at her briefly. She looked dead serious. No one was dead here — yet. Though judging by the poison-laced stares Maya was throwing at Nancy, that could change. 'Sure,' I said. 'Go ahead.'

'How did you all meet?'

The question was unexpected. I was certain she'd ask about yesterday — the figure drowning in alcohol, or the shoplifting Barbie. I wondered what had prompted her to ask.

Anyway, there wasn't much to it. 'Stirling University, 2014,' I said, spooning a bit of dhal into my palm and blowing on it, then tasting it. Not bad. 'That's when we came to the UK. Jay was doing his master's in chemistry. Dhruv, Shravan, Maya, Bala, and Bhoo were already there. Jay and I were the only couple.' I sniffed. Something was burning. 'Quick, pass me the oven gloves.' I wrestled the pot off the stove, narrowly averting disaster. 'Hmm. Where was I?'

'You and Jay were the only couple.' I had forgotten about Livi, chopping onions just behind us.

She always seemed to be listening. Slightly annoyed, I continued, 'Then Maya and Bala got together, though it was a good three years before they married. Nancy joined us the following year. Then we had three couples.' Dammit. I didn't mean to let that slip.

Jay was always warning me about my big mouth. 'One day, Smitha, you're going to land yourself in serious trouble with that mouth of yours.' Then he'd pause dramatically before delivering the punchline. 'And you'll drag me down with you.' And every time, I'd silently hope he was right. At least about him coming down with me.

'You mean Nancy and Shravan?' Leela asked. In the background, the chopping resumed, faster. I glanced at Livi. The onions were making her cry.

I turned back to the pot. How I missed the pressure cooker we had in India, with its blaring whistle that made you jump out of your skin. Seriously, pressure cookers should come with a warning: *Not to be used by pregnant women or those with weak hearts.* If timed just right, it could be useful. It could drown out an argument, for a start. When the noise of that whistle finally died down, neither party would remember what the row had been about in the first place.

The chopping ceased. 'All of you in a three-bed house?' Livi said.

So she knew part of it, at least. I wasn't sure how much Shravan had told her about his relationship with Nancy. 'Not all of us. Dhruv and Shravan had a place somewhere else, but they hardly ever went there.' Leela and I shared a glance. 'We had three great years, the eight of us. It was a blast. Every Friday we'd go out partying all night.'

Ah, those were the days. True, I did most of the cooking, and even then Maya was Miss Bossy Pants, but we had fun — the kind of fun you can only have in young adulthood before children and the mortgage arrive.

'Sounds fun. You met every week?' Livi asked.

'Week? Every day, more like. We practically lived together. Dhruv and Shravan only went to their place to sleep. Then Dhruv took a job in London and Shravan moved in with us.'

Thinking back, that was probably when Bala's drinking began to spiral. When Shravan moved in, citing 'space issues', Maya and Bala had conveniently shifted out. But even before that, Bala's fondness for alcohol wasn't exactly a secret. The slurred speech, the stumbling steps — they happened often. We just didn't realise how bad it was.

I sometimes wonder if it was all just an excuse. Was Maya trying to protect him? Distract us with her obsession with appearance while secretly enrolling him in rehabs around the world? But that wasn't what Bala needed. He didn't need coddling — he needed to face reality. In the end, it was the anonymous email that probably saved him.

Livi handed me the onions. 'Is that enough?'

'Plenty,' I said, setting the frying pan on the stove for the spices.

As the oil began to heat up, my thoughts drifted back to when Shravan moved in. He was supposed to be sleeping on the couch, but I often saw him coming out of Nancy's room in the morning. Nancy shared a room with Bhoo, who was often on a night shift. Shravan and Nancy's relationship developed into a roller-coaster of break-ups and tearful reunions, and I was cast as their designated go-between.

'Tell him, Smitha! His lecture on human behaviour is in one hour, and he's just sitting there,' Nancy would shout from the lounge.

'Tell her I don't need an assistant, Smitha. I'm perfectly capable of managing my own schedule.'

'What?' I'd ask, over the hum of the exhaust.

Both of them would answer, 'Never mind.' By the time I got back to the living room, she'd be sitting in his lap. *Living room*. Why did they call it that? As if we were supposed to be dead in the other rooms. In India we always called it the hall.

'It must have been awkward for Bhoo,' Livi said.

'How do you mean?' I asked.

'Being surrounded by couples,' she said.

I shrugged. 'It's all history now, anyway.' I wished she'd stop going on about the past. Who knows where that might lead us.

Shit. The onions were burning.

CHAPTER FIFTEEN

Day Three: Leela

I have always been afraid. It wasn't fear of the dark or other childish imaginings — no monsters under the bed. My phobia concerned the fear I saw reflected in the eyes of the people around me. Fear of me. The smallest thing could arouse their anxiety.

There was the incident with the squirrel. I found it one day sitting just outside the house, its cheeks full of the peanuts my stepmum had thrown out of the kitchen. Oh, the way its little teeth worked at the nut, its sharp little eyes glinting in the sun. I wanted to keep him so I could watch him whenever I wanted. 'Oh, look at the little squirrel. He'd make a lovely plush toy,' I exclaimed. No harm in that, right?

Wrong. It was as if all the joy had drained from the room. Everyone froze, wide-eyed, like I'd just suggested a massacre. It was just a comment — I thought they'd all smile. *I* was smiling. And yes, he *would* have made a cute plush toy. But no, it wasn't like I planned to skin him alive or anything. Their fear gave me power. The next day, I got a squirrel plush, wrapped and all. I hadn't even had to ask. Did they think I'd actually catch the real one and slice him up? After that, my stepmum never threw peanuts out again.

What I wanted to say was, a certain amount of fear is perfectly natural. We need it in order to survive. In the past, we had to be on the lookout for predators, now we're alert to the danger of thieves, or people wishing us harm. But my family's fear was excessive, unhealthy.

I'd lived far too long with fear. It was time I dealt with it. So I accompanied Dhruv on the white-water rafting trip. We were doomed to ten years of bad luck, but there was nothing I could do about it. I'd just have to let the goddess have her way.

As we made our way down the stone steps leading to the River Awe, I began to wonder if I'd made the right decision. A lone boat lay bottom up in the grass. I gazed at its rotting planks and peeling paint and put my hand on Dhruv's arm. What if it tipped over? What if there was a hole in the bottom?

'We're not going in that, are we?' I breathed.

'No, silly. That's a canoe. The rafts are a bit further on.'

I had no idea what a raft even looked like, just that it was some sort of boat. My family never went on holiday, not to the seaside nor to a river like this. On the rare occasions that Mum didn't have to work, and we were at home together, we spent our days holed up in the tiny house because she was exhausted from her many jobs.

Bhoo and Laxman had opted out, claiming they couldn't swim. I couldn't swim either, but that wasn't going to stop me. Smitha laughed when she heard Laxman wasn't coming. 'Of course. It would have meant forking out more money, wouldn't it? That's what Laxman is really scared of.'

After the incident with the dolls, no one was surprised that Maya and Bala had chosen to sit this one out. Other than Maya's brief appearance at lunch yesterday, where she ate quickly, glaring at the rest of us as if daring someone to say a word, they had been holed up in their room. She looked subdued, almost defeated.

It was another day of miserable weather. The river looked even greyer than the sky. It was flowing in murky sheets and white triangles, swirling and tumbling across the rocks with an almighty roar. I wondered how many people had perished on those rocks. How many bodies had the river swallowed, breaking them into fragments against its rocky bed and turning them into fish fodder?

Livi was checking her phone. 'Ah, they've already started the water release.' We were supposed to arrive before two, and it was now ten past.

Not only were the people in this country obsessed with the weather, they were also fanatics about time. It was totally foreign to me. Always looking at their watches or phones, how could they ever enjoy anything? Where was the thrill of the trip when it was always about the end?

But in this case, Livi had a point. At two, water from the dam just upriver was released in a rush. The rafting took place when that happened — at other times the water was still.

'There,' Shravan said, pointing to a large inflatable boat with red ropes along its sides. According to Livi, it had a capacity of eight, so all of us should fit in easily.

'Are you okay?' Smitha asked.

My thoughts had drifted back to the dolls, and I quietly raged at the fact of someone using things so sacred to make some petty point. It didn't help that Dhruv expected me to treat it as a joke. *Just you wait*, I thought. *You won't be laughing when the goddess starts taking her revenge.*

'Oh, I'm grand,' I said bleakly.

'You don't mind if I take Dhruv's place, do you? If I sit in the back I might get seasick.'

'Not at all,' I said. 'I think he's had enough of me by now.' I was only half joking. This holiday seemed to be driving a wedge between us, revealing aspects of ourselves the other wasn't yet ready to learn.

So, I was relieved when Smitha clambered in next to me. At least I wouldn't have to endure Dhruv's muttered criticisms for a while. The raft lurched ominously as each of us climbed tentatively in.

'Are you sure this is safe?' Jay said from the shore.

'Come on, Jay. The water isn't even knee deep. Besides, you're wearing a life vest,' Smitha mocked, though her own face was just as pale. She wasn't wrong — the water barely reached my knees.

'It gets deeper closer to the bridge, but don't worry, I've done this hundreds of times,' Livi shouted over the rush of the water. 'I'll be your cox. Just follow my instructions and avoid the rocks. Paddle when I say and lift it the rest of the time. And stay seated. It's important to keep the raft stable.'

Jay gave a stiff nod, clutching his paddle like it might save his life. His knuckles were white. If he'd had doubts before, now he looked like they'd trebled. Nancy and Dhruv were behind us, then Livi and Shravan, with poor Aswin having to drag Jay in at the rear.

We settled ourselves in our appointed seats. 'Ready?' Livi called out.

'Ready!'

'Okay. Here we go. Hold tight.' She removed the rope mooring the raft to the jetty, and we were off. The spray hit us full in the face, the waves sending us tossing about like rag dolls. My stomach lurched. But that was only for a moment. When we came back down, then up again, I was beginning to enjoy the ride.

When we were moving forward more steadily, Smitha turned around to face me. 'You must be feeling bad, huh?'

'What about?' I asked, knowing perfectly well what she meant.

'The dolls being moved, and all those old issues being stirred up.'

I wished she wouldn't keep needling me about it. Avoiding her gaze, I saw that the bridge was just a few metres away. Not long now.

But Smitha refused to leave the subject alone. 'I think it's Nancy,' she said.

Out of the corner of my eye, I saw a sudden movement. Before I knew what was happening, the raft gave a violent lurch, and for a moment I thought it might topple over. Dropping my paddle, I held on for dear life. Then, off to the side of the raft, I heard a splash. It was a moment or two before I realised that Smitha was no longer beside me.

CHAPTER SIXTEEN

Day Three: Nancy

The atmosphere was becoming unbearable. I almost preferred yesterday's stolen glances and hushed tones. After the first time the dolls were moved, Maya had dismissed the whole thing as a prank. She'd laughed as if she didn't care, though her eyes said otherwise.

But after the second time, it wasn't funny anymore. Whoever was behind it obviously had a personal grudge against Maya. The whispers grew louder, and the threats were no longer veiled. Forced to do something, I pulled Maya aside and pleaded with her not to let me down. Somehow, I managed to convince her that I had no reason to pull a stunt like that.

It wasn't my fault that Bala had a drinking problem. Maya had tried to hide it for a long time, sneaking him off to rehab with excuses like he was visiting his parents in India, or touring South Asia with a friend.

When Shravan had asked which friend, she'd said vaguely, 'Oh, his school friend. You wouldn't know him.' There was a time when he was supposed to be in Switzerland, and it turned out he'd been in a Swansea rehab clinic all along. According to the anonymous email, the only tour he'd ever been on was to different rehabs.

Anyway, Maya reluctantly agreed to come to today's gathering at the cabin. I couldn't let her suspicions fester like last time, when they had grown out of all proportion and it had ended badly. Very badly.

So Maya, Leela and I went to the wood cabin to visit the dolls, clad in bright red, the colour of the day. Mainly, I went to escape Livi and Shravan's whispered sweet nothings. Somehow, they were immune to the happenings, as if the moving dolls and the spilling secrets were but a minor inconvenience, a speck of dust in their la-la land of love and romance. It wouldn't have been so bad if they'd confined their smooching to their room, but they seemed to be omnipresent, spilling everywhere like a fat woman's bosoms. If I was heading to the bathroom, there they were, in the corridor. If I took refuge in the kitchen, there they were again, kissing and touching. Okay, so it was Livi's house, but there were other people there too. It's not like they didn't have a room — and theirs was the nicest, with an en-suite jacuzzi and a Victorian draped circular bed. But no, they had to flaunt it in front of the rest of us. Me, in particular.

After the rafting incident, the men made themselves scarce. Except for Shravan, of course, who clung to Livi like a limpet. Maya and Smitha mostly kept to their rooms. Who could blame them after what had happened? So, when Leela suggested we pay a visit to the dolls, I jumped at the chance. Maya came too, although Leela and I had to drag her out of her room.

Smitha was still shivering following her immersion in the river, though she'd long been dried. 'You go ahead. I'll be fine,' she said, her teeth chattering. The drama queen!

We walked to the cabin in silence. My thoughts returned to the raft. I still felt guilty. If I hadn't stood up, Smitha wouldn't have fallen from the raft. But it was her fault too. She shouldn't have gossiped while I was right behind her. Besides, something tripped me, I still felt it on my ankle — the bloom of a bruise, the sharp twist of something that caught me unawares. If I had fallen to the side instead of forward, it could have been me in the water. And on my side there were rocks, big bad boulders that would have cracked my head open like a nut. I was lucky, I thought, and corrected myself immediately. There was no luck in what was happening. Not for me.

Ten minutes after the three of us had arrived at the cabin, Livi and Shravan walked in, hand in hand.

Livi stared at Maya. 'Where did you get those?'

'Those' were a pack of funky-looking cards. Unlike typical playing cards, these bore pictures — angels, a sphinx, and other fantastical creatures swirling around against a background of stars and clouds. They reminded me of something, but I couldn't think what. At the centre was a wheel or compass that a wolf-like creature was carrying on its back, inscribed with what looked like hieroglyphs.

Maya looked like a shoplifter caught in the act. 'Oh, sorry. I didn't mean to take them. I was just looking for some sticky tape. The flower arch . . .' She gestured towards the arch above the dolls, which had come loose at one end. 'Sorry.' The posh, self-assured Maya had vanished, and she was again the girl from seven years ago, struggling under the weight of all the wrong decisions she'd made.

We had just managed to extract Maya from her self-imposed isolation, and now this. All our efforts, undone in a matter of minutes.

'I found them,' I said, stepping in front of Maya. 'I gave them to Maya to see. I thought they were just playing cards. I'll put them back.' It wasn't me, but Maya had suffered enough in the past couple of days. I wasn't about to let Livi treat her like a thief, Livi with her superior air and smug demeanour. As I took the cards from her, Maya gave my hand a grateful squeeze.

'No need to apologise,' Livi said. Actually, I hadn't, but never mind. 'It's not important, it's just that I hadn't seen them for a while. They belonged to my mother. She, er, used to consult them.'

Of course. Tarot cards. How did I not recognise them? A glance at the images instantly transported me to a place I never wanted to revisit — the days of my brief marriage to John. He'd had a deck of tarot cards, although his were fancier. He even did a few readings for me. Most of them were vague and could be interpreted in various ways, but occasionally they revealed something eerily close to the truth.

He once laid out a nine-card spread that he called a Celtic Cross. According to his reading, I was torturing myself with longing. At the time, he didn't know about Shravan, and I asked him what the outcome was. He drew the Death card. When he saw my reaction, he explained that it didn't literally mean death, but change, new beginnings. 'It's not what you think, Nancy. It never was . . .' His words still rang in my ears. And that was the last time he ever read for me. I wouldn't let him. He was getting too close.

'Nancy?' Maya said. I realised I had been staring at the cards as though mesmerised.

'Oh,' I said. 'It's fine.'

'What's fine?'

'Did I say fine? I meant it's late. Where are the men? And Bhoo?' The deck suddenly felt heavy in my hand.

'Ta-rot cards,' Leela read the name on the pack. 'Hmm.'

'It's pronounced *taro*, without the second "t". Take a look.' I thrust the cards at her as if they were burning my hand.

'What are they for?' Leela asked. 'Some kind of game?'

Livi stepped forward. 'You might call them intuitive tools. If you have a problem, or you're worried about something, you use the cards to guide you to a solution.'

'They predict the future then,' Leela said, 'like a fortune teller.'

'Not exactly . . .'

'Will you read mine? Pretty please,' Leela asked like a child asking for a treat.

'I don't know . . . I haven't done a reading in a long time,' Livi said.

'But you still remember how to do one,' Shravan said, almost as eager as Leela to see what would happen.

'Please, Livi.'

Livi shook her head, but then gave a resigned sigh. 'Oh, all right then.'

Holding her hand out for the cards, Livi dimmed the lights, and the four of us sat on the floor. Outside, dusk thickened, and inside the cabin, the sweet scent of incense curled through the stale air. We were huddled in a group on a worn yoga mat, its faded red threads doing little to soften the hard floor beneath us. Peering at the cards, we leaned in close — so close I could smell the mix of coffee and biscuits on their breaths. It felt more like a séance than a tarot reading. An image of Livi with her hair piled high in some elaborate bun, peering into a crystal ball, popped into my head unbidden. I giggled, which earned me sharp glances.

Livi shuffled the cards, and then handed them to Leela.

'Now, you shuffle them,' she said. 'And as you do, think about a question you want answered.'

'Must I say it out loud?' Leela asked.

'No,' I said, with a glance at Livi. 'A real reader should be able to work it out from the cards.'

Livi merely smiled at the barb.

Leela began to shuffle the cards with a little chuckle. 'Ooh, isn't this exciting!'

'Now, cut the deck and choose three cards,' Livi instructed.

Livi had barely finished speaking when Leela jabbed a finger at the spread. 'This, this, and that,' she said, with the certainty of someone picking tomatoes at the market.

Livi smiled as she retrieved the cards and turned them over one at a time. The first revealed a hooded figure, cloaked in shadows, a lantern held out in front, his back stooped. There was something in his eyes — something quiet, knowing. 'The first card stands for your past. The next shows your present and the last the future.' She tapped the cloaked figure. 'This is the Hermit. He's a seeker, often alone. It suggests loneliness in your past. A heartache, maybe. Or a desire to belong.'

'And you can tell all that from the card?' Leela asked, unaware that this was a trick used by fortune tellers the world over — throw out the net, and see what sticks. If Leela had said, *No, that's not true,* Livi would immediately have changed tack: *You were surrounded by people, but they didn't understand you. Jealous of your beauty, your wit, your success.* And who hasn't felt alone at one time or another?

The second card depicted a couple who, goblets raised, were toasting each other.

Given Leela's recent marriage, the meaning was pretty obvious, so Livi proceeded to the next card without comment.

'Your third card is the Queen of Wands,' Livi said, 'which indicates control.' She paused, tucking a loose strand of hair behind her ear.

'You mean me?' Leela said, looking quite overcome when Livi nodded. 'And what am I controlling?'

'It could be anything. You tell me,' Livi said, with a wink. But there was something in the smile she gave Leela — something that didn't quite land as playful, but was more like a challenge dressed in silk. She held Leela's gaze for a long moment.

No one spoke.

It was Shravan who finally broke the silence. Beaming at Livi, he said, 'A lady of many talents, my Livi.'

'Can you do a reading for me?' I said without thinking — it was the last thing I needed. But I was curious to see how she'd interpret my situation. More than that, I wanted a read on *her*. So far, I had failed. Would she take the bait or flat out refuse? Was she someone who shrank from discomfort, or did she rise to a challenge? It might be useful to know.

She glanced at Shravan, who shook his head slightly.

But Leela said, 'Oh, go on. I'm enjoying this, it's fun.'

'All right,' Livi said reluctantly, and pushed the deck towards me. 'Why don't you shuffle the cards and think of a burning question? If it's something you really want an answer to, the reading will be clearer.'

Ooh, this was interesting. I had to admire her guts. What if she didn't like what she saw?

My hands shook slightly as I shuffled the cards. Maybe this was a bad idea. Would Livi guess my question? Why had I even asked? I had never believed in the cards when John read them, so why should they give me any answers now?

No. She wouldn't know. She *couldn't* know. My question was mine alone. A secret I'd carry to my grave. I thought of the nightmares that clawed me awake. The *if onlys* that never let me rest.

'We will do the same three-card reading. Past, present and future. Now, think of the question as you cut the deck,' Livi said, her voice calm, almost hypnotic.

Almost automatically, my hand reached towards the middle of the deck. The card showed a regal woman wearing a headdress, something like a nun's wimple, with a crescent moon cradled between two horns. Her eyes held a calm, unreadable expression — the Mona Lisa of tarot cards.

'Don't touch them, just point them out and I will draw them for you,' Livi said. Her tone was clipped.

'Oh, sorry,' I said, reddening. Of course I had to go and make a fool of myself over a little game of cards. 'This,' I pointed at the card on the far left.

Livi drew it out and flipped it over. A blindfolded woman, her hands tied with cloth, stood surrounded by swords stabbed into the ground, like a cage or a warning.

'Interesting,' Livi said. 'And the second one?'

I didn't see anything interesting — just a woman completely unaware of the trap she'd walked into. She looked like she was shivering in her flowing robe. I much preferred the serene royal nun. My fingers trembled slightly as I pointed to the next card, this time at the far right. 'This one?'

'Are you sure? Go with your instincts,' Livi said.

My instincts were telling me to run. 'Yes,' I said, and Livi turned it face up.

On this one a tower was burning, with silhouetted figures tumbling out of it, escaping the flames. Great, just what I needed. 'Well, aren't you going to tell me what it means?' I said angrily.

'It's better if I read them all together so they give the full picture,' Livi said. The whole thing felt orchestrated, like the cards were stacked against me. Like this game was one I was never meant to win.

With a shrug, I pointed at the third card. This card bore the title 'Justice'. A man in a flowing robe was seated on a throne, with a sword in one hand and a scale in the other. I liked him. 'That looks better,' I said with a chuckle.

But Livi had turned pale. 'This is unusual. I don't think I've ever had a reading quite like this before.'

Suddenly, it no longer felt like a game.

'Well?' I said.

She pointed to the Tower and Justice. 'It's rare to have two cards from the Major Arcana together. And if we'd gone with your original choice for the first card, the High Priestess,' Livi said slowly, 'that would have been three for three. They indicate fate.' She paused and tapped on the tortured woman. 'Your first card, which signifies will or conscious action, is a Minor Arcana card.'

'And? What does that mean?' It came out more harshly than I had intended.

'Leela's cards indicated that she's in control of her fate. Yours, on the other hand, suggest that you're not. Your future is in the hands of fate. The card representing your past is a Minor Arcana card, so you were in charge back then, but that is no longer the case now.' She paused. 'And swords signify betrayal.'

'You should have picked my original choice. The Priestess, right?' God, I was starting to sound desperate, as if the card could save me from whatever was to come.

Livi shook her head. She looked almost, well, sad. 'Both your first choices, whether the Priestess or the Eight of Swords, indicate secrets and betrayal in the past . . .'

'You mean I was betrayed?' I asked.

'It could be,' she replied, but she didn't sound convinced.

'It could be John?' Maya said, 'He betrayed you. Back stabbed us.'

For a second, Livi's face twisted to an ugly purple. Then, it cleared.

I winced. The bit about fate and control was vague enough to be practically meaningless, but betrayal was too close to the bone. 'But that's in the past, right?'

'I guess so,' she said uncertainly.

'What about the Major Arc— whatever you call them?'

'The second card, the Tower, represents your present situation. It signifies, er, chaos.' Livi looked embarrassed.

I started to speak, but Livi was pointing to the third card, the future. 'Justice—'

With a cry, Leela fell to the ground and started jerking violently. Horrified, we realised she was having a fit. We stared helplessly at each other until, with a final spasm, she went limp and lay still.

CHAPTER SEVENTEEN

Day Three: Smitha

Bhoo and I made our way over to the cabin to join the others. As we approached it, I noticed the lights were dimmed. Above us, where the slanted roof met the cloudy sky, tendrils of smoke curled lazily into the air. My first thought was, *Great, no one's here.* Followed immediately by a flash of panic — Leela had probably left a tealight burning and started a fire. Not that she'd ever admit it.

For a second, I seriously considered going back for help. But then Bhoo tapped my shoulder and pointed to the cluster of shoes on the veranda. Maybe they were still here.

We arrived to find Leela lying on the floor, her head in Dhruv's lap. 'What's going on?' I asked.

'Leela fainted,' Dhruv said. 'Again.' He sounded guilty, like it was somehow his fault that his wife had a habit of dropping like a stone at the most inconvenient moments.

Again? Leela might as well carry a crash mat with her everywhere.

'Come on, Dhruv,' Nancy said. 'It was more than just a faint. She had some sort of seizure. You need to take her to a hospital. She needs to see a doctor.'

Immediately, Bhoo stepped forward, as if she'd only just realised that she was a doctor. 'Give her some air, would you? I'll see how she—'

She stopped. A look of utter horror spread over her face.

I looked at Leela. Surely she wasn't . . .

'Bhoo?' I said.

But Bhoo wasn't looking at Leela. Wordlessly, she pointed towards the dolls. Of course, the dolls had moved. Now, there was a new centrepiece.

The small figure of the doctor had been moved from her usual spot on the top step, and now stood alone on the middle one. In the hospital set, she had been holding a syringe. Now she had a scalpel, pointing towards herself. Both arms were covered in tiny scratches and there was blood on her white doctor's coat.

These weren't random cuts. They were battle scars. They were the weight of life-and-death decisions, made in the blink of an eye. Bhoo had often told me stories about the early days of her career when she was a trainee doctor in the emergency room. Stories of swallowing her tears while delivering devastating news, only to turn that pain inward. The day she failed to revive a baby who had been taken to the hospital when it was already too late. Or the night she spent keeping a grandmother alive just long enough to say farewell to her granddaughter. After experiencing many such tragedies, Bhoo had begun to cut herself. Each tragedy left its mark, a permanent reminder of what she saw as her failures. Two scars became three, then too many to count — her arms and legs etched like pages in a journal, each line a little longer, each cut a little deeper.

The first we knew of it was when someone began sending us emails about her. We hadn't noticed the quiet changes

— how she gave up wearing her Maya-approved halter tops in favour of a sweater. Always in long sleeves, sleeveless tops with cardigans, even in the heat of summer. There was a photo attached to the email. Now, Bhoo was frantically tugging at the sleeves of her blouse, tears running down her cheeks.

CHAPTER EIGHTEEN

Day Three: Nancy

It was late, and my bones ached from the burden of the day. But Shravan had called an emergency meeting. I hadn't felt like eating after what happened and had rushed straight to my room to hide. His message had been short, terse: *Come down, Nance. Everyone is here. An emergency meeting.*

That wasn't like Shravan. Not at all. He was a take-a-deep-breath type — steady, measured, the kind of person who'd talk you down from the edge with a cup of chamomile and a reassuring voice. He had to be, I suppose. It was his job. That sort of built-in calm came with being a psychiatrist. I stared at the message, debating whether to go. But if I stayed in my room, my absence would read like guilt, and they'd declare me the culprit. I couldn't give them more ammunition. Not now. Not with everyone ready to point their fingers at me.

Trudging down the stairs, I wondered what this was really about — this so-called *emergency meeting.* The smell of chilli and rice hit me halfway down, and despite myself, my mouth watered. There they were, gathered around the dining table, half-empty plates pushed aside like they'd been interrupted mid-bite. Not quite everyone, though. There was no sign of Leela, Smitha, or Aswin. As I entered, every face turned to me. Even Bhoo — red-eyed and wrung out from crying — looking like she'd rather be anywhere else. That made two of us. Maya sat beside Bhoo, her arm around her shoulders. She wore an expression I couldn't quite place — part defiance, part dread.

'She's here,' Maya said under her breath.

I sat down opposite Shravan — it was his meeting, after all. He had shaved off his beard. Without it, he looked naked. His eyes fixed on me, he cleared his throat. 'The things that've been happening these last few days, the dolls moving and all that. It's not fair. Not right. Livi was kind enough to open her house to us, is this the way we repay her kindness?'

'But—' Livi began.

Shravan held up a hand, 'This was supposed to be a holiday. We came here to relax and enjoy each other's company.'

'Why are we skirting around the issue?' Maya asked. 'Tell her.' As she spoke, she played with the diamond-encrusted 'M' ring she'd had for as long as I could remember — slipping it off and on like she always did when she was nervous. She'd lost weight and it came off easily.

'Come on, Maya. It could be anyone. We don't know for sure.'

'Do you even hear yourself? Tell me you're joking. You think it's me? Or Bhoo? Maybe Bala?' Maya said. 'Why would we do that to ourselves?'

The words were out before I could stop myself. 'It's a neat way to rule yourself out, isn't it?' I didn't mean it, but Maya was getting on my nerves. I had been protecting her, taking care of her, yet she was only too willing to throw me under the bus.

'Nancy—'

'Look, I'm sorry.' I was not. 'That wasn't fair. But believe me, I'm as clueless as you are. I don't know who's doing this. Or why.'

Jay, who'd been quiet so far, asked, 'But why? Why do we think they're doing this? I mean, it's not new.' He was right.

106

The first time, the reason for it had been clear. Nobody knew those secrets — the anonymous emails had revealed them. But now? Everyone knew the stories behind the doll set-ups. Maybe it was a copycat stalker, like those copycat killers you get.

Maya said, 'They clearly think it's all a big joke.' That didn't make sense. How could it be a joke? The faces around me were all staring into space, like they'd swallowed thunder.

'I'm not so sure,' Shravan said. 'This has gone far beyond a joke. And it's not just the dolls. Leela fainted. Smitha . . . the rafting incident. Something doesn't feel right.' For a second, I wondered if he was going to do a Leela and proclaim that it was all supernatural, with doom and death awaiting us. 'Whoever's doing this has something else in mind.'

'Like what?' I asked.

'They're trying to tell us something. Convey a message through the dolls.'

Maya laughed. 'That's not very original, is it?'

'True, none of it's news.' Jay sounded worried. He should be. It was his turn next. Last time he was the first. He'd been caught with his trousers down — literally. Man, was he embarrassed. The guys in his class had been ruthless. *Show us your thongs, Jay,* they'd shout. Sometimes they'd even draw a picture of him twerking on the board. In the end, he'd had to quit his job.

'It will come,' Shravan said.

I stared at him. 'What do you mean?'

'They're only setting the scene. Establishing that they're . . . that they know things. That they're telling the truth. Giving you proof of their insider knowledge.' He looked at me as he spoke. He thought it was me. 'And once they've done that . . .'

The defiance was completely gone from Maya's face. Bhoo was sobbing softly into her hands. Jay looked pale. Bala had his fists clenched as if he would like to punch something or someone.

'What?' I was the only one who seemed capable of speech.

'There will be more to come,' Shravan said.

'But there's only one more,' I said, and Jay put his face in his hands.

'You mean the old ones? What about the things that weren't put out there? New secrets.'

'I don't understand. What do they want?' Maya asked.

'If only we knew,' Shravan said. 'It could be something as simple as jealousy. Or revenge.'

'Revenge? For what? You don't mean . . . It couldn't be the letter, could it?' Maya looked around with a stricken expression. 'Do you mean he's here? Watching us, laughing at us?'

Surely she couldn't be talking about John. And what letter?

'Let's not torture ourselves with hypothetical scenarios. It might all be a bluff,' Shravan said, although he didn't sound convinced. 'It could be a prank gone wrong, and today's happening brought them to their senses.' He was staring at me again. 'I hope they do stop. Before it's too late.'

I shook my head. 'If there's one thing I'm sure of, this is not the end. It's just beginning.'

CHAPTER NINETEEN

Day Four: Livi

'Can I ask you something?' Leela said.

'Mmm . . . ?' I wasn't too happy about having my peaceful Sunday morning disturbed. I love waking up early on Sundays when everyone else is catching up on their sleep. Today obviously wasn't one of those quiet mornings. By the time I came in for my tea, Leela was already up.

She was holding a steaming mug of coffee in both hands. 'Chamomile? In the morning?' she said. 'Isn't that supposed to be a calming bedtime drink?'

I sighed. 'That's what they say, but I drink chamomile tea all day. Why not? Besides, it's a holiday, and we don't have any plans. Why shock my body with caffeine?'

And I wasn't going to make any plans either. What had I been thinking, inviting a bunch of virtual strangers into my holiday retreat? Bloody dolls festival. Who would have guessed they'd bring so much drama?

'So, no plans for today, then?' Leela said.

I was tempted to tell her that I had already provided them with free accommodation, so they could hardly expect me to put on daily entertainments for them as well. Not that they needed it — there was enough going on without me planning anything. But when I looked up, I saw she wasn't being pushy. She looked relieved, like she was pleased I wasn't about to drag her up a mountain or something. Poor Leela. 'Well, I said we could go for a morning walk. There's a lovely farmers' market in Oban on Sundays.'

'You mean, just you and me?' she asked, smiling like a little child.

'Yes, just the two of us. Before the others get up.'

'Deal. But only if I can have some chamomile tea first,' she said, pushing her mug of coffee aside.

Laughing, we ran out of the house. Quite unexpectedly, I found I was enjoying myself. I realised I hadn't laughed properly since Mum died. Maybe not even before. I noticed she looked a little surprised too. I wondered how long it had been for her since she laughed.

The streets of the sleepy town were deserted, still shrouded in mist from the night before. The cobbled streets shone like gold in the early morning light. The air was rich with the salty tang of the sea. Only the distant call of the seagulls broke the silence.

'I suppose you must really hate the weather here,' I said. In some ways, Leela and I were alike — both of us were outsiders, new to this group of close friends. We shared a love of storytelling, me a writer of short stories and Leela with her dolls. We're both spiritual, in our own way. Perhaps, in time, we might become friends.

'I like it here,' she said. 'It makes me feel free.' Her eyes followed the trail of smoke from the distillery nearby.

'Free?' I asked, intrigued.

'Yes.'

'Free from what?'

'Oh, I don't know,' she said. 'From judging eyes, maybe? In the gloomy days, I don't feel exposed like I do under the harsh glare of the sun.'

I'd never thought of it that way. I'd always thought the sunshine made you freer, but I could see what she meant. Bright light did tend to show up your imperfections. And hadn't I always liked to hide away in the shadows?

'Oh, listen to that bird!' Leela cried. 'Isn't it sweet?'

'Don't be fooled by the song,' I said. 'That's a grey shrike. They're known as the butcher birds. They impale their prey on thorns or barbed wire.'

'And so they should,' she said with a smile.

I stared at her. 'Poor little birds, it's not very nice to do that to them.'

She stopped walking and turned towards me. In the morning glow, she looked beautiful, her heart-shaped face framed by black curls and her high cheekbones burned to a natural rosy tint. When she batted those long eyelashes, she looked like a Disney princess. 'Have you ever heard of karma?' Leela said. 'In India, we believe in the cycle of death and rebirth. Your present life, as well as the manner of your death, are determined by your deeds in the previous one.'

I laughed. 'So the little birds deserved what was coming to them. They were bad in their previous lives. But how can animals be bad? They're innocent creatures, unlike humans.'

'Ah, but they could have been human in a previous life. Bad people, reborn as animals.'

'I suppose a belief in karma leads people to do good deeds. It even makes a twisted kind of sense. So, shrikes were better in their previous life than the birds they prey on? They couldn't have been very saintly, or they wouldn't have been reborn as an evil shrike.'

'Huh. Saints,' Leela scoffed.

'Now I really don't understand.'

'In my view, saints go against nature. They undo karma, and in so doing they only prolong the endless cycle of death and rebirth, which is suffering. The goal of life is not to have to be born again, and to finally find peace.' She paused to check her mobile. 'I left Dhruv asleep. He might be wondering where I am.' She typed furiously on her mobile for a few seconds.

Message sent, we continued the conversation. 'Anyway,' I said, 'back to the shrikes. I don't quite get where they fit into this, er, "cycle of death and rebirth".'

She beamed. 'Easy. Shrikes carry the burden of balancing nature, serving the karma.'

I shook my head. 'I thought this "balance of nature" was a natural process.'

'Oh, sometimes nature needs a little bit of help,' she said.

'How?' I asked.

'The thing is, if the consequences of what you do in one life aren't reaped until the next, and the memory of your past life is lost, you're more than likely to keep on committing more sins, aren't you?'

It made sense, I supposed. My head was full of half-formed questions that I couldn't put into words. Then the shrike called again. I shivered.

Leela smiled kindly at me. 'Enough silly talk. Let's go and take a look at this market, shall we?'

'Yes, let's,' I said, suddenly eager to move on before the next shrike took the life of some poor sinner.

CHAPTER TWENTY

Day Four: Leela

London's streets bear the stains of its guilty pleasures. They reek of piss and stale booze. They are never silent, never still. Oban is another world. The streets here breathe. You can hear the echo of your own footsteps. And in the background, like a distant orchestra, the sound of the sea. Sometimes it roars, at other times it whispers. The air smells of salt, and fish.

The farmers' market wasn't due to start for another half-hour or so, but the vans and SUVs were already parked up, with their rear doors open to display the different wares on sale. Some were crammed with home-made items — jars of golden honey, jams, candles, perfumed soaps, bottles of rosewater. Others held crates packed with freshly washed fruits and vegetables, while others showcased craft brews. In some places, canopies were raised. Under its cover, the vendors bustled about, setting up awnings and arranging produce on their tables.

Livi stood a short distance away, leaning against the trunk of a rowan tree full of berries. She seemed thoughtful, distracted, and strangely fragile—like she was made of paper, ready to blow away in the next gust of wind.

Perhaps I shouldn't have spoken as I did about karma. I thought she'd understand. After all, she was always full of tales about spirits. She burned sage and read those strange *ta-rot* cards. Our discussion about shrikes had obviously upset her.

I went and stood beside her and gazed up into the tree. 'It's a rowan,' she said. 'They're supposed to protect you against evil spirits and witches' spells.'

I bent down and picked up a fallen cluster of berries. 'Oh, look, a pentagram!'

'What?'

'Each of these red berries has a pentagram-shaped calyx,' I said, turning the cluster between my fingers. 'It's an ancient symbol of protection.'

'That's interesting,' Livi said.

'Your *ta-rot* reading was impressive,' I said. 'Where did you learn how to do it?'

She looked away, her gaze landing on a table beneath the shelter of a red canopy. An elderly woman was arranging jars of home-made jams and marmalades at the back, while a small boy set out little plastic cups containing samples for prospective buyers to try. For every spoonful he poured from the sample jar, he snuck two helpings into his own mouth. With a playful smile, the grandmother picked up one of the strawberries she'd scattered around the jars for decoration and tossed it at him. The boy giggled.

Smiling too, I glanced at Livi, hoping to catch her eye, but her thoughts were clearly elsewhere. She looked sad.

'Livi?'

'Mmm?'

'I was asking where you learned about the *ta-rot*,' I said.

'It's pronounced *taro*, Leela. My mother taught me. Mum was a natural, she could see things in them I'll never be able to, however much I practise.'

'It must be nice,' I said wistfully, 'to be able to share something like that with your mother.'

'It would have been if I'd ever really shared it with her. I used to laugh at her when she read the cards. My brother did — share it with her. He was sensitive like her. In fact, he became better than her in the end.'

In the end? Whose end, I wondered — his or their mother's?

'He could sense the slightest change in the way the cards fell — the position they were in, what it meant if they were upside down. Even the light on them. I could never do that. It wasn't until after — after they were gone — that I started taking the cards seriously. I've gotten better with time, but I'm still nowhere near as good as them. And when they left me,' she swallowed, 'there was no one to teach me. Poor mother. She never recovered from the loss of my brother.'

I looked at her and saw tears pouring down her cheeks. I wrapped my arms around her, murmuring words of comfort. 'Hush now, it's all right . . . I know just how you feel.'

With a jerk, Livi pulled away from me. Wiping her nose on the sleeve of her jumper, she said, 'No, you don't. You have no idea how I feel.'

So I told her something about me that few people knew. 'My mum and my little sister died in a fire. I was eleven. Mala was only seven, she had her whole life ahead of her. I had gone off to a dance class. My mother didn't want me to go, she disapproved of dancing, but I went anyway. When I got back, the house was on fire.'

I had never danced again after that.

Livi touched my arm. 'Oh my God. I'm sorry. So, so sorry.'

'It was arson,' I said shakily. 'Someone poured kerosene over a pile of papers lying on the floor in the kitchen and set them alight. The door was locked from the inside, so the police concluded that it must have been suicide. People said my mother did it to get back at my father for leaving us.' I looked at Livi. 'And do you know what the worst of it was? The rest of the family blamed me. Me! An eleven-year-old child. My uncles, my grandparents, the neighbours, all of them. They said I brought bad luck. None of them were there for my mum when she needed them — after Dad left. After the fire, they couldn't get enough of me. They revelled in it — said I was born under a bad sign.'

'Bad sign?' Livi asked.

'The way the stars were aligned at my birth. They said it was an evil omen. It was . . . You see, the stars had only been aligned that way once before. When Maa Kaali was born.'

Livi stared at me, wide-eyed, then she looked puzzled, as if she didn't quite grasp the significance of what I'd just said. 'What happened to you afterwards?'

'I was sent to live with my grandmother. She didn't want to take me in, but someone had to. My uncles and aunts all had their own children, and they didn't want me bringing my bad luck on them. I spent four miserable years with her, abused, denigrated and treated like a slave. When she died, they said it was my fault.'

'Oh, that's so unfair,' Livi said, sounding genuinely shocked. 'And then?'

'The relatives got in touch with my dad and practically forced him to take me back. He had no choice, really — India doesn't have a system of foster care like here. So I went to live with him and my stepmother.'

By now, the farmers' market was in full swing. 'Shall we take a look?' I asked.

'In a while,' Livi said. 'I'm still taking in what you just told me. So, were things better after you went to live with your dad?'

I grunted. 'Worse, if anything. My stepmother didn't want me there at all. She behaved like I didn't exist, and my father took his cue from her. She was a rising movie star, and I think he was rather in awe of her. A year and a half after I went to live with them, my dad fell down the stairs and broke his back. He's paralysed from the neck down, totally reliant on others to feed and clean him. Not wanting to interrupt her career by being forced into the role of nurse, my stepmother kept me on as his unpaid carer. I didn't mind. It meant I could continue my education and, more importantly, it meant I could be near my dad. I wanted to watch him suffer. I enjoyed seeing him helpless and remorseful, totally dependent on the daughter he had neglected.' I let out a shaky breath. 'His situation became harder and harder to bear, until he begged me to help him die. Naturally, I refused. He wasn't going to get off that easily.'

Livi stared at me, taken aback by my words. And then her lips spread in a smile.

It's always easier to open up to strangers than to the people you're close to. And Livi knew all about pain.

'Do you know what the strangest part of it all was?' I asked. 'Despite what my family believed about me, when he fell down those stairs, nobody blamed me. Even though one of the pearls I wore had caused him to fall when he put his foot on it and slipped.'

Livi stared at me.

'When my stepmum moved on to a younger and fitter model, some even said he had it coming. Karma, they said. All this time, there's been one question that won't leave me alone,' I said, staring at the ground. 'Why didn't my mum wait for me to come back? I knew she didn't exactly shower me with love, but still, I thought she loved me enough to take me with her. Or at least to say goodbye.'

Looking back, I should have realised what she was planning. My mum — who could barely scrape together enough money for a proper dinner most nights — handed me a whole ten rupees for a treat. I was over the moon. I just grabbed it. Didn't think twice.

Livi gently rubbed my shoulders and pulled me into a hug.

CHAPTER TWENTY-ONE

Day Four: Nancy

Nightfall. The curtain was coming down on another gloomy day. As usual, I was thinking about Shravan, and where I had gone wrong.

He took me too much for granted, that was the trouble. I was his safety net, the best friend who'd talk him through his break-ups. The buddy who always cheered the loudest when he won an award. I was always there, maybe that was the problem. It was why I had started seeing John, in the hope of making him jealous. If I made myself scarce, I thought, he'd realise what he'd lost. I even got engaged in a desperate bid to force Shravan to act before he lost me. Time passed, until one day I found that somehow I seemed to have agreed to marry John. You'd think that would have made me come to my senses. Instead, I fanta-sised about Shravan storming into the wedding ceremony and carrying me off. But life isn't a romcom. How stupid can you get? By then, it was too late to back off my engagement.

Far from carrying me off, Shravan said he was happy for me. Happy? Did our relationship mean nothing to him? But what relationship had we ever really had? One kiss, for which he apologised profusely. Stupid me, I told him to forget it, while all I wanted to do was scream. I didn't need his apology. What I needed was for him to kiss me like he meant it. The way a boyfriend kisses his girl — full of passion.

Anyway, he quickly moved on, pretending it never happened. The trouble is, I couldn't get that kiss out of my mind. Now, in a last desperate gesture of hope, I decided to put on the same ink-blue saree I had worn then. It was just another evening visiting the dolls, nothing special. Bhoo was keeping to her room, still upset by the cruel way her secrets had been laid bare.

Smitha, too, had decided not to come, which was totally unreasonable. I mean, it wasn't like she'd drowned. The water was barely knee deep. She claimed she'd hit her head on a rock, but if she had, it hadn't left a mark.

Smitha was like that, though. Anything for a bit of attention. This time, her moment of glory had been snatched away from her. So, she was sulking.

I could have stayed silent and let her have her moment. Instead, I said, 'Of course you wouldn't have drowned, Smitha. Not even a toddler would with that life jacket you were wearing.'

All hell broke loose. She screamed at me, unleashing years of resentment at the way she was taken for granted, treated like a maid. I have to admit she had every reason to feel that way, but her anger was misdirected. I had always been supportive, it was Maya and Bhoo who deserved her fury. But Smitha was too afraid of Maya, of the power she wielded over the rest of us. Smitha was well aware that with a snap of her fingers, Maya could exclude her from the group. Now that Smitha had let it all pour out, she was probably wondering how to make it right. It would be hard to act as if everything was just like it used to be.

I thought long and hard about whether I should go. My room had become a refuge from the tensions of this disastrous holiday. It was larger than my tiny flat in Sheffield, with a king-size bed and a jacuzzi, no less. Why not just stay here and make the most of it? But after last night's emergency meeting, what kind of message would that send? They all thought it was me, that much was obvious. And this morning had been no different. They didn't say so, not in words anyway. But they didn't have to. The way their conversations trailed off the moment I entered, how they suddenly found the weather fascinating.

Which meant it was left to me to uncover the culprit. Last night, I'd been sure it was Leela. She had the easiest access to the dolls, she kept the keys to the cabin. But why? Unless she knew what I'd done and somehow took it upon herself to prove my guilt. But how could she possibly know that? And all that talk of ill omens, the frantic prayers when the dolls were moved — was it all a performance? If it was, give her the Oscar already.

The more I thought about it, the less likely it seemed. But I had plenty of other suspects. Smitha, for one. In a way, I hoped it was her, because her motive would simply be to gain attention, nothing more sinister.

Or Maya. She had never trusted me after what John did, and would be pleased to see me banished from the group. But would she go as far as implicating herself? Two of the three secrets so far had been too close to home. Would her spite carry her that far?

No, I had to be there. I needed to find out who was behind this. Watch their next move, and catch them red-handed if I could. Resolutely, I made my way over to the cabin. I was about to open the door when I heard Maya speaking. She had to be talking about me.

'Don't you think it's too much of a coincidence?'

'Nancy? But why?' Leela said.

'Who else could it be? Well, that's it, I'm calling her bluff. This is the last straw. I've had enough of her antics.'

I pressed my eye to the keyhole. Maya was pointing at the dolls. Was it some new revelation?

'Is the door locked? Or do you always go around looking in keyholes?'

'Oh, Shravan! You made me jump.' I stepped aside to make way, surprised not to see Livi with him; she was usually glued to his side.

As he went in, Shravan said, 'Next time, just knock and enter, will you?'

I went in after him, disappointed to see Livi already there.

'Oh, hi Nancy,' Maya said.

'I found Nancy outside,' Shravan said. 'She seemed to be having trouble opening the door.'

Blushing, I turned to look at the dolls. 'So, what is it today?' They all appeared to be in their usual positions. The doctor doll was now cleaned up and free of scratches. The Barbie was back pushing the trolley, and the football player was no longer inside a glass, but happily reunited with his teammates.

'There.' Leela pointed at the post box. A pair of black metal peacock feathers were dangling from the letter slot.

'Are those earrings?' I asked.

'Yes, Bhoo's. Remember?' Maya said. 'The ones that were taken as a token.'

Now I remembered.

'A token?' Shravan asked.

'Oh, come on, Shravan. Don't pretend you don't know. You were there,' Maya said.

'No, that's not what I meant. I posted them, didn't I? I sent them to John, along with that vile letter you wrote, Maya. I told Bhoo we never found them, but we did, didn't we?'

'I'm lost,' I said. 'Who posted what to John? What for? Can someone please explain? Maya?' I turned towards her.

Maya sighed. 'When we found out about John, you begged — pleaded with us — not to go to the police. But what were we supposed to do? Just let it go? Allow him to walk away unpunished? He wrecked our lives, Nancy.'

Come on, I thought, *that's a bit of an exaggeration*. Typical of Maya, though, always overdramatic. Her whining was starting to grate on me. It was always someone else's fault, never Maya's. *If only the traffic lights hadn't turned red, why hadn't the child looked before crossing? Careless parents, what business did they have leaving a ten-year-old unsupervised on the streets?* It was never, ever, Maya's fault.

'So?' I asked.

'So we decided to post these to him,' she said, holding up the earrings. 'To remind him of what he did. A token of his criminal activity. Something that will be a constant reminder of the scars he left.'

'You mentioned a letter,' I said.

'Yes, I wrote him a letter to go with the earrings. Shravan posted it, since he was the only one who had John's address,' Maya said.

Shravan. Of all people.

'I mean, what was I supposed to do? She was going to report it to the police otherwise . . .'

CHAPTER TWENTY-TWO

Day Five: Smitha

I woke up to the sound of feet and the thud of heavy suitcases being dragged down the stairs. The rain was still falling. I'd spent the whole of the previous day locked in my room, refusing to open the door even to Jay.

I'd had enough of them, hounding me with questions, their dismissive sympathy, their smug little jokes. The endless *Come on, Smitha*s and *It can't be that bad*s. As if I were overreacting, as if my pain were some kind of punchline. Their smirks and tone-deaf tweaks of my truth scraped at my nerves until I wanted to scream.

I needed to clear my head. For God's sake, I fell into that freezing river. That should count for something, surely. The shock of it — the icy cold of the swirling river against my skin, the jarring bump as I hit the slimy rocks, and then the brutal yank of my hair as Shravan and Aswin pulled me into the raft.

Locked in my room like some tragic soap opera heroine, I kept replaying it all in my head. What actually *had* happened? What could I have done differently?

One moment I was just sitting there, chatting with Leela, minding my own business. That blasted bridge — the finish line — was just ahead. I remember feeling proud that I'd made it. And truth be told, it hadn't been nearly as terrifying as I'd expected. At least I wasn't passed out on the raft floor.

Then the raft shook. Just a little. Nothing dramatic. I glanced back and saw Nancy stand up. That alone should've been enough to set off alarm bells — she's built like a statue and just as subtle. She looked furious. Could she have heard us whispering? No. Not above the roar of the water. Besides, it was all harmless talk. Stupid, maybe. But not vindictive.

I half turned, and saw Nancy sway dangerously, teetering, about to topple. *She'll capsize the raft.* I reached out a hand to steady her, half rising from the bench. Did she take it? I don't remember. What I *do* remember is her coming towards me. Automatically, I ducked, lost my balance, and fell headfirst over the side. I gasped, breathing in ice-cold water, and began to choke.

What use is a life jacket when your head's underwater, and the current is so strong? Helpless, it carried me along, arms flailing, hitting rocks, so that I had no idea which way was up and which way down.

What angered me the most was Jay's utter lack of concern. 'You had a life jacket on and still managed to drown? You should lose some weight, you know. Shravan and Aswin nearly dislocated something pulling you out.'

Oh, very funny.

I wasn't going to let him get away with that, but first, I needed to regain my strength. I'd nearly died, for heaven's sake. Meanwhile, Leela had quietly taken on the role of house-maid, leaving trays of food and mugs of too-sweet milky coffee outside my closed door.

Annoyed at being woken, I threw off the duvet and went over to the door and opened it a crack. At the top of the stairs was Laxman, a holdall over his shoulder, Bhoo trailing behind him carrying a shopping bag.

I opened the door wider. 'Where are you going?'

'Home,' Bhoo said. She looked exhausted, her eyes were red, and from the state of it, her hair hadn't seen a brush in days. Bhoo had always been the sensitive one in our group, quick to react, usually with tears.

'Has something else happened?' I asked.

'Yesterday . . . the dolls. It was the final straw.'

'What about yesterday?' A chill ran down my spine. There was just one more photo left from all those years ago. Was that it, then? Everything finally out in the open?

Bhoo hesitated before pulling out the peacock earrings from the shopping bag. She held them up. 'These were with the dolls.'

'Are those what I think they are?' I asked.

Bhoo didn't respond. The earrings were her favourites, the ones with peacock feathers and tiny bells that used to jingle whenever she turned her head. She held them out in her palm.

Then I saw it. A small blood-red smudge.

Bhoo nodded. 'The very same. From all those years ago.'

We had assumed that whoever was messing with the dolls was playing some twisted game at our expense. But these earrings — snatched seven years ago by John and never seen since — had taken things to a whole new level.

The earrings were the only items we never recovered. Not the real ones. There was a fake pair with the other keepsakes. When we asked John, he claimed he had no idea where they were, which was puzzling, given that when we saw them, all the other things — Maya's ring, Bala's Fitbit, and Jay's glasses — were in the box that Shravan had accidentally found under John's recliner. The earrings were identical to Bhoo's but it was fairly obvious that they were only a replica, a bad one.

That's when it all started to make sense. The stalking, the anonymous emails revealing our secrets, the random things inexplicably missing, all pointed to John. It came as a relief, honestly. At least we weren't imagining the whole thing.

John had protested his innocence. Swore up and down he was being framed. But the emails magically stopped after

Shravan found the box. According to Shravan, stalkers often took trophies, little keepsakes of what they'd done.

I stared at Bhoo. 'But what does it mean?'

'It means John is back, Smitha.' Her voice was flat, like she was reading out a weather report. 'Whatever the reason, he wants to pick up where he left off. The whole thing is starting again.'

'But that doesn't make sense,' I said. 'He can't be here. How would he even know where we are?'

Bhoo shrugged. 'Who else could it be? Until these turned up—' she shook the earrings — 'Maya was convinced it was Nancy.'

'And why now?' I asked.

'Maybe he didn't like the thought of us getting back together,' Bhoo said. 'You know, stirring up old resentments.'

'He can't have been watching us all these years, can he?' I said.

'You know what comes next, don't you?' Bhoo said. 'The secret.'

'It follows. If it is him,' I said.

'You should leave too. Before . . .'

'No,' I said. 'I am not leaving. That would mean he wins. He wants us to run away. It would mean he has power over us again.' It was only part of the truth. I wanted something else too. I wanted the next secret to come out. *Jay's* secret. I wanted him humiliated. It would serve him right.

'Suit yourself. We're leaving, in any case,' Bhoo said, and turned to go.

'Wait!'

Bhoo stopped and looked back.

'What about Maya?' I asked. 'She's not leaving, is she?'

If anyone could convince Bhoo to stay, Maya would. She'd held the strings since day one, and Bhoo had always danced to her tune. She'd always been dazzled by Maya's self-assurance — the kind that comes from growing up with Rolls-Royces and closets full of designer labels. Maya used to say that she didn't even *know* how many shopping malls her family owned. Her father once offered to buy us a house near campus. Maya turned down the offer, but not before making sure we all knew about it.

It wasn't just Bhoo, either. We were all Maya's puppets. Having Maya for a friend meant you didn't have to live off soggy canteen food, or spend your Friday nights watching box sets. You got a free pass to clubs, designer samples. You felt like you were living the life.

None of us had the courage to confront her with what she really was — a bully — until John came along. In fact, many of us were secretly happy when the anonymous video landed in our inboxes.

'What about Maya?' Bhoo asked.

'Does she know you're leaving?' I said.

'Oh, Maya left last night,' Bhoo said, and headed downstairs.

I was shocked. For all her flaws — and God knows she had plenty — Maya wasn't one to run away. Even when the video of her shoplifting that hideous bracelet and the campus gossip burned her reputation to ash, Maya held her head high.

She didn't need to be at university. She could easily have lived off her dad's money, and enjoyed a life of brunches and yachts. But she stayed.

So, why run away now?

CHAPTER TWENTY-THREE

Day Five: Leela

An acrid smell filled the air. Something was burning in the room next to mine, Maya's room. But Maya had left last night, after the argument. The room should have been empty.

As I stood wondering what to do, my mind went back to the argument I'd overheard the previous evening. I couldn't make out everything that was said, only that the tone had been acrimonious. I did hear Maya mention something about a ghost seeking revenge, which immediately reminded me of Maiden Island. Perhaps it was Mhairi who was moving the dolls.

Shravan had laughed.

'Like, seriously. It could be—'

'Honestly, Maya. Did you hear what you just said? It's ghosts now, is it? Come on, you're just scared.'

That was enough for Maya, apparently. She declared she was leaving, and that the rest of us should leave too. Whoever this joker was, she'd had enough of their stupid stunts. A few hours later, she was gone, scurrying away in the middle of the night while everyone was asleep. I heard her and Bala dragging her suitcases down the stairs . . .

I came back to the present with a jolt. Tendrils of smoke were now curling under the door. I couldn't ignore it any longer. Running to open it and found Livi inside. She was holding a tiny brass burner from which smoke was streaming.

She beamed at me. 'Morning! Sorry, did the smoke wake you?'

'I thought the room was on fire,' I said.

'Oh, this,' she said. 'It's sage. I was just cleansing the room. You know, with Maya leaving last night and the earrings and all that, I wanted to get rid of some of the bad energy. Even Shravan was talking about an evil presence.'

I wondered how much Livi knew. I wasn't sure how much I knew myself, come to that. I'd been told that John had waged a hate campaign against the friends, sending out anonymous photos and videos that exposed their secret vices. They said he'd stolen small items from them as trophies. But that was seven years ago.

Apparently, Maya had made Shravan post a vile letter to him, along with Bhoo's earrings. None of the others knew about this until yesterday, when the earrings turned up amid the dolls. The whole thing was a mystery to me, it just didn't add up. Suddenly I began to feel dizzy.

'Are you okay?' Livi asked.

I shook my head. 'I'm fine.' For a moment, I thought I might faint, but it quickly passed, thanks possibly to the sage.

'Here, sit for a while,' Livi said, and led me over to the bed.

I sat on the white coverlet, debating as to whether I should confide in Livi. I hardly knew her, but she was the only person here that I felt some connection with. Just as I was about to speak, Smitha burst into the room.

'Bhoo is leaving,' she announced.

'Oh? Why?' Livi asked.

Smitha shrugged. 'She didn't say, just that Maya had gone.'

'Yes, but that's no reason for Bhoo to leave,' I said. 'Didn't she say anything else?'

'She's spooked. The earrings . . . it's made her worried,' Smitha said.

'But that's just another of those nasty pranks, right?' Livi said.

Smitha looked at the floor. 'She seemed to think it was more than that.'

'What made her think that?' Livi asked.

'You see, the earrings were never found. John had them. He never gave them back. And now they turn up here . . .' Smitha shivered.

'They might not be the same ones,' Livi said. 'The prankster, whoever they are, could have easily bought a pair that looked just like the original ones.'

'No, it was the same pair,' Smitha said. 'One of the earrings had a spot of red paint on it. It was there on the ones we found.'

'Who would know about the mark?' I asked.

'Well, I certainly didn't. Not that it was red or anything like that,' Smitha said. 'Bhoo said it got there because she'd been using red paint when she put them on once. And she touched it accidentally, leaving a smudge.'

Livi asked, 'The ones we found. Did they have the same mark?'

'Yes,' Smitha said. 'In the exact same spot.'

Livi hesitated. 'But could it really be the exact same mark?'

'Bhoo's a doctor. She should know,' Smitha said. 'She's the one who noticed it in the first place.'

'But doctors aren't forensic experts,' I pointed out. 'Just because she's a doctor doesn't mean she can identify a thing like that.'

Fear does strange things to people. They were clearly spooked. When your nerves are frayed and the shadows start creeping in, maybe every little paint smear starts to look like proof. Maybe you start seeing patterns where none exist.

Or maybe this was just another of Smitha's endless stories. Dhruv had a name for them — *Smitha's tatty tales*. Apparently, she had a flair for the dramatic, spicing up the ordinary with a bit too much flavour.

'She's harmless,' Dhruv had said. 'A bit like an annoying relative that you're really quite fond of. She means well.'

But still, this wasn't the kind of thing you over-drama-tised. Not when feelings were running so high.

'When the missing things were found,' Smitha said, 'there was a pair of earrings, just like Bhoo's, among them. But there was no paint smudge on them. Bhoo knew they weren't hers.'

'So, what happens now?' Smitha asked, her gaze darting between us.

I began to get worried. Maybe we should leave too. Dhruv had been part of the group, but he'd been working in London when it all happened. He hadn't met John, or even attended the wedding. At the time, I believed him. He hadn't given me a reason not to. Now, I wasn't so sure. If he was keeping something from me, I'd rather hear it from his lips than from the dolls.

The dolls! I thought about the Navaratri. I couldn't disrupt that. Not until day ten. It would bring more bad luck.

'Well, I'm not leaving,' I said. 'But you go if you want.' If everyone left, maybe the festival could continue uninterrupted, and there'd be no more bad luck. With no one left, maybe the dolls wouldn't need to move.

'I'm staying too,' Livi said. 'I'm not running away from my own house, that would be crazy.'

'If you're staying, I am too,' Smitha said. 'I thought everyone was going.'

We fell into a thoughtful silence. My gaze wandered to the door, and I gasped. Around the frame were blue and red marks clearly visible on the white paint of the door. One side had blue marks, the other side red. Above the blue marks someone had written the initials 'JD', while the red side bore the letters 'OJ'.

'What are those?' I said, pointing at the marks.

Livi's face took on an expression I couldn't quite read. I wondered if I'd asked something I shouldn't. But then she smiled. 'Oh, those. My mum made them. She used to measure our heights every summer when we came for the holidays, to see how much we'd grown during the previous year. The red one's mine. The blue was Dexter's.' Her brother. The one she'd lost.

CHAPTER TWENTY-FOUR

Day Five: Nancy

After the discovery of the earrings, I found that I was once again part of the group. Although no one had actually apologised — that would have been nice — they began returning my smiles. And I was included in the conversation again, at least on the periphery. With Maya gone, taking Bala, Bhoo, and Laxman in her wake, I thought things should be easier. Four fewer people meant eight fewer eyes watching me, waiting for me to slip up.

The initial shock had faded, particularly after Shravan admitted he'd posted Maya's letter to John. He should have known better than to do as she asked. Anyway, if she'd found out that the letter hadn't been sent, who knew what she would have done. And Shravan. Shravan did it for me, to protect me. He might pretend otherwise, but I knew better. Who goes that far for someone they don't love? I could see cracks beginning to show between him and Livi. Fewer touches. No more fond glances. Maybe there was a chance for me after all.

So, when Smitha had suggested that we all head out for a walk, to perform our evening ritual of visiting the dolls, I was pleased. I didn't even mind when she reminded me that we ought to wear yellow for the day. Yellow's cheerful. Yellow suited me. Jay and Aswin opted out, which left the six of us — me, Smitha, Livi, Shravan, Leela, and Dhruv. I was just happy to have been included.

Stepping out of the house, Livi said, 'One for sorrow.'

'What's that?' I asked.

Livi pointed at a lone magpie, hopping about on the unmown lawn in search of worms.

'All right, but why sorrow?' I asked.

'It's a rhyme,' Livi said. 'People recite it when they see a magpie.'

One for sorrow,
Two for joy,
Three for a girl,
Four for a boy,
Five for silver,
Six for gold,
Seven for a secret, never to be told.
Eight for a wish,
Nine for a kiss,
Ten a surprise you should be careful not to miss,
Eleven for health,
Twelve for wealth,
Thirteen beware it's the devil himself.

'Poor magpies,' I said. 'They're such cheery little birds. What did they do to cause people to think of them like that?'

'Ah, well, you see magpies are notorious thieves, and they're particularly fond of bright, shiny objects — like jewels,' Livi said.

Or earrings, I thought. It all came back to the earrings.

'I wonder why black is always associated with evil,' I mused. 'Black cats, magpies. People who wear black.' It wasn't aimed at Livi — not really. For the bullies at my

133

school who'd tormented me for years. Called me a witch, a raven — even tar-face — just because of my skin tone. Only if they could see the beautiful swan that ugly duckling had morphed into.

'Magpies are black and white, actually,' Livi said. 'And black cats are considered lucky in parts of Britain. Depends on where you are from.'

'Oh, it's all right then,' I snapped. That fixes everything, doesn't it? Years of being treated like an omen, a warning, a shadow in the corner — but hey, as long as someone, some-where, thinks a black cat might bring a bit of luck, it's all fine.

By now there was a whole flock of magpies on the grass. Smitha counted them. 'Seven. What does that mean?'

'*A secret, never to be told,*' Livi said.

'A secret, eh?' Smitha said.

For a second, I was sure someone would turn and look straight at me and shout, '*Gotcha!*' But no one did. As we rounded the corner, I glanced back. The flock had grown larger. They flew dangerously close to the metal trap — too close.

Suddenly, the metal teeth snapped shut. I screamed.

'Don't worry,' Livi whispered. 'It wasn't caught. Magpies are too clever to get trapped like that.'

I shivered.

Earlier that day, we'd taken a trip into the nearby village, a few miles from where we were staying. Smitha had suggested chaining a bell to the key for the cabin, so we would hear it if anyone sneaked in. It was getting dark by the time we returned. The trees looked different in the fading light — qui-eter somehow, like they knew something we didn't.

It wasn't a bad idea to attach a bell to the key, but it was also a bit pointless. Leela kept the key knotted in her saree, and now every time she moved, there was a jingle.

As I watched her march along, arms swinging, with that 'I own the place' air she had, I couldn't shake the thought that it had to be her. Who else could sneak around unseen, move the dolls when no one was watching?

Last night before we left the cabin, Smitha had smeared mud over the handle so that we would know if anyone had been inside. As far as we could tell, the mud hadn't been touched.

Inside, Leela made straight for her dolls.

Reaching the display, she suddenly stopped and put a hand to her mouth, pointing at the middle tier.

This time, it was the bridegroom doll that had been used to make a point. He had been removed from the wedding scene, and now lay submerged in a makeshift bathtub fashioned from a biscuit tin filled with water.

The tiny figure, obviously drowned, looked deeply sinister.

So far, the dolls had been arranged to show us things about ourselves that we already knew. It was why we had been able to dismiss it as some kind of sick joke. This, on the other hand, looked more like a premonition. And who was the target?

As soon as Livi set eyes on the drowned doll, she gave a cry and burst into tears. Shravan put his arms around her, while the rest of us looked on helplessly. Between sobs, she gasped, 'My brother . . . That . . . It's my brother!'

Eventually, she calmed down enough to tell us about what had happened. Her brother, Dexter, had only just got married when his new wife suddenly announced she wanted it annulled. She accused him of things he hadn't done — things he wouldn't even have dreamed of doing. He fell into a deep depression. Their mother tried to help him, but nothing she tried seemed to make any difference, and she feared the worst. At the time, Livi was in Brazil, studying Portuguese. By the time she got back to the UK, her brother had holed himself up in their holiday home — the very house we were now staying in.

When she couldn't get through to him, Livi immediately came up to Scotland. Arriving at the house, she got no response to her frantic knocking, then she found the back door open. The house appeared to be empty. She wandered from room to room, calling out his name, until she came to the bathroom attached to the room I was now staying in. He was lying in the jacuzzi, and had obviously been there for days. The coroner ruled it death by misadventure, the result of an overdose. No one could say whether it had been deliberate or not.

Livi was still talking, but she lost me at the jacuzzi. All I could think was, her brother had been found dead in the jacuzzi — the same one I'd soaked in this morning. An image flashed on my mind, a limp hand resting on the wet grey panels, the same ones I'd traced random swirls on. My stomach flipped.

I glanced at Shravan. It was clear from his expression that he knew nothing of this. Why hadn't Livi told him?

CHAPTER TWENTY-FIVE

Day Six: Nancy

Soft pops of bubbles sounded from the far corner. I couldn't see that far, my eyes were still adjusting to the dark. Curls of steam rose from the surface, the white clouds forming a criss-cross pattern — and as I watched, they turned a bright shade of blue. My eyes must have been playing tricks on me. I rubbed them, but the blue vapor only deepened, shifting to an aubergine purple.

Out of it emerged a darker shape, the size of a fist. Hands instinctively raised, I turned sideways and crouched, bracing for impact. Nothing came. Slowly, I opened my eyes and looked around. The bubbles were now crimson, but instead of the soft hiss, they made a raspy cawing sound. The bubbles grew larger and larger, inflating until they splattered into a bloody mess like they'd been tethered and then cut loose.

Warily, I stepped closer, feet dragging, pulled forward by something I didn't understand. I peered down at the now clear liquid, white froth swirling in the centre. Before I realised what was happening, I was floating in it, embraced by the warm water, my muscles loosening, the tension melting away. I sank a little deeper, my shoulders relaxing, my eyes closing. For a brief, stolen moment, it was bliss. I let my head drop back, wetting my hairline. Salty water stung my eyes. But it wasn't just water anymore, it had darkened a deep red, with big, fat bubbles forming all around me. As they swelled, they pulled me under. Slowly, steadily. Suddenly I realised I couldn't breathe.

I thrashed about, splashing wildly, swallowing mouthfuls of liquid. Finally, I broke the surface, panting. Just then, a bubble shot up like a balloon on a string and burst. From it, a clump of black and white emerged — a magpie. Wings tucked in, it soared into the air, then glided down to perch on the edge of the jacuzzi. More bubbles popped. More magpies appeared. I counted seven.

As I said the last number aloud, one opened its beak and instead of cawing said, *'Seven for a secret, never to be told.'* The popping grew louder, more urgent. Soon there were nine, ten, eleven of them. The thirteenth one tilted its head and asked, *'Do you know who the devil is?'*

'You can't talk. Magpies don't talk,' I said. The terror that had wrapped itself around me shifted, just slightly, into disbelief.

The thirteenth magpie cackled — a strange, shrieking laugh — and as it did so, its face changed into Livi's. Her lips moved — deliberate, mocking. *'Magpies don't talk, do they? But I'm no magpie.'*

'What do you want?' I asked, my voice rising with the steam.

'That should be my question. What do you want, Nance?' she — it — replied.

'Hey, don't call me Nance,' I hissed.

'Oh? Does it remind you of Shravan?'

'Don't talk about Shravan,' I snapped, trying to stand. Water splashed out as the magpies fluttered then flew out the open window, vanishing into the dark woods.

'Aw, did I hurt your poor little feelings?' Livi-Magpie called, tailing the flock.

'Wait! Tell me who the devil is!' I shouted. But my fingers caught only air, and I stumbled forward—

And woke up. I lay panting in bed, half expecting magpies to launch themselves from the ceiling. The temperature had dropped overnight, made worse by the old wooden-framed windows that let in far too much air. My heart pounded, wild and relentless. Taking deep breaths, I told myself again and again that it was just a dream. I reached for my mobile. It wasn't on the bedside table.

I switched on the lamp. Light poured across the floor. No phone. The empty carpet stared back at me. The window rattled. It should have been shut. I didn't remember opening it, but the wind was stronger now. I would've noticed if it was open. Then came a soft *ping*. The sound of my phone. I turned, and the screen glow blinked from the oak-panelled corner. Breadcrumbs. The cold bit at my legs as I moved, floorboards sharp beneath my feet. My hand closed around the phone — it pinged again.

The lock screen displayed a text from an unknown number: *I C U*. With it, a winking eye — large, round, brown, ringed with white dots. Not human. My instincts screamed at me to throw the phone away, but instead I tapped it. The eye sharpened. Then the rest of the face. And the body behind it. This time, the shiver had nothing to do with the wind.

CHAPTER TWENTY-SIX

Day Six: Smitha

I wondered who could be up and baking in what I now firmly considered 'my' kitchen. Sure, some of the others — the women, naturally, because we were born with a ladle — had helped now and then, but I was the one who did the bulk of the cooking. The heavy lifting. The actual planning. There should've been an apron embroidered with *MASTER CHEF* just for me. Maybe even a hat. One of those tall ones.

So, when I smelled something warm and sweet drifting down the hallway, I was immediately suspicious. Someone was playing house in *my* territory.

I walked in and found Livi, still in her pyjamas and wearing oven gloves, crouched by the open oven door, pulling out a baking tray with a large cake on it. She looked proud.

'Mmm . . . that smells good,' I said.

'Oh!' Livi jumped, almost sending cake and tray crashing to the floor. 'You startled me. It's nothing, just a good old sponge.'

'It was nice of you to get up early to make it,' I said, wondering what the occasion was.

For a moment, I wished Veena were here. She loved baking. Always had. From the moment she was able to string a sentence together, she began pestering me to let her help me bake. The trouble was, I didn't know the first thing about baking, couldn't tell a tart tin from a tyre iron. I didn't have the patience for it, there was too much fiddling around for my liking. It's a maddening science — too many rules, too much faff, and absolutely no room for improvisation. You get the measurements wrong, and the whole thing is a flop — literally. I'd lost count of all the hard, flat sponges I'd had to throw away. It's worse now Veena is older:

'My friend Lily's mum baked an amaaazing unicorn cake. You never make cakes like that. Can't we do one? Pretty please . . .'

'Why don't we do samosas instead? I bet Lily's mum doesn't make samosas.'

'No. I like cake.'

And so on.

I eyed the cake, now sitting on a plate on the kitchen island. It looked simple enough. And before I knew it, the words were out of my mouth: 'Would you share the recipe? My daughter would be so pleased.' Maybe I'd even try it. But more likely, it would be filed away in the ever-growing 'because it was polite to ask' list of recipes I had no intention of actually making.

'Of course. How old is she?'

'Six. She'll be seven in December,' I said, shamelessly picking remnants of cake from the tray and popping them into my mouth.

Livi smiled at me. 'I hope Shravan likes it, that's all I can say.'

'He'd better.' I grin. 'I'd forgotten that today's his birthday.'

'Yes. I had planned to bake it yesterday, but . . .' Livi shrugged. It must have been hard for her, I thought. Until then, Livi had been a spectator, watching us get torn apart, one by one. But, yesterday, after the doll representing her drowning brother, she'd become part of our drama. One of us.

'I'm not sure if I'll have time to decorate it, though,' she said.

'I'm sure Shravan won't mind,' I said.

'What won't I mind?' It was Shravan, standing behind us, smiling.

* * *

'Happy birthday to you!'

When our ragged chorus fell silent, Jay continued, 'May God bless you, dear Shravan.'

Jay could be so embarrassing at times. What were we, nursery kids? Honestly, it was like living with a toddler in a grown man's body. I found myself wondering when a doll set-up showing him would finally appear. I already knew what it would show — Jay in a thong, bent over, his trousers down, in front of a semi-naked stripper.

It should have been yesterday. But for some reason, last night's was different. *A deviation*, as they say. The big reveal should have been about him, about *that*, but instead, it was Livi's brother.

And he was dead. *Dead*. In this very house. A bloody shock, really. If we'd rented this place on Airbnb, I'd have filed a complaint by now. Surely they're supposed to disclose things like, I don't know, *previous occupant found dead in the bathtub*? It should be somewhere in the fine print, right? *No pets, no loud noises, no dead bodies.*

Shravan blew out the single candle and looked around for a knife.

As Livi turned to get one, Nancy stood up, her expression grim and unsmiling. 'Happy birthday, Shravan,' she said, extending a gift bag towards him.

Shravan blinked, startled, making no move to take it. He just stared at the bag, as if it might explode.

Livi nudged him gently. When he still didn't react, she reached out and took the bag from Nancy herself, then held it out to him, one eyebrow arched, like *what the hell?*

142

Reluctantly, Shravan accepted it from Livi, his smile faint and uncertain. 'Thank you.'

Shravan fished in the bag and pulled out a long serrated knife with a ribbon tied in a bow on the handle. There was a card with it, which Shravan quickly read and stuffed in his pocket.

'I guess I can use this to cut the cake.'

'A knife? As a gift?' Leena said. 'That's bad luck.'

Oh, for heaven's sake. Hadn't we had enough of her endless prophecies of doom?

Evidently Dhruv agreed with me. 'Cut it out, Leena. Will you just let him cut the cake?'

Before Shravan could pick up the knife, Livi, with a kiss, handed him a gift bag of her own. 'Happy birthday, babe. Don't worry, there's nothing sharp inside.'

With an awkward chuckle, Shravan tore open the bag and pulled out a pair of brown leather gloves. They looked pricey, I spotted the designer label as he held them up. Of course, they were personalised. An 'L' dangled from a key-ring on one glove, and an 'S' on the other. Livi and Shravan. Because nothing says true love like monogrammed accessories or matching tattoos.

I found myself idly wondering what would happen to the gloves if they broke up. Would she reclaim hers? Would he awkwardly scratch off the 'L' or pretend it stood for 'left' (even though it was on the right glove)?

'Thank you, darling,' he said, giving her a lingering kiss.

'Now, you'd better not lose those,' Livi said, wagging her finger at him, 'or I'll come and get you.'

CHAPTER TWENTY-SEVEN

Day Six: Leela

I'd had enough. Of the holiday, and the people I was forced to share it with, especially the one playing this stupid game with my dolls. What did they think they were achieving by it? Even when I pleated my green saree, I wasn't thinking of Goddess Katyayani, or her prowess, not of the way she sat on the glorious lion and forged a path when there was none, or that the colour of the day was leaf green, not the bottle green that I was wrapping myself in that made me look like a lit-up Christmas tree. I was thinking of how someone could think all this was a big joke. From where I was, it certainly wasn't funny, and when it came down to it, most of these 'terrible' secrets were pretty mundane. They were certainly nothing to the one I carried. Good that I'd stopped myself from revealing it to Livi that day.

Last night, I'd been sick with worry, certain the scene in the bathtub was a warning, and that Dhruv was the bridegroom. Panic had gripped my chest so hard I thought I'd pass out. Then came Livi's guttural cry, snapping me back, keeping me conscious. Only when she explained about her brother's wedding, how it was all tied to his death, did my insides unclench. It wasn't Dhruv. It wasn't a premonition. Not this time. But then came the guilt. Because part of me had felt relief. That it was Livi's sorrow, not mine. I wasn't sure I had it in me to survive another one like that.

My father used to say that people who claimed to have no secrets were often the ones with the most to hide. He wasn't usually right, but on this occasion, he was spot on.

Tonight, even before I went into the cabin, I knew that the dolls would have been moved. It was inevitable. Even so, it took me a moment to piece together today's reveal.

At first glance, they all seemed to be in place. Then my eyes fell on the wedding scene on the bottom step. The car was missing. It now occupied the middle tier, taking centre stage. Instead of the groom in his wedding attire, the man driving the little car wore a suit.

I stared at the tiny figure at the wheel. Okay, so what was the big reveal? I stepped back and took in the scene and saw that there were more figures. A mother and child from the school set-up had been placed on a pavement, just in front of the car. Then I saw that the car had mounted the pavement, and was heading straight for the two little figures.

Which one of the men in our group had run down a child? Had it died? Surely not Dhruv! I recoiled in horror at the thought that it could have been my husband.

I heard the door to the cabin open and turned round to see Shravan. His expression told me all I wanted to know. He stood transfixed, gazing at the scene with a look of dismay on his face.

Dhruv was just behind him.

Wordlessly, I pointed at the dolls.

'The girl was fine,' Shravan said. He stepped forward, his eyes on the dolls. 'I didn't kill anyone.'

'When did it happen?' Dhruv asked. It obviously wasn't one of the secrets John had revealed in the anonymous photos and videos he'd sent, or Dhruv would have known.

'Before,' Shravan said.

'You mean before John?' Dhruv asked.

Shravan shook his head. 'No, it was . . . then.'

'Oh?' Dhruv said. 'So, how come—'

'That was what led to the accident. One of those damn anonymous emails,' Shravan said. 'I was with Nance when she got the photo, the one with Jay.'

'The strip club one?' Dhruv asked.

I remembered Dhruv telling me about that photo. The group had received it when she first started seeing John, the first reveal by the self-proclaimed digital warrior, a messiah of truth. Sometimes, truths were best left alone.

'Nance, John, and I were going somewhere — I can't remember where — when Nance showed us the picture. I remember that John shrugged. 'So what?' he said. 'It's no big deal. Men go to strip clubs all the time, especially on stag nights.'

As we were talking, Smitha and Livi had come in. Taking in the scene before us, Smitha asked, 'So, why didn't John send us a photo of that?' She pointed to the tiny car. I couldn't tell if she was relieved or disappointed that it wasn't Jay's. 'And what about yesterday's scene? None of us knew Livi back then. How does it even fit in?'

'Yeah, it doesn't make sense,' Dhruv said. 'I mean, you said John was right there when the accident happened. If anything, John should have had more reason to expose you.'

Shravan nodded.

'So, why didn't he send us a photo then?' Dhruv said. 'It doesn't make sense.'

Smitha stepped forward. 'He wasn't even there for Bala's stag do. That was when you went to the strip club, wasn't it? He was out of the country visiting his sister. But that didn't stop him from sending us that photo of Jay, did it?'

CHAPTER TWENTY-EIGHT

Day Six: Nancy

Three knocks on the door. I moved away from the window, wondering who it could be at this hour. The house was steeped in darkness; it had been hours since the sun had gone down. I couldn't sleep, the scenes from the past playing out in my head. The scene the dolls had depicted tonight (or was it last night?) refused to leave me.

I had been there with Shravan when the first of the anonymous messages landed in my inbox, and as Jay's half-naked photos loaded, I still remembered the squeal I had let out. The car had been speeding well into the forties through a school zone. 'What?' Shravan had asked, one hand on the steering wheel, the other reaching out for the phone.

There were countless times I had replayed it in my head — should I have said it was nothing? Maybe put down my phone rather than handing it over like it was a hot lump of coal? But before Shravan's hand reached it, his eyes had already taken in the image, the implications, and then the car had lurched. By the time we realised what was happening, the car had mounted the pavement, a child underneath it. Thank God the car had slowed — she was fine, nothing major apart from a few scratches and bumps. Oh, but the mother had been furious, ranting and raging.

The knocks came again, more urgent this time, followed by Shravan's voice. 'Nancy, you up?'

Suddenly, I found myself hoping it was still the same day — Shravan's birthday — and that, just like old times, we might go for a walk, my hand tucked into his, speaking of nothing in particular but laughing all the same. One last walk, for old times' sake.

But as I opened the door, the look on his face confirmed my fear. It wasn't going to be one of those walks. In his hand was the note from earlier, his birthday gift from me, the ribbon still attached, curling down towards the floor. He didn't step in. Just stood there, arms stiff by his sides, as though he were holding himself back. 'Come down,' he said. 'Let's go for a walk.'

I didn't ask why. Glad that I was still getting a walk, I just grabbed a jumper from the chair, pulling it over my head as I followed him down the corridor.

Carefully closing the front door so as not to wake anyone, he walked beside me. Outside, the moon flaunted six days' growth behind a silver cloud. A fine drizzle fell — so fine it was almost invisible, revealed only under the golden spill of the streetlights. The Shravan I knew — my Shravan — would have noticed that I wasn't wearing a jacket. He would have shrugged off his own and draped it around my shoulders, murmuring something stupid and tender. But this Shravan — Livi's Shravan — walked on, oblivious, his only concern to avoid being seen. Only when we were far enough from the house, swallowed by the dark, safely beyond the reach of any watching window, did he stop.

Turning to face me, the note crumpled tightly in his fist, he said, 'What the hell, Nancy? What is all this?' A muscle in his jaw twitched, and for a moment, it seemed he might say more, but he bit it back. I resisted the urge to reach out and stroke his jaw, to feel the thud of tension ease under my thumb — like it used to, once.

'Did you not like my birthday wish? I'm gutted.'

'What's wrong with you?'

'Don't you think it's a little late for that?'

'After everything I've done—'

'Cut the drama, Shravan. We've both done a lot for each other,' I said, giving him a pointed look. 'That's what people in love do.'

'It . . . This is not love. This is toxic. Unhealthy.'

I reached out and grabbed his hand. Shravan shuddered but didn't pull away. He looked sad. A part of me wished to stop, to wipe that sadness off his face, to tell him I was sorry. But the other, bigger, part of me knew this was essential — the pain before the birth was always the worst. 'Listen,' I said. 'We. You and me, we're meant to be. We belong to each other. There's no one else who understands you better than I do.'

It was almost like my words had stung him. Pulling his hand away, he said, 'That's not true. Livi knows me. With her, it's easy. It's natural. I've never loved anyone like this before.'

I searched his eyes for signs of a lie. Surely he was saying this only to put me off. But he meant it — every word. It was easy for him to say, but hearing it from him nearly broke me. And I had to give some of it back. 'Oh really?' I asked, 'Did she know about the car crash? I mean, before today?'

'Yes.'

'Did she now? Did she also know how you ran? Reversed and drove right off. Didn't even stop to check on the girl? Was she there to hear the mother's screams as we sped away? The new car, the registration still pending, no CCTV footage . . . convenient, wasn't it? Does she know all that?'

Shravan remained silent; his head bowed. 'Does she know about this?' I pointed at the note in his hand. 'What you did to Maya?'

'Nance, please—'

'Don't "please" me. Answer me, does she know about this?'

'No.' He sounded weak, almost defeated.

'I didn't think so. Would she still love you if she did? The way I love you, have always loved you, huh?'

'Nance . . .'

'Do you know Maya has memory gaps? Because of what you did. You broke her mind!'

'That's not true.'

'Oh, it very much is. Ask her. Call her now,' I demanded. When he stayed still, refusing to budge, I raised my phone. 'You know what? I'll call her. We can ask her together. Maybe it'll even encourage her to come back.'

'No,' he snapped, grabbing the phone from my hand.

I laughed then, but it was manic, brittle, an *I didn't think so* laugh.

'Please. Listen to me. The past is the past. We should look ahead. Build a new life. We've all made mistakes. It's time to move on.'

'Right,' I said, my voice cold. 'That's what I want too. Let's leave the past behind. I made one mistake. One stupid mistake.'

He looked at me, incredulous, like he wanted to say it was more than one mistake. I held his gaze, almost daring him to challenge me. It wasn't like he was innocent either. The car crash, Maya, John's letter — the odds weren't exactly in his favour either. Perhaps sensing that, he said nothing.

'How long are you going to hold it against me? Hate me for it?' I moved a step closer, the space between us shrinking. The smell of mint and lemon, the familiar scent of him, made my heart dance. All I wanted was to lay my head on his shoulder and inhale him, to feel like everything could be okay again.

Instinctively, he took a step back. '*Us* doesn't exist, Nancy. It never did.'

I thought of the kiss, the soft brush of his lips against mine, the slow, almost hesitant start, followed by the urgency that came after. I also thought of his hasty withdrawal, his hurried apology. 'You didn't give us a chance. Not properly,' I said.

'We don't,' he replied, shaking his head. 'I mean, we aren't good for each other. With Livi, she brings out the best in me. When I'm with her, I'm kind, I'm funny. Sensitive. With you . . .' He paused, looking down. 'With you, I was different. Dark.'

'With me, you were yourself,' I told him. 'You didn't have to pretend. You didn't need to put on a mask and smile. You were real with me. Why can't you see that? We belong together, Shravan. We completed each other's sentences and laughed at each other's jokes even when no one else did. We were meant to be.'

'I don't know, Nancy,' he said, his voice quieter now. 'I wish I could see it that way. I wish I could believe we were what you say we were. But it's like I lost myself when I was with you. I don't even recognise the person I became. And I don't know if I want to go back there.'

Each word he spoke felt like a knife twisting in my chest. 'You're scared, Shravan,' I said, stepping closer. 'You're scared because you think that loving me means losing yourself. But you never lost yourself. You just forgot what it felt like to be loved unconditionally. You forgot how to be free with someone who understands you without judgment. We had that, Shravan. And you're throwing it away because of—'

'I love Livi.'

Something inside me snapped. I'd poured my soul out to him, and this was his response? He loved *her*? The soft touch wasn't going to work now. 'You have three days,' I said, my voice steely. 'Three days to break up with Livi and tell her you love me. Actually, scratch that. I need you to tell the world that you love me. I want a ring, flowers. I want you to get on your knees. I need a proposal. If not . . .'

'What?' His voice trembled, as if he didn't want to know the answer to his own question.

'I'll tell them the truth. The whole truth. At this point, I don't care. I'll happily go down with you. But remember, you have more to lose than me. Livi, your licence, your friends, the life you've carefully built over the years.' I made a sweeping gesture with my hand. 'They'll all be gone. You'll lose everything. Except me. Then you'll have no choice. You'll be mine.'

'Over my dead body.' With that, he turned and walked back towards the house, leaving me standing there alone. I waited, hoping he'd turn around, realise his mistake, come back to me. But he never did.

Over his dead body? *Or hers*, I thought. If only I could get rid of her, he'd see things clearly, no longer blinded by the early days of love. One way or another, he would be mine. And if I couldn't have him, neither would Livi.

CHAPTER TWENTY-NINE

Day Seven: Nancy

> *'An unseasonal "Beast from the East" is set to sweep across parts of Britain over the next two days. Temperatures are expected to plummet overnight, followed by fierce winds and thunderstorms. Conditions will be particularly severe in the north-eastern regions of Scotland. A red weather warning has been issued for Argyll and Bute . . .'*

A frumpy-looking girl, dressed in what appeared to be a mismatched assortment of her granny's wardrobe, stood before a map of the UK, the map splattered with red spots like the face of someone with a bad case of chicken pox.

> *'People are advised to stay away from the coast and avoid non-essential travel. The storm is predicted to be the most severe in fifty-six years, with a force comparable to Hurricane Low Q of 1968, when thirty lives were lost.'*

Oh, fantastic, just what we needed — a hurricane. If the weather reporter was out to cause general panic among the population, she was certainly doing a fine job. This was her ten minutes of fame, and she was milking it with everything she'd got. She was now droning on about how the army was deployed for the cleanup operation after the 1968 hurricane.

Define non-essential travel! I wanted to shout at the screen. *Go on, define it.* Because from where I was sitting, leaving this wretched place and escaping the dreary company I was stuck with felt absolutely essential — life-preserving, even. But there she was, safe in her studio, smugly advising us to stay put. I had half a mind to reach through the screen and wipe that grin off her face. She was clearly basking in her rare moment of glory. After all, it's not every day you get to announce a hurricane in the UK. There haven't even been all that many thunderstorms — I could count the number I'd seen of those in the past decade on the fingers of one hand.

There was something Shravan had said this morning that kept gnawing at my brain. He'd asked, 'It was only us, Nancy. In the car when the accident happened. You, me and John. Nobody else knew. Well, it wasn't me who moved the dolls, and John, well, he's obviously not here. So there's only one person who could have done it.' The implication was clear: he thought it was me. Only, it wasn't. Why would I kill the goose that laid the golden egg? Automatically, my eyes darted around the room. Could it be as Smitha said? Could it really be John?

Shravan had been angry then, the only time he'd shown some passion towards me since we came here. I almost preferred that to this indifference. Now, he was slouched on the sofa, his normally clean-shaven chin dark with stubble. All the weight of the last few days had begun to tell, and he looked so exhausted I doubted he'd slept at all. It was all I could do not to reach out, caress his face, and soothe his tired, red-rimmed eyes. I wanted to hold him, whisper that everything would be all right, that we'd get through this — like we always did.

But I suppressed the urge. I knew how he'd react. There was no *us*, certainly not after the note, not after last night. He'd thank me later though, once all this was over and we were back together. Just like we were always meant to be. That little blonde witch would be gone for good. There would be a time when he appreciated everything that I'd done for him. The extent I'd gone to, all for him. Him alone. I'd waited seven years. What was one more day?

I had only seen him like this once before, about seven years ago, give or take. It was on that fateful day when he came to visit me at the flat in Glasgow. John wasn't home — he'd gone out somewhere, I can't remember where. It didn't matter. Not as much as Shravan's visit did.

I told him not to sit on the recliner, which was broken. It had been like that since the wedding. 'Just leave it,' I said, forgetting that Shravan was the fixer. Shravan repaired everything, from minds to malfunctioning furniture. I guess he saw it as a challenge.

All it took was the five minutes I was in the kitchen making tea, and he was calling out, 'Ah, I knew it! Something's got jammed in there. A small box. I wonder what it is.'

Dropping the tea filter, I rushed to him, hoping, praying that it wasn't too late. The secret was still safe. It was only twenty feet from the kitchen to the lounge, but it was the longest walk of my life.

'Box?' I asked, my voice trembling.

'Maybe the previous tenants left it,' he said, fiddling with the lid of a small black metal box.

Before I could come up with an excuse to stop him, he had taken it off, sending the contents spilling out across the carpet. After that, all hell broke loose. We considered every possibility, but nothing could explain how Maya's ring, Bhoo's earrings, Jay's glasses and Bala's Fitbit had ended up in that box, stuffed into the reclining chair, in our house, under *my* couch.

Jay's secret was the first to come out. A short, grainy video from Bala's stag do — him in a strip club, laughing too loudly, waving notes. There was a photo too, of Jay with his trousers halfway down, pooling around his calves, his back thrusted out like he was twerking. I had only just started seeing John then — what were we? A two-week-old couple at best. I often wondered what triggered it. Jealousy? Resentment? Or something deeper, more rooted — a fear, perhaps, of other people's happiness. Of their easy laughter and effortless intimacy. When everything between John and me felt so forced. So fake. Because it was fake, wasn't it? How else could I explain it?

Maya's secret followed soon after. Maybe two weeks later, days after her wedding. The shoplifting video — a bracelet she hadn't paid for casually slipped into her bag, all the time glancing over her shoulder. It went viral overnight, pinging from WhatsApp groups to Instagram feeds, looping endlessly. It was everywhere. For two days, Maya stayed in, curtains drawn, crying rivers and calling in favours. Somehow, she managed to scrub it off the internet. Every single copy. But even she couldn't undo the damage. Couldn't make people unsee it. After a while, she didn't care. She came back — and how! Tossing her newly styled hair, rocking a Sabyasachi. Laughing too loud, talking over everyone. Picking up exactly where she left off. Like she'd never been gone. Like none of it had ever happened. As if the scandal was just a minor inconvenience — an administrative hiccup in her otherwise curated, cashmere-lined life.

Then came a lull. A quiet stretch of maybe a month. As if that had been enough. Mission accomplished. Whatever it was. People stopped whispering. The laughter started creeping back. Smiles were no longer faked. We began to believe it was over.

That's when Bhoo's secret dropped. This one didn't cause ridicule. Instead, it drew sympathy. Concern. She was caught in a rare moment with her sleeves rolled up, her arm looking like a zebra's — cuts and marks all over. Details that should never have seen the light. But the reaction was unexpected. Everyone rallied around Bhoo — supportive, gentle, protective. Not what the stalker had likely planned.

And maybe that was the problem. Because then — for months — there was nothing. We started to breathe again. We even believed that the stalker had grown bored. Having failed to get the chaos they craved, they'd lost interest.

Finally, it was Bala's turn. This time, it came with a not just one video or a photo. Chilling, time-stamped footage. Spy-level detail. His entry and exit from multiple clinics were stitched together into a meticulous timeline. His hunched posture. The tremor in his hands. Close-ups of his red-rimmed eyes. It must have taken months to pull together — a slow, methodical unravelling. A hatred so precise it looked professional.

That was when we understood — the stalker hadn't stopped. They'd only been warming up. And then came the trophies. All of this was playing through my mind at numbing speed when Shravan called out.

The world crashed around me. The reality of what he was holding and what it meant. There it was — the trophies. The keepsakes. The ones the stalker took. The ones that ruined my friends, tore through their lives like wildfire. And they were here. In Shravan's hands. Found in my house. Our house.

The following days passed in a blur. Shravan took charge. All I could remember were the tears, the recriminations. The screaming. Nothing could have prepared me for it.

For a long time, we'd tried to keep it a secret from the others, but I could see it was eating Shravan alive. Like a parasite, it would kill him, bit by agonising bit.

And now Shravan looked just like he had back then.

'Just a little longer,' I urged him silently. Two days at most, and then he would be free — *we* would be free. Free to be together, just as we were always meant to be. For now, I was simply content to have him sitting on the couch with me, the two of us alone together, like old times.

'We should leave,' he said, running his fingers absently over the stubble on his chin. Worry lines creased the parts of his face not overshadowed by stubble or exhaustion.

I nodded, but before I could answer, Livi wandered in. She placed a protective arm around Shravan, as though shielding him. 'We can't.' She went over to the window and yanked the curtains open. Sunlight streamed in, so warm and golden it could almost have been summer. 'You know what they're like, they're always overly cautious. Besides,' she added, tapping Shravan's head lightly, 'we can't move the dolls, remember? It's best to let it pass. No use trying to avoid it. Some storms need to be weathered.'

I wondered if she was really talking about the weather. With Livi, it was never just what it seemed. The enigma that she was, I no longer knew where the mask ended and the face began. After that big revelation about her brother, I'd expected her to retreat — to grieve, or rage, or maybe unravel in some spectacular way. But by the very next day, she was back in the kitchen, humming and measuring out flour, dusted in sugar like nothing had happened. In a past life, I would have found it stoic, admirable even. But now I found it eerie.

And to her credit, she'd taken the story of Shravan's hit-and-run in her stride — unlike Dhruv and Smitha, who had been relentless, grilling Shravan on why he hadn't revealed his secret before. They had a point, I suppose. John did have more reason to seek revenge on Shravan, — the veiled glances, the almost-touches, the kind of tension you could feel between Shravan and me. That sort of thing doesn't go unnoticed. It would make sense. It would even make him more human — jealous, passionate, wounded — everything that John was not. But they were asking the wrong question.

Shravan squinted as the sunlight hit his eyes, and he held up his hand to shield them. 'Hardly looks like a storm, does it?' He sounded disappointed, as though he'd been hoping for an angry sky, giving him a more plausible excuse to run. Little did he know, there was nowhere for him to run. Nowhere left to hide.

CHAPTER THIRTY

Day Seven: Leela

'It doesn't make sense,' Smitha said. *Huh*. Smitha wouldn't see sense if it jumped up and hit her in the face. She was crouched next to the steps, looking at today's centrepiece with squinted eyes. It was a grey day, on the outside and in — the excitement long gone, replaced with something dull and miserable.

'The dolls are never wrong,' I said, refusing to take her bait to move closer, to look again.

'Then what does this mean?' she asked, pointing to the set-up for today. It was another scene from the past. This time a hut from the village set had been moved centre stage, a doll standing outside and peering into the window. 'But the stalker wasn't a woman,' Smitha said. 'It was John, wasn't it? So, what does this—?'

Next to me, Nancy had gone rigid, her lavender perfume now undercut with another smell — fear.

Smitha stared at her. 'Nancy?'

'This is getting ridiculous,' Nancy said, her voice cracking. 'Who *is* this person anyway? The one moving the dolls. Why are we giving them so much power over us?' She stepped back and leaned against the wall, as if she were afraid of losing her balance. 'Can't you see what they're doing? They're turning us against one another.'

Smitha looked from me to Nancy, puzzled. It was just the three of us here — watched by the glassy eyes of the stuffed deer's head above the doorway.

'But why?' I asked softly.

'How should I know?' Nancy retorted. 'In fact, I should be asking you. You saw what was happening, so why did you insist that we stay, endure these cruel displays? Or wait — was it you all along? You say you didn't know what happened back then, but Dhruv could easily have told you. He knew. Did you do it just to watch us squirm? Enjoy your twisted little game, did you?'

Smitha turned to look at me, her eyes saying, *Was it you? Your dolls, your tales.*

I could see what she was doing, but it wasn't going to work, not with me. I had seen plenty like her. Shaking my head, I said, 'Don't try and deflect the blame onto me. Look at what the dolls are saying. Now's your chance to come clean, put an end to all this.'

'How can I come clean when I didn't do it?' Nancy said and burst into tears.

'Do what? Move the dolls?' Smitha asked. No, not the dolls.

Nancy sniffed and wiped her nose against the tip of her saree. 'What nonsense. There's no logic here. For argument's sake, say I did the first few. Which—' she paused, putting out a finger — 'I didn't. But let's assume I did. At least I knew those secrets. But the ones after — Livi's brother, for instance — how could I have done those? I didn't even . . .'

Smitha didn't flinch. She continued to stare at me. 'You knew,' she said to me. 'Nancy didn't know about Livi's brother, but you did. I was there when she told you. In Maya's room. We saw the doorframe markings. Don't tell me you didn't!'

'You're right, Smitha,' Nancy said. 'You've seen them, her and Livi. Always together, whispering. It's a shame the men aren't here to see this, so we can sort it out, once and for all.'

But the men had had enough. 'Carry on with it if you must,' Dhruv had said, 'but leave me out of it.'

Jay and Aswin had stopped coming days ago, claiming this whole drama with the moving dolls made them uncomfortable. I suppose Jay was worried it could be his secret next. Livi and Shravan had gone into town to get provisions for the coming storm and weren't yet back. Maybe they'd had enough too. So it was just the three of us left to face this latest doll set-up and decide what it meant. With both me and Nancy trying to place the blame on the other, a lot rested on Smitha and how she chose to interpret it — whom she decided to trust. I couldn't believe that she hadn't figured it out yet. This wasn't about who moved the dolls. It was about what they were saying. Who they implicated.

I tried to get Smitha to meet my gaze, but she kept her eyes averted.

'Look at me,' I said. 'How could I possibly have known about Shravan's accident?' Was it yesterday's revelation, or the day before? I was beginning to lose track of them. 'Only three people knew about it. Two of them are here. And before you say anything, I don't think Shravan is behind this. And that leaves . . .' I gestured towards the dolls.

Before I could finish, Nancy jumped in. 'Anyway, if it was me, why would I use a female doll to represent the stalker? I'd only be implicating myself. After all, the trophies were found in my house,' Nancy said, regaining some of her composure.

Smitha was still watching the two of us, as if she were trying to make up her mind. 'Nancy's right, it can't be her, and it's definitely not you. There was no way you could have got those earrings,' she said to me. 'Which means . . . Oh, God, it must be John. It's the only thing that makes sense. John was the one with the earrings.'

Could that be? Could I have got this all wrong?

'But how would he know where to find us?' Nancy involuntarily glanced towards the window, as if he might be standing there, looking in.

Smitha shrugged. 'How should I know? He's the stalker, right?'

So many questions hung in the air, each more tangled than the last, but none felt as immediate as the looming reality that the three of us would soon have to venture out into the woods — with a potential stalker lurking somewhere in the darkness. The very thought made me dizzy.

The last thing I remember before the blackness swallowed me up was the door slowly opening, a tanned leather glove on the handle. It must be him. It must be John.

CHAPTER THIRTY-ONE

Day Seven: Livi

The fire was dying down, until just the glowing embers lit up our faces. The old firepit creaked under the quiet crackle, its once-orange frame now blackened with soot from all the summers it had seen. On either side stood Mum's beloved V-sticks. She'd skewer a whole chicken and roast it slowly over the flames. Dex and I would take turns spinning it, careful not to drop it, arguing who was going to get the best piece the whole time. We'd sit around with lemonade, Mum sipping rosé, talking about nothing and everything. Those were the good days. Days untouched by grief or guilt. Days before life showed its teeth and ripped us apart.

This was not quite the campfire I had envisioned. There should be music, marshmallows, mulled wine, laughter, and silly games. I had pictured myself sitting on Shravan's lap, not facing him across the burning logs as if we were the opposing parties in court. A sigh escaped me. My heart felt hollow, aching for what could have been.

I forced myself to look at Shravan. He hadn't said a word since we'd lit the fire. The house had felt suffocating. I craved fresh air, yet lacked the energy to walk. On a cold, windless night like this, a campfire should have been the perfect remedy. It was just the two of us out here — Leela needed rest after her latest fainting episode, and Dhruv had stayed behind to keep an eye on her. Smitha was too frightened to venture outside in case John was lurking out there, and she refused to let Jay or Aswin come out either. As for Nancy, I didn't bother inviting her.

It should have been nice, just the two of us. We could have had a little party. Instead, the mulled wine sat untouched, and the marshmallows were nothing but blackened lumps covered in ash. Shravan was lost to the world, head bowed and rocking slightly. He had been like this since the trip began, totally disconnected. Not the Shravan I knew or had grown to love. It was astonishing what seven short days could do. Just a week ago, I had been full of hope that this holiday would be a chance to reconnect with the past, to come full circle. Or something. Whatever I truly expected, it certainly wasn't this.

When Shravan finally looked up, it was only to gaze into the distance. He seemed torn between a need to unburden himself and the desire to tuck everything away, to pretend it wasn't there. Maybe he thought that if he maintained the illusion that everything was fine, it would eventually just go away, and we'd be back living our mundane lives, where the biggest problem was deciding whose turn it was to do the laundry.

But then he shook himself. 'This is insane.' He was balling up scraps of papers, tossing them one by one into the fire. Each piece flared briefly, lighting up his eyes, then vanished into ash.

I nodded, although I had no idea how to respond. My thoughts were a tangled mess of threads that no amount of trying could possibly untie. These people had secrets, which nearly seven years ago had been exposed by some nameless outsider. Nancy's ex had been wrongly blamed and had been cast aside, never to be seen again. For quite some time, I'd had a fair idea of who the real stalker was and her motivations, and any doubts had been dispelled by tonight's display with the dolls, and the whispered conversation I'd overheard a few days ago. The dolls never lie!

Then there was the letter Maya had written, and which Shravan had posted to John. This led me to the question of what Shravan's role in it all was. Just thinking about these things hurt my head.

The silence stretched on, punctuated only by the hiss and splutter of the dying embers. Finally, Shravan seemed to pull himself together. 'Listen, I'm sorry for dragging you into all this.'

I couldn't help wondering why he was apologising to me, and not the man who had been wrongly accused.

'I had no clue that this was going to happen. I mean, it's been seven bloody years. Why open the can of worms now?'

'Closure, maybe?' I suggested.

'Nonsense,' he said. 'Closure from what?'

I shrugged. *You tell me. It's your mess.*

'It's jealousy,' he said, looking at a point just above my shoulders, unable to meet my eyes. 'That's what it's always been about — Nancy's stupid jealousy.'

'When you found the trophies, in Nancy's house . . .' I paused, not sure if I really wanted the answer.

'Mmm?' he said.

'Did you, even for a minute, think it could be John?'

He blew into the fire. It dimmed for a heartbeat before crackling back to life, louder. 'John? No way. There wasn't a single bad bone in his body.'

'Are you saying it was Nancy who moved the dolls?' It made sense — it was patently obvious that she was still desperately in love with Shravan. Clinging on to the hope that maybe one day he would be hers. 'But why would she implicate herself?'

'So I'd have nothing over her,' he said. One of the paper balls he threw bounced in and out of the firepit, catching fire and rolling off like mini firefly.

'I don't understand what you mean.'

Shravan sighed. 'I knew right from the start — even before I found the box of trophies. Don't ask me how, I just did. But I didn't want to face it, bring it out in the open. What good would it have done? Anyway, I had no proof, so I continued to pretend that I didn't know. Then I found the box. How I wish I hadn't. If only I'd let sleeping dogs lie. Nancy might have gotten bored or run out of things to expose. Dammit, she might have even found happiness — somehow. She never was happy, you know.'

I watched him. This must have been new for Shravan. Normally, it was he who encouraged his patients to confront their demons. It is easier for Catholics, they have the confessional. The rest of us have to turn to a therapist, someone like Shravan, who has the skills to guide others through the process without them breaking apart.

'She was bullied as a child,' he said. 'Made to feel unwanted. Her mother couldn't even bring herself to give the child a name. She never felt good enough or that she deserved to be happy. As soon as anyone tried to get close to her, show her a bit of love, she would bolt or sabotage it.'

'That's no excuse. Not everyone who's bullied turns into a stalker or tries to destroy their friends' lives.' I tried to stay calm, but my voice didn't cooperate.

'No, it's not that simple. I mean, take the case of child abuse. Not every victim ends up becoming a killer. But if you look at the profiles of all serial killers, most of them have suffered some abuse as a child.'

'How is that even related? Child abuse is about power.'

'So is this.' He looked uneasy, as if he was debating how much to reveal. I didn't think Nancy had ever been his patient, so his hesitation wasn't about patient confidentiality. Maybe some misplaced loyalty. I waited for him to say more, but he never did.

Instead, he poked the fire with a stick, watching sparks flutter up like angry insects. 'You're right,' he said finally, voice low. 'It's not an excuse. But it's a start. A way to understand what broke inside her, and why she tried so hard to control everything around her. Even people.'

After all that had happened, Shravan's first instinct was to defend Nancy, and at all costs, even to the point of justifying the damage her actions had caused. His face took on a look of tenderness when he spoke of her. It was almost like that of a doting father when he looks upon his little child. For some reason, I didn't feel threatened by it. If they hadn't framed an innocent man, my heart might have gone out to them.

'She loved you,' I said softly.

Shravan looked down at his hands fiddling uselessly on his thighs. He couldn't deny it.

'And you loved her. Just not in the same way.'

For a moment, he seemed about to protest. Then he said, 'I tried.' I understood what he meant. He felt responsible for failing to give Nancy the one thing she most craved, his love, thereby sending the dominoes toppling one after the other — a trail of destruction which had finally ended here, at my house.

The sorrow on his face tugged at my heart. I wanted to give him a hug, whisper in his ear that everything was all right, and I was there for him. It was the least I could do, after the support he'd given me when I was on my path to self-destruction following the deaths of my brother and my mum. I wanted to be the girlfriend he needed. But was I the girlfriend he deserved?

This conversation wasn't really about Nancy. It was about him and his role in all this. The hiding. The lying. Pinning it on an honest guy. In a way, he'd enabled Nancy's behaviour — providing her cover when what she needed was to confront her problem. She was a junkie — her drug, other people's secrets.

'Why didn't you just hide the box and carry on as if everything was the same?'

'Because John walked in. He was a decent chap, and he couldn't let it go. He told Nance the least she could do was apologise and promise never to do it again. *The truth will set you free,* he said. When Nance refused, he said he would do it for her — beg for forgiveness.'

'So you put the blame on him?'

'The straightest trees always get cut down first,' he said. Still, he would not meet my gaze.

I felt a wave of disgust wash over me. He did this knowingly. It wasn't a mistake or an accident. They worked together to implicate him. This wasn't the Shravan I knew. Not the kind, caring man I'd fallen in love with. This was a stranger — a selfish, corrupt one who'd do anything to get what he wanted. Yet, I didn't have all the pieces. The birthday card. 'She must be holding something over you. What is it?'

'What do you mean?'

'She implicated herself so you wouldn't have anything over her. So she's free to use whatever she has on you without fear of retribution. The note, the one she gave you on your birthday with the knife. What did it say?'

'Are you insane?'

I let it go. I could find out myself if necessary. And I wasn't even sure I wanted to know. 'Okay, then Maya's letter to John. Why send it if you knew it wasn't him?'

Shravan shrugged. 'What else could I do — short of telling Maya the truth? She was threatening to go to the police.'

I couldn't believe this. Not one expression of regret, not one apology to John. He simply did it to save his own skin. I struggled to reconcile this Shravan with the one I had met and fallen in love with — the kind, considerate man who had rescued me from myself. They seemed like two different people. Jekyll and Hyde. The trouble was knowing which one was standing before me.

'I'd like to know what you would have done if you were in my position,' Shravan said coldly.

'Well, I certainly wouldn't have thrown an innocent man under the proverbial bus. And if Maya had asked me to post the letter, I would have thrown it away and told her I'd sent it. Anything but what you did. I would have gone to John and apologised. You must have done that at least. Did you?'

He hung his head. 'I didn't have a chance.'

Still not looking at me, Shravan put his hand in his pocket, pulled out a crumpled piece of paper, and dropped it into my open palm as if it were a burning ember. It looked like a printout from an online article. I read the title: *OBITUARY FOR JOHN D. WILLIAMS.*

CHAPTER THIRTY-TWO

Day Eight: Livi

The thing I remember most about that day is the silence. Not a single bird chirping. Even the leaves in the trees were still. The sky outside was a uniform grey. There were no gathering clouds to signal what was to come. It wouldn't be the first time the forecasters had got it wrong. The weather reports for Scotland were always pretty hit or miss.

I woke to a dull ache in one of my upper arms. Closer inspection revealed a big blue-green bruise, which hurt when I pressed it. I had borne the brunt of Leela's headlong fall last night in the cabin. Shravan and I had only just managed to catch her when she landed like a felled log on top of us. She'd insisted that she didn't need a doctor. It was normal for her to pass out, she'd said. She did it all the time. Fainting every other day doesn't sound normal to me, but she wouldn't be persuaded.

Beside me, Shravan was sleeping peacefully. I resisted the urge to push his tousled hair off his forehead. Let him sleep. He was having a tough time. He tried to hide it from me, but I could see that what was going on was affecting him badly.

What had I been thinking, bringing these people here? It felt like ages ago that I'd planned this trip — it felt like another life, a happier, more innocent time.

My throat was parched, so I slipped out of bed and tiptoed down the stairs. The sky was just beginning to grow light. Expecting the others to all be asleep, I was surprised to find Leela in the kitchen, sitting at the table, her head in her hands. I felt sorry for her. These last few days must have been hard for her. She'd set such store by those dolls, they meant so much to her. She truly believed moving them brought bad luck. I hesitated a moment, and then turned to leave her in peace. I could always get a drink of water in the bathroom.

But she had seen me. 'You're up.'

'Good morning to you too,' I said brightly.

But there was no answering smile. 'I'm sorry about yesterday. I didn't mean to faint.'

I went over to her and put my hand on her arm. 'I don't think anyone intends to faint.' I gestured to the chair beside her. 'Do you mind?'

'Go ahead,' she said.

She was looking at the horizon, at the quietness of it, the utterly unremarkable dull grey of the autumn sky, the stillness hanging in the air. 'The storm is coming,' she said, eyes fixed straight ahead.

'You think?' I wasn't so sure. My luck had been rotten for so long, it felt like it had to turn.

'I don't think,' she said, finally turning to me. 'I know. This is the calm before the storm. The birds — they're cleverer than us. They know when to fight, and when to retreat. Unlike us humans. We always have to take a bad situation and make it worse. Don't we?'

Was she still talking about the storm? 'Sometimes we don't have a choice,' I said. I was thinking of Shravan, his words from last night, his helplessness.

She placed her hand lightly on my thigh. 'We always have a choice,' she said, her voice quiet but certain.

We sat for a while in silence, then she said abruptly, 'Smitha thinks it's John moving the dolls and exposing all our secrets. She thinks he's back and looking for revenge.'

'What do you think?' I asked.

'Who cares what I think?' she said bitterly.

'I do.'

Our eyes met. Then she looked away. 'I don't think it's him.'

'I don't either.' I wondered how much Leela really knew. Was she playing me, feigning ignorance while she prompted me to tell her what *I* knew?

'It could be him, though,' she said. 'It would make sense.'

'I suppose so.'

'But you're not convinced.'

'It's not him.' I left it at that, not wanting to elaborate further.

I was still rattled by what Shravan had told me last night. John was dead. It was Shravan's fault — unknowingly, but a death nevertheless. All those months of listening as I poured out my deepest, darkest moments, and he'd never said a thing about himself. I'd caught him at odd moments gazing into the distance, his eyes filled with pain. Well, the loyal girlfriend that I was, I wasn't going to rat him out — not until I'd got it all straight in my head. Even then . . . maybe it wasn't my story to reveal. His guilt. What was it that he used to tell me? *Guilt shared is guilt halved.* Yes, that was it. That's what he used to say. All that burden he carried — halving it wouldn't be so bad when he was ready. I now had all the pieces of the puzzle, but they weren't yet fitting together. Perhaps I was just too scared of what the final picture would reveal.

Leela was tracing patterns on the table. It looked like a pentagram. Who was she protecting? From what?

'Are you scared?' I asked.

'Should I be?' she said, looking me directly in the eyes.

I shrugged. 'How would I know?'

She smiled coldly. 'It's not about me, is it?'

I didn't know how to respond.

'It's not about you either.'

I shook my head. 'Who do you think is moving the dolls?' I asked.

'Well, it's not me, that's for sure,' she said. 'And I don't believe it's you either.' Leela put her hands on my shoulders and shook me gently. 'We're both outsiders. This . . . mess has nothing to do with us. Whatever happens, it's not our problem. Let them sort it out. Let them pay the price for their misdeeds. We're better off out of it.'

CHAPTER THIRTY-THREE

Day Eight: Smitha

I'd had enough of all the silly games and pointless pranks. Honestly, it was like living in a deranged escape room designed by emotionally stunted adults. And as if that wasn't drama enough, Leela kept fainting like she was some Victorian maiden. All I wanted was to go home, back to my Veena and all her little foibles — the socks on the sofa, the obsession with Peppa Pig, the way she talked to plants. I'd been far too long away from her. At first, I enjoyed having my days free from parental shackles. No packed lunches, no midnight wakings, no constant soundtrack of 'Mum? Mum? Muuuum?' But the charm wore off quickly, especially as the cracks began to show and the masks of my so-called friends began to slip, I found myself missing her. At least I knew where I was with Veena — she told it like it was, unlike these bitter pills hidden beneath a coating of sugar.

When Jay announced two days ago that he wanted to leave, I wanted to wait so I could see his secret being revealed. Then, when I changed my mind, he decided we should stay. 'Only two more days, Smitha. Anyway, it'll look bad if we leave now.'

Oh yes, heaven forbid we do something wrong in front of his friends. Wouldn't want to upset the stalker.

That hadn't stopped him wanting to leave when he felt like it. Then, I'd practically had to pin him down to stop him. Now that he'd figured out that his secret wasn't coming. Whatever this whole creepy set-up was, it had moved on from his silly twerk, and he'd decided he'd much rather stay after all. This was deeper, darker — and definitely not about him or his minor indiscretion (as he called it). Plus, to spite me. He knew I was keen to leave before the storm broke. 'That's precisely why we should stay put,' he said. 'We can't risk driving in that.'

Three hours — that's all it would take us. We'd be gone before the storm hit, but it was no use arguing with him. He'd made his mind up, and once that happened, logic could go take a hike. I agreed on one condition: he would come with me to the eighth-day ritual at the cabin. Dhruv and Shravan were going, so why should he be spared the agony? Whatever tonight's secret would turn out to be, he had a bigger part to play in it than me.

With the storm predicted to strike at any moment, we had agreed to meet earlier, before darkness swallowed the woods whole.

'How do I look?' I asked Jay, pulling in my stomach. I was wearing my Anarkali salwar suit. Purple always suited my skin tone, and this one, adorned with black stones, was my favourite. It was beautiful, and I wouldn't have minded Jay saying so.

He didn't even glance my way. 'Fine.'

'You didn't even look,' I said. 'Today's colour is purple—'

'This isn't a fashion show,' Jay said abruptly. He cast a quick glance at me and snapped, 'Nice. Happy?'

I wondered if all married men were like that — never paying attention to their wives until they felt like having sex. Then his legs would be rubbing against mine like a nail file. Even then, it was over in seconds. A few grunts, and he'd roll onto his back and start to snore. With other women it was a whole different matter, the compliments rolled off his tongue like honey off a spoon. It was different with unmarried couples. Shravan only had eyes for Livi, and Dhruv was still on his honeymoon, so he didn't count. For the sake of my sanity, I decided that all husbands were the same.

We had agreed to all go together as a group, so that no one could sneak in and move the dolls around before the rest of us got there. I had taken the precaution of spreading sand on the patio and dust on the door handle. Last night, nothing had been touched, yet the dolls had still been moved. It had to be Nancy — at least that's what Bhoo had implied. Who else could it be? She was bitter, lonely, scorned by the one she loved. Well, if she thought she could win Shravan back this way, she had to be mad.

Or could it be Leela, as Nancy predicted? She had the keys, and the dolls were hers. Could she be the one moving them around and crying wolf? I didn't know what to think anymore. The only thing I was sure of was that it couldn't be the men. They lacked imagination. Too wrapped up in themselves to pull off something like this.

After the usual small talk about the weather, the walk to the cabin passed in an awkward silence. Inside, the air smelled of smoke and sage. There were no indications that someone had been inside — no footprints in the sand, no smudges on the doorhandle, yet we all knew that some new revelation would be waiting for us there.

We didn't have to look hard to see it. The postman, in his red uniform and matching cap, who had been on the bottom step in the corner, was now in the centre of the middle step. His raised hand, where the wooden post should be, held a notecard with a ribbon tied in a bow.

Next to me, Nancy had come to a halt. It was her birthday note to Shravan, waved by a tiny postman, inviting anyone who wished to read what she had written. It can't be her, then, I thought. Poor thing, she must be terrified. I glanced at her. Far from looking horrified, the corners of her mouth had twitched upward. It took me a moment or two to comprehend, then it hit me. This was for Livi. Nancy wanted her to see it.

In two rapid steps, Livi was by the postman and reaching for the note, her hand trembling slightly. I was right behind her, and leaned over her shoulder to take a look. I just had time to read the first word, *Devil*, before Shravan's voice rang out. 'Livi!'

She jumped. Shravan snatched the note from her hand.

CHAPTER THIRTY-FOUR

Day Eight: Nancy

I liked to watch — like birdwatching or meteorite spotting, except I watched people. People who went about their perfectly mundane life, doing things everyone does, until they got bored. Bored of being perfect, staying in their lane, Sunday church, charity donations and generally of being model citizens. Citizens who, when they thought no one was watching, slipped, but . . . But I watched. Watched and waited, patiently, for those unguarded moments, for the mask to slip and when it did — I . . . I snatched. Snatched those moments before they vanished, before they corrected themselves. Before they remembered how to be good again. Before they were gone, lost, slipping away into the mask, pretending to be someone else.

Sometimes I wondered how it was different. David Attenborough travelled the world, hiding in bushes, planting himself in the shadows, watching animals at their most private moments — mating, birthing, dying in the jaws of predators. No dignity, no consent. And he broadcast it for the world to see. All in the name of awareness. Education. He got knighted, while all I got were side-eyes and jibes.

To be honest, I did them all a service. I showed them a mirror, forced them to seek help. Pretending everything was fine, pretending there was nothing wrong, wasn't going to save them. Sooner or later, Maya would've been caught — and then what? Bala's liver would have given out, or he would have killed himself, or worse, someone else in a drunk-driving crash. He might have thought he was functional, but he was far from it — most days he could barely hold himself up. A slap in the face was what he needed, and I gave him that. They should be thanking me. Instead, they blamed me, as if it wasn't them that was the problem, but my revelations.

I had learned early on, back in my school days dealing with bullies, that knowledge was power. At first, I went quiet, thinking if I dissolved into the shadows, made myself part of the furniture — small, insignificant — they'd stop noticing me, stop having fun at my expense. But with my height, and my top rank, it became impossible. That was when I learned, almost accidentally, that one of the bullyboys was still wetting his bed. The next day, I scrawled it outside the boys' toilet, and by afternoon, I had one less bully. He was too busy scrubbing the toilet wall. The announcements moved from walls to blackboards or anonymous notes to parents, but the effect was the same every time. Like clockwork, I lost a bully — or handed them a different victim.

Watching my back, tracking every move around me, became second nature. I liked leaving crumbs behind, subtle reminders that no one was truly unseen. I don't remember when watching stopped being enough — when I crossed over and started taking pieces of them with me.

A ring left carelessly by the sink. An earring tossed around like it didn't matter. A torn bracelet snagged on a door handle. Small things. Things they wouldn't even notice were missing. At first, it was harmless. A secret thrill, knowing I held a piece of their life between my fingers. But secrets have a way of growing, festering, demanding more. And I was no exception.

Secrets that were so thrilling they deserved to be shared. Carefully, reverently, like sacred offerings. This wasn't idle gossip — God, I hated that word. Cheap. Demeaning. Like I was just another bored housewife whispering over tea. No, what I did wasn't gossip. It was more. It was necessary. It was holy.

Shravan knew all this. He knew me better than anyone else did — maybe even better than I knew myself. That was why I wasn't concerned when he knocked on my door, asking me to come down to the kitchen for a meeting. 'Livi and Leela are out,' he said. 'Stocking up for tomorrow. Ahead of the storm.' *Which storm?* I wondered.

When I came down, it was only Smitha, Jay, and Dhruv — but there was anger enough for an army. I thought Smitha of all people would get it. Maybe even thank me for stepping in before it got ugly, for letting her know about Jay's straying before it got too far. But she was the worst. 'It was my life!' she screamed, her voice shaking with something wild and ugly. 'You had no right.' Then the best part, the ridiculous, almost laughable part: 'Even if Jay was cheating, which—' she jabbed a finger in the air, trembling with rage — 'he was not, what if I didn't want to know? Not from you. Not like that.'

As if ignorance ever saved anyone. As if pretending made the truth go away. I almost pitied her. Almost.

'Did you know?' she asked Shravan. He gave himself away by staying too quiet, shrinking into his chair, pretending to be invisible. Not jumping in, not playing his part to sling mud at me. Mud he knew would come right back at him.

'No,' he said, but he didn't sound convincing. 'I would have told you otherwise.' He would never choose them over me.

Smitha knew that. She just didn't care. 'It makes sense,' she said, voice tight. 'Your secret was never shared. Because you played along. Because Nancy cared about you.' Smitha wasn't about to let it go.

'Why would I post the letter to John otherwise? Why would I blame him? I was tricked, just like you. I didn't know. Please, trust me.' I let him be for now. He had until tomorrow to break up with Livi and become mine. There was no point in breaking the pot before the butter had fully formed.

Smitha was dubious, but Jay was reasonable. 'He has a point, Smitha. Let's not take it out on each other.' Reluctantly, she gave in, turning to me. 'Why did you do that?'

What could I tell her? That I was helping them? She'd only laugh in my face. So, I decided to keep up the farce. 'I don't know what you're talking about.'

'Don't,' Dhruv interjected. He'd been quiet up until then, as he should have been. He wasn't involved — then or now. But it was Leela's precious doll, and he was her warrior husband.

'It has nothing to do with you, Dhruv.'

He didn't take it well. 'You are evil!' he screeched.

I ignored him, turning to Smitha. I just had to take her down, and the others would follow. 'Hey, listen to me. What's the proof? A bunch of dolls? And you believe whoever's behind that over your friend of ten years?'

There was confusion in her eyes, but it quickly dissolved into fury. 'That's you too, right? Moving the dolls. Last time it was pictures, videos, and now it's the dolls.'

'Listen to yourself,' I said. 'Yes, I knew the first three secrets. But so did you. And everyone here.' I paused for effect. 'Shravan admitted he posted Bhoo's earrings to John. How could I have gotten them? Livi's brother — how could I know that? Why would I even implicate myself? None of this makes sense.'

This time, I didn't have to fake my anger. Whoever was behind this, their intentions were clear: they wanted to make me fall. But I wasn't going down that easily — not without taking them with me.

There was a moment when I wondered if it was Shravan who was moving the dolls. Had his guilt gotten too much? Maybe meeting his angelic girlfriend triggered some sort of epiphany in him. He said he'd posted the letter to John, with the earrings. But we only had his word for it. He could have kept the earrings after all. Of course, he knew about the accident — what better way to remove himself from the list of suspects? 'Poor me', playing the victim, worked just fine, as long as the secret wasn't as bad as mine. The only problem was tonight's note, the one in the postman's hand. Why would he try to reveal that? That was one secret he couldn't afford to let slip.

Smitha placed her head in her palms, 'If it wasn't you . . . who could it be?' She scanned the room, only to find equally puzzled faces staring right back.

'Could it be Maya?' Dhruv asked. 'It's rather convenient, isn't it? For her to just up and leave like that? She never does. But suddenly, the earrings appear and the next day she's gone. Not when her secrets were exposed, but after the earrings.'

He had a point, Maya never runs. Shravan shook his head. 'It doesn't make sense. How would she have the earrings? I posted them to John.'

He kept talking, but my mind had drifted. It always came back to the earrings. Even then, I'd been surprised when Bhoo insisted the ones in the box weren't hers. How could they not be? I was the one who put them there — along with Maya's ring and Jay's glasses. Later, I added Bala's Fitbit to the collection. I knew they were hers. But Bhoo had been adamant, and then she explained how hers had a paint smudge.

What if Maya had kept the originals? She was the first one to see the box. After we'd ummed and aahed for a bit and got our stories straight, Shravan had wanted to test it on Maya. He'd said, 'If she gets doubtful or asks too many questions, we can regroup and fix our narrative. Once we had Maya, she will do the rest.' He called her, and she came alone.

What if she swapped them at some point between Shravan showing her the box and when the others got to see them? When she'd heard everything and right after she'd insisted that the police should be involved, she'd declared, 'The box stays with me,' snapping the box shut and pulling it towards her, 'I don't trust either of you.' She had plenty of opportunity to buy an identical pair of earrings and replace the originals. That made sense, I could see how it would appeal to her kleptomaniac tendencies. The question was: *Why?* Why would she do that?

Unless . . . that was it. It was all coming together. I'd always wondered how Maya figured out that it was me. Not at first. But the earrings must have triggered something, a small seed of doubt. It had been stupid of me to wear them, even if it was just that once, before Shravan found the box at my place. But the thrill was intoxicating. To flaunt them in front of Bhoo, to hear her say, 'I have some exactly like this.' Oh, how I'd wanted to correct her. *You had. Not anymore. They're mine now.*

It had taken all my self-control not to say it. Bhoo was fooled. But Maya? She always noticed things, cared enough about material things to note the tiniest difference. When she saw the same pair of earrings in the box and heard me swear I had no idea about how they got there, she must've suspected, maybe not fully, but enough for her to want to keep them. Maybe that's when she swapped them, taking the originals and replacing them with fakes. She probably meant to replace the originals back again later but never got to do so. Not until two years ago, until . . . the photo. That's it!

Gripped by sudden clarity, I now scrolled through the WhatsApp group, going back two years, to the event before everything exploded. Once I passed the last burst of reunion nostalgia, there wasn't much and I found what I was looking for. The proof that Maya needed, the missing piece of the puzzle, the one that pointed at me, that it was me all along who was the stalker, not John. Dhruv had posted the photo. *Happy Friendiversary*, or something equally cringy. A collage. And there it was — a photo of me, arms around Bhoo, wearing those earrings. I zoomed in. There it was, the tiny, unmistakable dot of red paint.

It all made sense now. The frantic call from Maya on an otherwise unremarkable night a couple of years ago. The way she'd shown up at my door with a guilty-looking Shravan trailing behind. The shouting. *It was you*. The knife. It all made sense. She'd pressed the earrings to my face between the '*I knew its*'. I remember briefly wondering about Bala, where he was — if he'd checked back into rehab. Maybe that's why she hadn't told him, in case it tipped him over the edge again. And after that night? We made sure she never did. Not even to herself.

And if I was right, Shravan had a much bigger role to play in all this. All I knew at that time was he gave her something to calm her down and hypnotised her to make her forget about the incident. He'd come out smiling. 'That's fixed.' As if Maya was the problem to be fixed, not me. And I didn't question him. That must be when he planted the false memory, made Maya believe in the lie once more. One that triggered her to write the letter and use it as a ploy to get rid of the earring, just in case it jolted her memory later. Reminded her once again of the true chain of events.

'What's funny, Nancy?' Dhruv broke into my thoughts. I realised I was smiling and quickly rearranged my expression to something more acceptable.

'Sorry, I was thinking it through,' I said. 'I don't think it was Maya.' This time I meant it. 'The dolls, they're still being moved, even after Maya's left. It can't be her, surely.' Unless she came back. Could she?

I touched my hand, my fingers brushing the ring — the one with the diamond 'M' that now felt like it was mocking me. Did she really leave it behind? Or was that just part of the plan — a perfect little trap, with me right in the centre?

I was sure all of us had our theories. I, for instance, thought it was Leela. But if asked for proof, I wouldn't be able to explain how she could have laid her hands on Bhoo's earrings, or my note to Shravan.

Maybe she found both in the same place — with Shravan? Still, I couldn't risk placing the blame on her. Not with Dhruv around. It could backfire on me spectacularly.

Not getting anywhere with it, she manoeuvred. 'What was in the note? The one you wrote to Shravan?'

'Happy birthday?' It came out more like a question, and she wasn't buying it.

'A happy birthday wish that started with "Devil"?' she pressed. 'And if it was just that, why did Shravan not want anyone to read it?'

I shrugged. 'I can't answer that. Maybe you should ask Shravan.'

'What?' Shravan asked, throwing his hands out as though he was exasperated. 'Okay, if you must know, there were things there I would rather Livi didn't see. Things that Nancy had written. About us. Together.'

Cleverly played, but: 'What things, Shravan? Things that start with "Devil"? I wonder what could it be? Livi's not here. Maybe you can show us now?' I asked sweetly.

'I don't have it.'

'You did earlier tonight. You took it from Livi.'

'Not anymore I don't. I tore it up.'

'Maybe I can help,' I said, locking eyes with him. '*Devil's Breath*—'

'Stop it, Nance.' His voice dropped, low and warning.

Ignoring it, I took a step closer. '*Do you remember?* I spoke, quoting from the note. '*I often think about it.*'

'No, Nancy.' His voice cracked, desperate, pleading.

Another step. '*Sometimes I fantasise about telling Maya.*'

'Enough.'

Then the power went out, plunging the room into darkness. Smitha screamed.

CHAPTER THIRTY-FIVE

Day Eight: Leela

The wind was picking up, its thrusts stronger, its howl louder. At the edge of the car park, leaves and a plastic wrapper spun into a frantic whirlpool. Maybe Shravan had been right and this wasn't such a good idea, coming out when a storm was brewing. But Livi insisted we needed batteries for the torches, and we were running low on milk. So there we were, at a twenty-four-hour Asda, one of the few places still braving the storm. I grabbed a trolley — partly out of habit, partly to have something to hold onto in case the wind picked up even more.

Livi was lost in thought, her silence punctuated by sighs — not the resigned kind, but sighs that trembled ever so slightly, as if bracing for what was to come.

She looked tired. Who could blame her? After Shravan had snatched the note from her hand, he'd rushed off before anyone could stop him. He was gone a long time, and by the time he came back, we'd almost finished our dinner. That was when Livi suggested we head to the shops. When she returned, she had a whole conversation ahead of her — and it wouldn't be a pleasant one. I wondered what was in that note. And, if it was worth all the hassle.

Pulling her hat down, she walked in silence, and I followed. I was surprised when she asked, 'What do you think the dolls showed last night?'

That was last night, not tonight, not the note, but the stalker. She seemed keen to avoid talking about tonight. 'You mean the woman stalker?' I asked. She *ummed* but stayed quiet. 'It's rather obvious, isn't it? That it was Nancy, not her ex, who was the stalker. Don't you think?'

Another sigh. 'Do you believe it? Could it be true?'

'There's no reason not to. It's been right so far, hasn't it? Even the new ones — your brother, Shravan's car crash.' I left the note out. Something told me Livi didn't want to talk about that. Not yet. It was too raw.

'That's so twisted, isn't it? And to think Maya believed it was John, and the letter she wrote . . .' She left out Shravan's part. 'That's cruel,' she said, shivering — maybe from the cold air in the chilled section, maybe not.

I took three cartons of milk. We'd need it for two more days. Placing them in the trolley, I said, 'It's not fair. But Maya didn't know. She thought she was wronged, that John was the stalker. If she'd known . . .'

Livi gulped. I thought about her words — about ghosts and revenge — and how scared she must have been. Was it just fear, or was it guilt?

We crossed the aisle and came across a whole section for garden and outdoor supplies, filled with tools and plants and other things I had never seen in London. In London, it was all plastics and processed foods. Livi was turning over a pair of shears when the lights blinked. They came back on, but weaker, buzzing like a dying wasp.

'Do we need it?' I nodded at the shears.

She shook her head and placed it back. Picked up a roll of industrial duct tape instead. 'For the bins. We should move them and tape the lids.' I nodded though I wasn't sure if the tapes would hold.

I glanced towards the storm-streaked windows. 'The mains power's out,' Livi said. 'Hmm. I hope it's still on at the manor house.' Her phone rang before the words had even left her mouth. A burst of noise spilled through — screams, scattered words. Livi tried to pull sense out of the chaos, barking instructions. 'The generators,' she said, her hand cupped over her mouth. 'Go outside. Around the house. The shed. There are diesel generators there. Call me when you're there!'

The line cut out once. Then again. When Shravan finally got through, he was shouting over the roar of the wind, frustration bleeding through every word. 'He can't get it started,' Livi said, panic flashing across her face.

'Tell him to find Dhruv,' I said. Dhruv could handle things like this — last month, when the boiler failed and the landlord shrugged us off, Dhruv had pulled it apart and fixed it himself, one eye on a YouTube tutorial, the other on a battered screwdriver. He was constantly tinkering at something, an old laptop, the TV discarded outside the apartment.

The fluorescent lights above us buzzed again, dimmer still, shadows thickening between the aisles. Then, at last — a low, coughing roar came across the phone line. The generator had started.

We beelined to the nearly deserted till, the only customer ahead of us an old man stacking bottles of whisky and toilet rolls like he was preparing for a siege. I glanced at our own trolley, lined with toilet paper, batteries, milk, eggs, and tools. Maybe we were too. The lone shop assistant kept throwing worried glances at the window. The storm was rising — the whooshing deeper now as the wind poured through the gaps. Every few seconds, it slammed into the windows with a force that rattled the whole building.

'Doesn't look good.' The shop assistant shook her head as she scanned our items. 'We'll be closing soon, I hope. Before it gets too bad. Never seen anything like this — and it's not even supposed to start till tomorrow. You have far to go?'

Livi shook her head. 'We're up in the Williams manor house.' Something flickered in her expression — a brief shadow, a tightening around the mouth. Maybe it was just the lights dimming again.

'Stay safe.'

'What about?' Livi asked.

'It's close to Dunollie Castle, ain't it? There was a fire there last year. Some eejit thought it was clever to have a barbecue and just leave it burning. You know how they keep a stash of diesel there? For emergencies, that's what they call it. God knows why. Luckily, the fire didn't reach the cellar, but it raged for hours. You'd think they'd have learned their lesson. No. The diesel's still there. Now, with the storm and the lightning . . .' It reminded me of the thunderstorm when I was young, the peepal tree that blew up into a torch, and I shuddered.

Thanking her, we made a hasty retreat. Braving the storm, our hoods our only armour, we stayed silent. There was no point speaking — our words would be swallowed whole by the wind.

But my thoughts were whirling, looping, in a tangled mess of worry about what would come next. Only once we were back in the car — water pooling around our feet and warmth slowly seeping back into our numb fingers thanks to the heating — were we in any state to talk. 'You think it will be okay?' I asked.

Livi must have thought I meant the storm. 'We're stacked. The manor house has back-up power. So does the cabin. As long as we stick together and stay indoors—'

'No, we can't,' I said, more forcefully than I intended. She threw me a puzzled glance, our eyes locking in the mirror. 'I mean, we need to visit the dolls. Tomorrow . . .' I stuttered. 'Tomorrow is the big battle. The day when the goddess kills the demon. We can't abandon them.'

She looked worried. 'But the storm's supposed to be at its worst then. There's a red warning from noon to nine.' Livi said it like it was a choice, something we could avoid. But it wasn't. The dolls needed to be visited. That was the truth of it.

I was fully prepared to defend myself in case Livi laughed or poked fun at the rituals. But she wasn't like that, not like the others. She understood. In fact, she didn't talk right away, and when she finally did, it wasn't about the visit. It wasn't even about the storm. 'What do you think tomorrow's secret will be?' The way she said it, with that quiet certainty, made me pause. It wasn't a question anymore — it was a statement. She had realised what I already knew. There would be another secret, and it was coming, whether we were ready for it or not.

'Every time there's a new secret,' I said, 'the stakes get higher.'

'How do you mean?'

'It started small — shoplifting, self-harming, drinking. Jay's secret didn't even make it to the list. Not worthy of the dolls,' I said. The sky rumbled, not the deep, thunderous roar of an Indian monsoon, but something more like a hungry stomach — low and insistent. I didn't even notice the lightning. 'Then the earrings. That was a shift.'

She glanced at me, then back to the road. 'How?'

'Earlier, it was about the secrets themselves. The earrings were different — it moved the focus from what to *who*. Who could have got the earrings? Who is moving the dolls? It forced everyone to wonder what this is all really about.'

Livi smiled tightly. She leaned forward, her hands gripping the wheel, her eyes never leaving the road. The rain was properly lashing now, the visibility down to maybe a hundred metres.

'That was when the blaming started,' I continued, 'and people left. Until then, it had been a game.'

Seeing me watch her, Livi nudged me. 'And?'

'From then on, the stakes got increasingly higher. A suicide, an attempted murder—'

'An accident,' she corrected me. Semantics. Accidents were between two cars, not when you drive onto a pavement and hit a child.

'Stalking, and then last night! That was a threat.'

'A threat?'

'What else could it be? A blackmail note, clearly.'

'About what?' Livi's voice shook. I shrugged. I didn't know, but what else could begin with *Devil?* And it came with a knife. It was a threat. 'What do you think is next?' she asked. Her look suggested she already knew. But like her, I didn't want to voice it, in case the angels were listening and decided, *so be it.* But what else could it be if not a murder? The question wasn't *what.* It was *who*!

CHAPTER THIRTY-SIX

Day Eight: Livi

By the time we got back from the shops, everyone had gone to bed. The power was still off, but I could hear the low drone of the generator. Aswin and Dhruv must have managed to start it. Taking leave of Leela, I headed to our room. Shravan lay on the bed, curled in a foetal position. I watched him, a dull ache in the pit of my stomach, pity and disgust mixed with nausea. 'Are you okay?' I asked.

I should be comforting him, like he did, back when I was falling apart. But something held me back. Somehow, my heart just wasn't in it. Before last night, things were different. Better. His friends were no good — especially Nancy and Maya — but I already knew that. It hadn't bothered me. Shravan wasn't the company he kept. He was my anchor, the kind soul who'd pulled me out from the depths. I wished I could turn back the clock. Take us to a time before the confession, before the letter. It wasn't just the way he'd snatched Nancy's note from my hands. It was the secrets. All of them. And where they came from. I had the sinking feeling there were more. The man I loved had caused a death. The question was whether I could look past it, whether I could still imagine a future that held any kind of happiness. The past tense did not escape me. *Loved.* I hadn't meant to use it. But there it was, and it saddened me.

Shravan sniffed. 'I'm fine.'

He had a lot to deal with, this psychiatrist, things he had never confronted. From the time he found out that Nancy was the stalker and helped her to hide it, keeping silent while she blamed it on John, even posting Maya's vile letter to John, he had known he was responsible for the death of an innocent man. It was a heavy burden for one person to bear. With years of therapy and a bit of luck, he might make it through to the other side. But first, he had to acknowledge what he'd done, own his mistake. Even now, I wasn't sure he was really ready to take that first step. Willing to acknowledge the depth of his deeds.

An awkward silence fell between us. He had been the talkative one in our relationship, always knowing what to say and how to say it — ever the therapist. That was what had drawn us together in the first place: me, wallowing in self-loathing after the deaths of my brother and mother. Regretting all those times I had been too busy to take their calls. For what? A foreign language placement in Brazil that I promptly gave up. Would things have gone differently had I been here? Perhaps. Perhaps not. That didn't stop me from self-blaming. Survivor's guilt.

When my thoughts became too much to bear, I sought relief in strenuous exercise, always pushing myself to the limit of my endurance. I became obsessed with climbing mountains. It was how I met Shravan, backpacking in Wales. He noted the blistered feet, the bleeding cuts, the way I marched on as if I didn't dare stop. On and on I went, alone within the group, hoping to meet my end on some lonely crag. I chose to trek in a group so that someone might find me and bring me back home to have my ashes scattered with those of my brother and mother on Maiden Island. I was afraid of being alone, even in death.

I was still angry with my brother for not considering those he left behind when he chose to end his own life. Deep into the night, I used to wonder — did he ever, even once, think of me when he took the drugs? Think of the impact it would have, the unbearable consequences? Did he regret it afterwards, as he lay alone in the bathtub, chest-deep in water as the drugs took effect, dragging him under? Did he think of me — of the people who loved him? Or was it only her that filled his mind? Just her, and what she did.

It was what prevented me from taking the same path, even though that was what I sought, out hiking in the mountains. It would have been too easy to end it all. Somehow, Shravan saw this. He never said much, but he walked beside me, step for step, as if he knew. Matching me stride for stride. Not pulling me back, just being there.

At first, I barely spoke to him. I rarely engaged with any of the others in the group beyond the basic courtesies. Until one day we were making our way up Ben Vorlich, and he said suddenly, 'I keep thinking about my sister. She was only six when she died. I'm climbing for both of us.'

After this, it became easier to speak of my own loss. I told him about Dexter, and how I lost him a couple of years ago. Climbing had always been our family's favourite activity. It took many climbs, but in the end he knew more about me than I knew about myself.

After a few more ascents, heart-to-heart chats, warming to our mutual loss, we had begun meeting outside of our treks. The King became our favourite watering hole — they did a mean Sunday roast. At one of these lunches, I had just taken a bite of their pulled pork when Shravan said, 'I knew you were suffering. At first, I thought it was a bad break-up, but it seemed too intense for that. I mean, walking with both feet bleeding — unless your ex was an Adonis.'

I smiled. 'Oh, it's not that bad.'

'No, seriously. At one point, I thought you really wanted to die.' He reached forward to wipe a spot of sauce from the corner of my mouth. Then, without a second thought, he brought it to his lips, sucking it off his finger. I blushed. It was the first flicker — something shifting between us. A quiet, undeniable spark. Before, it was just talks. Light, careful, dancing around the edges. But not from lack of wanting — at least, not on my part. 'You were punishing yourself, I could see that much.' He paused. 'I have a confession to make. I made up the story about my sister. I was an only child. No sister, never had one.' He'd put out a hand to stop me from interrupting. 'Before you get mad, hear me out. My intentions were good. It was to get you to tell me about your loss, what was causing you so much sorrow.'

I was furious, so much so that I stormed out of the pub. Maybe that should've been a warning of things to come. The secrets he could keep. The twisted lengths he would go to, just to get what he wanted.

In the days that followed, he begged me to meet up with him so he could explain why he'd lied to me like that. He left me voice notes, messages explaining the psychology behind it. If two people have both experienced a trauma, it makes it easier for them to connect, because the other person knows what you've been through. Eventually, I relented and agreed to meet him at a Starbucks, of all places.

'Take Alcoholics Anonymous,' he began. 'It works because everyone has been through the same sort of experience, and so no one is going to judge anyone else. Livi, please understand. I lied because I cared.' He kissed me, and ever since then, the smell of latte and almond cookies have reminded me of our early days together. Our first kiss.

Now, I no longer recognised this man. This was not the caring Shravan I had loved, but a liar. And those cold, vile lies had cost a life. Part of me believed it was my turn to stand by him as he once had stood by me. To see past his one mistake. But it wasn't just one mistake. He'd had plenty of opportunities to fix things, so many moments when he could've chosen truth over silence. He hadn't. And another part of me whispered that this was a coffin he'd built for himself out of lies, half-truths and silence. I had no rope strong enough to pull him from this mire.

As I gazed at him in revulsion, he awoke and reached out for me, pulling me towards him. Every instinct told me to push him away. Sleepily, he planted a kiss on my upper thigh. I went rigid.

'I'm sorry,' he said, sensing my discomfort. 'I should never have dragged you into this mess.' What was he talking about? It wasn't the mess he should be apologising for, it was his part in it.

'Is that the only thing you're sorry for?' I kept my gaze averted, unable to bring myself to even look at him. He had always been able to see through me, and if he looked into my eyes now, instead of love, he would find only disgust.

He sat up. 'What do you mean?'

If only things could be as they were. If only time would wash away the hurt. But time is like sand, sucked from beneath your feet by the waves, until you can no longer stand upright. So, I said, 'You know what I mean. What you did — or rather, didn't do. Why?'

He stared out through the window, into the darkness beyond, where the storm clouds silently gathered, ready for battle.

'I had no choice, did I?' he said bitterly.

'You always have a choice, Shravan. Those were your words, remember?' It was something he often said to me when I shed guilty tears over my loss. 'You can choose to wallow in sorrow, or to rise above it and move on.' That was before he told me, over that campfire, that he didn't have a choice. He had to pin it on John, blame him for Nancy's deeds. Was it only last night? It felt like a lifetime ago. This man had changed. Or had he always been like this, and I had been the one fooled? Fooled into believing the good in him, fooled by the charm and well-meaning words, fooled by the image he wanted me to see.

196

'Nancy.' He spoke as if the very word burned his tongue. 'I couldn't betray her, I couldn't.'

Excuses. I was getting tired of them. My response sounded harsher than I had intended. 'So you stayed silent. You let her blame it on her husband. Fair enough. But why post that vile letter from Maya?'

'You don't know Maya,' he said.

'What is she, a demigod? Are you that easily bullied?' Suddenly, it became impossible to sit there and listen to his feeble excuses. I stood up, not knowing what was the best thing to do.

'Don't go,' Shravan said. 'Please. Hear me out.'

'All right, I'm listening,' I said. I owed him that much at least. I remained standing, unable to bring myself to touch him, to comfort him. I shivered, suddenly cold. The power had been out for a while now, and we had been using the generator to keep the lights on, but the heating was off.

Shravan seemed to be casting around for the right words. Eventually, he said, 'No, you're right. I did have a choice. I shouldn't have let Nancy put the blame on John.'

'And? Go on,' I said. I sounded condescending, as if Shravan was a child I'd caught doing something he shouldn't.

My tone made him defensive. 'What's the point? You couldn't ever understand. You're not one of us. Never will be.'

CHAPTER THIRTY-SEVEN

Day Nine: Leela

'Leela, wake up. Look at me.' Dhruv was patting my frozen cheeks. He placed his finger under my nose, checking that I was still breathing, and heaved a sigh of relief. 'Oh, thank God! Are you okay, Leela?' He gathered me up, lifting me in his lap, placing me carefully into a crumpled heap, all dangling arms and sloppy shoulders.

For a moment, all I could focus on was the numbness in my limbs. Gradually, I made out the shape of Dhruv looking down at me. 'I'm . . . I'm all right,' I whispered. My voice was hoarse. I didn't want to move, not yet. Dhruv's lap was comfortable, and my head was still spinning.

I rubbed my eyes, which were wet. Dhruv must have splashed water on my face to bring me around. Then it all came back to me — the lightning, the badger, the dolls, the knife, the blood. Every image from before I fainted hit me all at once. My head spun, and I pushed myself up, unsteady. 'No! No!' I screamed. I didn't want to look. I knew what awaited me.

'Shh . . . It's okay. We managed to get the generator started. The power is back on. Everything's fine,' Dhruv said. I saw Aswin hovering anxiously in the background.

'No, it's not fine! There's . . . Someone is dead.' I pointed at the gruesome sight in the corner. How could they not see it?

'That . . . that's not a person, Leela. It's just a doll. And it's not blood. Someone is pulling a prank.' Despite his reassuring words, Dhruv sounded anxious.

Aswin cleared his throat. 'But . . . everything the dolls have shown has actually happened, hasn't it? You said so.'

'But those were past events,' Dhruv said. 'Weren't they?'

'But they're getting more and more recent,' Aswin said. 'The last one, Shravan's birthday note, that was from just days ago. What if—'

'Oh, don't be ridiculous. Are you saying the goddess has slain one of us?' Dhruv asked, glancing nervously at the tableau before us.

There she was, Maa Durga, in all her fury, her tri-headed spear plunged deep in the torso of one of the dolls. There was so much blood it was almost impossible to identify which doll had been 'killed'. It pooled on the white cloth carpeting the step. A drop fell onto my foot, and I screamed.

'Hey . . . hey.' Dhruv put his arms around me, dabbing at my tear-streaked cheeks with the end of my saree. I rested my head on his shoulder while he stroked my hair.

'You must call the police,' I told him.

'And say what?' Dhruv retorted. 'That there's a broken doll? Come on, Leela. It's just a prank.' He turned to Aswin, eyes pleading for support. But Aswin said nothing.

'Just a prank? Don't you think this has gone too far? What about the blood?'

'It's just paint,' Dhruv said.

'You know it's not. Surely you can smell it.' The stench was unmistakable, that mixture of rust and decay and something else that smelled like death. This wasn't paint, and he knew it.

'Listen, let's go back to the main house. See if we can find out what's going on,' Dhruv said.

Where was everyone? Why weren't they here? They must have heard me scream. Surely they heard.

CHAPTER THIRTY-EIGHT

Day Nine: Leela

The wind whipped at the trees, which crashed and groaned above the narrow path. We were only a few hundred metres from the main house, but it felt like miles. Taking a deep breath, I stepped forward, Dhruv's supporting arm around me. Together, we pushed through the darkness, side by side. He'd wanted me to stay back, safe in the cabin.

But I was having none of it. 'Wherever you go, I go too,' I'd told him. So, now we walked. Him and me. We left Aswin behind in the cabin, just in case someone came by.

Immediately, my foot slipped on the wet leaves, and Dhruv tightened his grasp. 'You okay?'

'Yeah, it's just slippery,' I said. I didn't have the heart to say that I was pretty sure I saw something moving, slithering from beneath my feet. He was trying, I could see that. Trying to be strong, to protect me, to protect us from whatever this was. But he wasn't built for this. Not that he was weak, no. Just . . . untouched. He'd lived a cocooned life, wrapped in silk-threaded comfort and quiet certainties. Not in a money sense. But in the way that comes from growing up safe, loved, unquestioned. All this darkness, this evil, it was alien to him.

All our phones died long ago; the power had been out for a while. Without it, we felt like we'd slipped back into the Iron Ages — cut off, silent, no messages, no calls, no way to check if the others were okay. We thought we'd run out of diesel for the generator until Aswin found a can in the wood cabin. Maybe it would last long enough to charge the phones.

The rain stabbed needles into my face, and my fingers were numb with cold. Every creak made me jump. We battled our way towards the house, our feet sinking into the mud. Each step was an effort. My jacket, now drenched and heavy, clung to me like a second skin. I longed to rip it off, scratch that itch, but it was the only thing between me and the storm, so I let it be. I glanced at Dhruv — he looked just as miserable. My beautiful green saree must be brown by now, I thought. That was the least of my troubles. The path seemed to have disappeared under a layer of leaves and sludge.

'You're shivering,' Dhruv said, pulling me closer. 'I told you we should have left days ago.'

'We'll go first thing tomorrow,' I said.

'As early as possible,' he promised.

We were supposed to put the dolls to sleep the next day and remove them the day after. But at this point, I didn't care a damn for tradition. At least the battle would have finished by the time we put them to rest in the car.

I reckoned we should soon be reaching the flower patch. From there, it was not far to the house. I couldn't even catch a glimpse of the house for the rain in my eyes.

Straining to look for its dark shape, I tripped and nearly took Dhruv down with me.

'Careful! You nearly had us both d— Oh. What's that?'

Then I saw it. A boot. It was one of Livi's. She must be nearby — she couldn't have gone far with only one boot on.

I called out her name. The sound of my voice was lost in the wind. 'I suppose it got stuck in the mud and she just pulled her foot out of it,' I said.

'But it's not stuck,' Dhruv said, picking it up. In a sudden flash of lightning, his figure, boot on his hands, almost leapt out of the dark. With a cry, he dropped it. Everything went dark again and I heard the thunder.

At first, I thought there was something wrong with him, a wasp or a scorpion, hiding in the boot from the rain and this godawful wind, had stung him.

'What happened?' I cried, running my arm over him, looking for a bump or a bruise or something that ought not to be there. Unable to find anything, I asked, 'Is it the boot? Is there something inside it?' I bent down to pick it up.

'Don't!' he screamed.

He didn't get to do that. He shouldn't 'Don't' me. Not like that. The wind, which had howled and clawed all night, suddenly dropped, holding its breath. Waiting. Watching.

I tipped up the boot, pouring out muddy water, and slid my hand inside. I pulled out what felt like a piece of sodden fabric. It wasn't a sock. I held it up. Another flash of lightning, and I saw that what I was holding was a rusty red colour. Its edges were marked with dark peacock green — the unmistakable hue of a saree. Or, at least, a part of it. A saree similar to mine. Was it Livi's? But the insides, soaked in . . . that was when I realised. The inside of the boot was soaked in not mud, but blood.

CHAPTER THIRTY-NINE

Day Nine: Leela

The manor house was shrouded in darkness. With each flash of lightning there were shadows across the walls — a dancing woman, a scarecrow with wild electric hair, a demon — each changing from one to the other as if they were in a game of relay. As if they were slave dancers and the lightning their whip-wielding master. It felt like I'd been waiting. Waiting for them to descend, unleash their fury. Ever since the dolls were moved.

I heard a small voice, the voice of a child. A sound from long, long ago. The night is a dangerous place, Leela.

Is that why you set the fire? I'd wanted to ask. It had been too late then, and it was too late now. I must have said it out loud. Or was it simply because I'd stopped moving?

'What?' Dhruv said impatiently.

I pointed to the shadows, still leaping across the walls.

'Oh, come on, Leela. It's the trees,' he said.

But it wasn't the trees, those shadows were signalling the danger that was to come. They were warning of death.

I recalled the day my mother took me to see the astrologer. I had been only about ten, but my mother was worried about me because I was born under the evil star, the star of the Goddess of Death.

The astrologer, a renowned shaman, had examined my horoscope thoughtfully for several minutes in silence. Then, he'd become possessed. Something took hold of his body, throwing him forward and backward in a frenzy. He gave a guttural cry and went still. Then he began to speak:

When the earth is plunged into darkness and the sky bleeds, as the cries of a million demons are carried by the wind and God's tears soak the land . . . believe no one, Leela, for you are all alone. Follow the path of the holy goddess, and if you must, slay the demon. For both the goddess and the demon reside within you. One must go for the other to thrive. Choose wisely, and you might live. Choose wrong, and death cannot be stopped.'

When it was over, his body jerked thrice. Tears were streaming down his cheeks and with trembling hands, he thrust my horoscope away. 'I'm sorry,' he mumbled. 'I can't do this. You should go now.'

At that, I ran, but my mum stayed for a bit. For many nights after, I'd woken choking on my own screams, haunted by the thought of what I hadn't stayed to hear. I'd begged my mum to tell me, over and over, but every time I'd asked, something in her seemed to break a little more. Her face would freeze, her eyes darken — not with fear *for* me, but fear *of* me. It had been a terrible thing to see. After a while, I learned not to ask. I'd swallowed the nightmares whole until they rotted inside me in silence.

My mother had never spoken of it again. Then, there was the fire — the night my mother and sister died, I thought that was what the shaman spoke of. The sky glowed red with flames, their cries twisted like demons. I'd believed it was my fault. That I had somehow chosen wrong. If only I hadn't gone to dance class . . . if only I hadn't taught Mala how to light a match. The guilt has gnawed at me ever since. But maybe it wasn't then. Back then, there was no rain. No God's tears soaking the earth. Now, though, it was pouring.

'Come on, Leela. Let's join the others,' Dhruv said. I caught it — the same flicker of fear in his eyes, the one my mother had carried every time she'd looked at me, right up until the fire devoured her. By then, I had long stopped screaming. I had learned to bury my terror so deep that it hollowed me out, left my head light and my body weaker. The fainting spells had started soon after. I'd discovered something then, that fainting was forgivable. It made me look fragile, breakable, human — not the danger that I really was, not the curse that clung to me, destroying everything I touched. As he pulled me gently in the direction of the kitchen, I saw a light in the second-floor window — Maya's room. But I knew she wasn't there.

In the kitchen, a lone figure was seated at the island. My eyes scanned for the others, for Nancy. For Livi or Smitha. Even Shravan. Where were they?

'Hey, you're back.' It was Jay. He was glad to see us. 'Where's Livi?' he asked, peering behind us, as if we could be hiding her there — like now would be a good time for hide-and-seek. When he didn't find her, his smile faltered. 'Isn't she with you?'

Dhruv shrugged. 'We thought she was with you.'

'She said she was going to help you. Get some diesel or something,' Jay said.

'When was this?' He ignored my question.

'She was there for a bit, but then she came back to fetch you,' Dhruv said. 'We found her boot on the path.' He didn't mention the blood.

'So, where is she?' Jay said. 'Lost?' His tone was accusatory, as if it was somehow my fault.

'She can't be lost. Not in her own place,' I said. 'She must know it like the back of her hand. They always came here for their holidays.'

'Well, she can't have walked off either. Not with one boot.'

'Did you ask any of the others?' Jay said. 'Smitha?'

Dhruv looked around. 'Where *is* Smitha?'

'She went to the cabin with Nancy,' Jay said.

'Neither of them came while we were there,' Dhruv said. 'And why didn't we cross paths with them when we were on our way back here?'

And where was Shravan?

CHAPTER FORTY

Day Nine: Leela

The dying wind moaned, like someone exhausted and without hope. The rain had stopped for now, but the clouds amassed on the horizon promised more to come. Frogs, brought out by the damp, filled the night air with their mating calls.

Dhruv wanted me to stay in the house while he searched the forest. Just like how he wanted me to stay in the cabin. He said he wanted me to be safe. But I didn't believe him. He just didn't want me fainting out there in the dark. But the voice from my childhood, that of the shaman, was impossible to ignore: *Follow the path of the holy goddess. Believe no one.* So I told Dhruv I was afraid of being left alone with Jay. Of course, Jay was perfectly harmless, but I had to find some excuse for going out. What better excuse than a damsel in distress? If I'd told him I would do better in the dark, he'd have bristled and gone all weird. But this was safe, a coy smile and distressed eyes always did the trick.

Aswin was waiting in the cabin in case the women or Shravan returned, while Jay was in the main house for the same reason. With our phone batteries out, there was no way to communicate.

'So, which way do we go?' Dhruv asked. 'We'll probably get lost out there too, and then what?'

I remembered Jay's words: *She was going to help you. Get diesel or something.* Suddenly, I knew exactly where they'd gone. 'Dunollie Castle,' I said. 'We'll start there.'

'What would they go there for?' Dhruv asked.

'They might be looking for diesel,' I said. 'I remember Livi mentioning that they used to store diesel there for the heaters.' Before Dhruv could raise any more objections, I hastened forward along the path that led up to the ruined castle.

Dhruv jogged up beside me, panting. 'You think Livi and Nancy went together? Think they would go off like that? Together?'

Too many questions. I didn't answer right away, because honestly, I didn't know. All I knew was, I couldn't just stand there and do nothing. Even with everything that had happened, the idea of Livi teaming up with Nancy felt far-fetched — implausible in the way nightmares sometimes do when daylight breaks. But then again, there was the diesel. That had to be it. They'd gone looking for fuel and were probably already on their way back. Anything else was too hard to even fathom. 'Maybe,' I said. 'We'll find out soon enough.'

He glanced around, uncertain. 'First, we have to find the path to the castle. The last time we went there, it was overgrown — bushes, thorns everywhere. And it was in daylight. Is this really a good idea?'

He had a point. But what was the alternative — sit and wait? 'What do you suggest?'

He exhaled, almost in relief, like he'd been waiting for me to ask. 'We go back,' he said with sudden certainty. 'Charge our phones. Call the police. They'll send someone.'

Strange. It was his idea to come looking. What changed? Just then, the distant call of a shrike sliced through the dark. My resolve hardened.

'You wanted to go alone,' I reminded him.

'To the cabin. Maybe the flower patch. Check if they're there,' he said quickly. 'Not into the woods. Just to charge the phones and get help.' So that was it. He'd never meant to search. Just pretend to.

'I heard a thud,' I said. 'When you and Aswin were fixing the generator.' The image hit me: the lone boot, the blood-soaked rag. 'What if it was a tree? And they're trapped under it?'

I could see him pause, genuinely consider it — a giant oak or a wind-wrenched birch collapsing in the storm, limbs like bones snapping as they fell. Crushing them. Smitha and Nancy, unconscious. Livi, pinned, screaming herself hoarse in the dark. I shuddered.

Dhruv snorted. 'And the tree flung Livi's boot all the way to the flower patch?'

I didn't respond. The logic was thin, but fear doesn't ask for logic. We fell silent. The torch beam wavered as we walked, barely making a difference. Then we found it — the fallen tree. Not far from the cabin. Split clean at the base, its trunk lay twisted like a body in mid-spasm.

'See? No one here,' Dhruv said.

He was right. The ground beneath the tree was bare — no signs of struggle, no footprints, no scraps of clothing or dying glow of a weak torch. When we looped around the cabin and headed towards the castle, I was surprised that he didn't resist.

'Where is Shravan?' I asked.

He shrugged but looked uneasy. 'I'm sure he'll be fine.' Shravan had been with us in the cabin — quiet, brooding, but present. But at some point, he must have slipped out. When Aswin found the diesel, Shravan hadn't been there. Just gone. Vanished into the night without a word. Dhruv hadn't wanted to leave me alone, so they'd called out for him, searched the immediate area. In the end, they'd headed out themselves. I wondered where he could have gone in such a hurry.

We stumbled on in silence, until the dark shape of Dunollie Castle loomed ahead. My eyes on the castle, I almost tripped over something too soft to be a tree branch lying on the ground.

'What?' Dhruv said. 'Why've you stopped?'

'There's something there. Look, on the ground.'

I felt around, and my fingers encountered something metallic. It was a torch. I tried switching it on, and to my surprise, it lit up. Though its side was cracked, the beam was stronger than that of our own torch. Now I could see the object clearly. Face down at my feet was Smitha, a deep gash just behind her ear.

CHAPTER FORTY-ONE

Day Nine: Smitha

I was back in the main building, huddled next to the heater with a mug of hot chocolate. Thank God the power was back on — at least I thought it was, I couldn't hear the generator. When I came to, I couldn't remember what had happened, only that I was drenched, soaked to the bone. And that my nose was less than inch from the mud. My legs and arms were numb with cold. Dhruv had had to almost carry me back to the house. It was a long way too, and he wasn't careful, dragging me through the bushes and rocks like a rag doll. A hot bath had restored some feeling to my fingers.

'Are Livi and Nancy okay? Where are they?' I asked. I scanned the group around me, such as it was — just Leela, Dhruv, and Jay. Then Aswin walked in as if he'd been summoned.

They exchanged glances. Aswin shook his head. 'We were hoping you'd tell us,' Leela said, turning back to me.

'Come on, Smitha. Tell us where they are,' Jay said impatiently. 'This isn't a game, you know.'

Yeah, some game. One where I knocked myself out, almost drowned myself and hoped someone found me lying in the dark. For a professor, Jay could be remarkably dense sometimes.

'What were you doing out there, Smitha?' Leela said, with a warning glance at Jay. 'Maybe we can start there. You and Nancy were going to the cabin. Is that right? So, how come you ended up near Dunollie Castle?'

The wound at the back of my head throbbed. Gingerly, I touched the dressing that Leela had applied; at least it wasn't oozing anymore. 'Mmm . . . I remember the generator ran out just as we were leaving. We took the last big torch — those others aren't much use, are they?'

'Then what happened?' Jay prompted. Leela silenced him with a look. I need to learn how to do that.

'We met Livi on the way.' I took a sip of chocolate. Instantly, warmth spread through my insides.

'See, I told you,' Dhruv said, only to receive another sharp glance from Leela. The effect was almost instantaneous, his mouth clamped shut and he dropped his head.

'When I told her the last of the diesel had run out, she said she'd head to the castle, where they used to keep a stash in the cellar.' I fiddled with the dressing, which appeared to have come loose, and in its wake was sending sharp shooting pains.

'Here, let me,' Leela said, and tightened the bandage. Holding it in place, her hands were steady, while the men were all quivering wrecks.

'And so you decided to join her,' Leela said.

'I, er, yes.' I paused, glancing at Jay. His face said it all: *Really? In that storm?* Though, of course, he wouldn't dare say it aloud. Not with Leela watching. Trying to get my thoughts together, I said, 'I told her it wasn't a good idea, and that we should send the men. We were all wearing sarees, which isn't the best thing for finding your way over rough ground in the pitch dark in the middle of a storm. But Livi insisted.'

'And you went with her,' Jay repeated.

'I've told you, yes.' By now, he was really beginning to annoy me. He could show a bit of sympathy. After all, I was his wife, and I'd just survived a murderous attack. Instead, he was sitting on his high horse and questioning every word of my story.

'So, what happened next?' Leela asked.

'We followed Livi. She knew the place and where she was going. She let Nancy and me have the torches and went on ahead in the dark.'

'This the torch you took?' Dhruv asked, holding it up.

'Nancy had that one. I had the red one,' I said.

We all looked at the torches on the floor. There was no red one.

'Go on,' Leela said.

'When we got to the bottom of the hill that leads up to the castle, I didn't want to go any further. The path was slippery, and I was afraid I might fall.'

'So you stayed behind to wait for them,' Leela said.

'I watched them go up until they vanished in the dark. Shortly after I lost sight of them, I heard them shouting. I couldn't make out much of what they were saying, but at one point I heard Nancy yell, "You ruined my life! You took everything from me, and now this!" It sounded like Livi was trying to calm her down. I didn't hear what she was saying.'

'But they were definitely having a fight?' Dhruv asked. 'That what you're saying?'

'Yes,' I replied. 'I wondered whether I should go up and try and calm things down, but then I heard someone come crashing through the undergrowth, followed by a loud scream. At that point, my torch went out, the battery had died. I stood there, listening, but there wasn't a sound. Then . . .'

Leela put her arm around my shoulders. 'It's okay. Take your time.'

But time was what we didn't have right now. They should be out there, searching for Livi and Nancy. I took a breath. 'Then I decided to go up. I couldn't see a thing, of course, but I reckoned if I just went uphill I might get close enough to hear them. I'd just started to feel my way forward when I heard someone behind me. It was definitely a person, I heard them breathing. I stopped, thinking it was maybe one of you out looking for us. Then I was struck on the head. I don't remember anything after that.'

'What are we waiting for? Let's go,' Aswin said. At last, I thought, someone's decided to act.

'Wait,' Leela said. 'What about the boot?'

'What boot?' I said.

'We found one of Livi's boots,' Dhruv said. 'There was a piece of bloodstained material in it.'

I squeezed my eyes tight shut, willing myself to remember. 'Oh yes. When we met Livi, she was kneeling down, holding something in her hand.'

What was it, in her cupped hand? It must have been the knock to my head, but my memory was fuzzy. 'Yes. It was a squirrel, it had been injured. Almost dead. There was blood everywhere. I asked her what she was doing. It wasn't safe. With the storm and all. Livi said—'

'She didn't want it to die alone,' Leela said.

'Yes, that's right,' I said, surprised at how certain she sounded. 'Livi said it had been caught in a trap near the bins. She'd had to wedge one of her boots between the teeth to stop it from snapping shut. Then she tore off a piece of her saree and wrapped the squirrel in it. The poor thing was shivering. So, she took off the other boot and placed it inside. I offered to go back to the main building to get her some shoes. Nancy came with me. When we got back with the shoes, Livi wasn't there. She eventually limped out of the bushes, saying she'd buried the poor thing.' My finger traced the top of the mug.

'So that explains the boot,' Dhruv said.

'And the blood,' Leela said.

Then we heard a voice from the doorway. 'We need to leave now and find Livi,' Shravan said. We hadn't noticed him come in. His coat was dripping with rainwater. His eyes were an angry red, and his matted hair stuck out in all directions. It was obvious that he had been out. Where, I wondered.

Walking closer, he put a hand on my shoulder, the psychiatrist in him coming to the fore. 'You've done well, Smitha. Now you should rest.'

I nodded, and picked up my mug, the forgotten hot chocolate now cold. As I lifted it, my thoughts wandered — back to the footsteps behind me, soft but deliberate. The flash of a gloved hand. The smell of mint interwoven with the wet dampness. The blow. The mug slipped from my hand and broke into pieces on the floor.

CHAPTER FORTY-TWO

Day Nine: Leela

Finally, Smitha calmed down enough for me to lead her up to her room, where I put her to bed. After what she had been through, she needed the rest. First, with the incident during the white-water rafting and now this. The devil must have been smiling down on her.

'What was that all about?' Dhruv asked when I came back down.

'A panic attack. Poor thing, she's been through hell,' I said. 'Anyway, Jay's with her now.'

'A little late to react now, isn't it?' Dhruv said. 'She was perfectly fine a minute or two ago. Anyway, it's Shravan who should be having a panic attack, it's his girlfriend who's missing.'

His words seemed to galvanise Shravan. 'We should go and look for her. We can't just sit here doing nothing.' Almost in the same breath, he asked, 'Did you see my gloves? The ones Livi gave me.'

'How could we? It's pitch dark out there, we have no idea where to even start looking,' Aswin said. He was kneeling on the floor, sweeping up the pieces of the mug Smitha had dropped.

'Ow!' One of the shards had pierced his hand. As he pulled it out slowly, something about it made me want to gag. I looked away.

'We can try Dunollie Castle,' Shravan said.

'But that's where we found Smitha. There's no one at the castle. Right, Leela?' Dhruv asked. 'You went in to check after I left with Smitha.'

Yes, I had. After we'd found Smitha, I went back to check if Nancy and Livi were still there. Dhruv had wanted to come too, but Smitha looked bad — her pulse was weak, her skin cold — and I was afraid she'd lose consciousness. So I sent them off and went in alone. But could I really be certain no one was there?

I remembered the sound — the crunch of rock underfoot, the footsteps that had spooked me before I ran back. Someone *had* been there. I just didn't know who. I hesitated. How much should I say?

'Well, it's a wide area, Dhruv. And it was dark,' I said reasonably. That much was true. I'd let Dhruv take the brighter torch. The last thing I wanted was to hear him say, 'I told you so.' Why was he always so negative? The slightest suggestion and he had to put it down.

'See?' Dhruv said as if I'd agreed with him.

'But you did find the sleeping bag and the cans,' Shravan said. 'Someone is camping there.'

'Yes. That's why I waited around for a bit, to see if anyone would turn up,' I said.

'Well, what are we waiting for?' Shravan said. 'Every second we waste could be dangerous. Livi could need help!'

I noticed how he had left Nancy out of the narrative, as if he knew something we didn't.

'We should call the police,' Aswin said over his shoulder, tipping the broken pieces in the bin. 'Someone else could get lost out there.'

'So we just sit around and wait?' Shravan demanded.

'That would be the most sensible thing to do, Shravan,' Dhruv said. 'The wind's picking up again—'

'I can't believe this. Livi could be hurt, lying somewhere, helpless,' Shravan said. He appeared genuinely distressed, but I couldn't shake the feeling that he was hiding something. For instance, he hadn't yet volunteered details about where he'd been. Why he'd suddenly disappeared without telling us.

'All the more reason to bring in the professionals, like Aswin said. Look what happened to Smitha,' Dhruv said.

'Well, I'm going,' Shravan said. 'If you're too scared to come with me, fine. Stay here, then.'

'No, Dhruv's right,' I said. 'It isn't safe. The last thing we want is for you to go missing too. For a start, our phones are all dead, so if anything did happen to any of us, we couldn't call for help.'

'I'll put them on charge now,' Aswin volunteered. A tactful way to say, *I'm not coming.*

'Then can you call the police?' I asked. 'Once the phones are charged. Call emergency and tell them two people are missing. Give them the address.'

But Aswin had already left the room, his phone in his hand, apparently having forgotten to collect ours.

I looked at Shravan. It was obvious that he was going, whether we agreed or not. 'We could go in the car, I suppose. Obviously, it's not straightforward, but I believe it would take us to the front of the castle,' I suggested.

Shravan nodded eagerly. 'Dhruv?' I prompted.

He shrugged. 'Okay, okay.'

'You still have your phone? We can charge it in the car as we go,' I said.

'Well, what are we waiting for?' Shravan said. 'But where are my gloves?'

His girlfriend was missing, and he was worried about gloves — this was the second time he'd asked. I wanted to ask him where he'd been, what he was doing out there in the storm. But that would sound accusatory. And right now, we needed him.

'Never mind. I'll look for them later. Let's go.'

I was wearing Livi's coat. Mine, still wet, was discarded on the bathroom floor. The rain had eased off to a misty drizzle. The worst is over, I thought. But maybe not. Heads down, hoods pulled up just in case, we made a dash for the car—

And stopped short, staring in horror. The wind had uprooted a large willow tree, which had fallen onto the car, crushing it. As we watched, not knowing what to do, a badger ran out from under it.

CHAPTER FORTY-THREE

Day Nine: Leela

The rain was pelting down again, and with both Shravan's and Jay's cars having been crushed by the fallen tree, we had no choice but to take ours. The little old Honda was hardly equipped to handle the rough terrain, or the storm. When Dhruv started it up, the engine coughed. He had to try several times before the engine finally turned over.

Inside, it smelled of tobacco and wet tree bark. My chest was still rising too fast, breath catching from the leftover adrenaline. I rolled down the window. The sweet, clean wind rushed in, the rain, cool against my face. For just a moment, I closed my eyes and pretended everything was fine. As if saying it to myself enough times could make it true. Maybe it could.

It was hard going. The car swung about and the wheels spun in the mud. Dhruv leaned forward, peering over the top of the steering wheel, trying to see ahead through the rain and the dark.

Thunder crashed in the distance. I shivered. When the next rumble came, it sounded farther off. At least the storm was moving away. I remembered a similar storm in the monsoon season when I was about nine. A young peepal tree next to our house had been struck by lightning, and the green bark had lit up like a phosphorescent beacon. It had burned for hours, just twenty feet from our thatched hut. According to my uncle, the burning tree had been visible for miles. By some miracle, our hut had remained untouched. The next day, all that had been left of the tree was a pile of ash and a gaping hole in the ground.

I often wondered if it was that incident that pushed my mum to consult the shaman. Even before then, there had been whispers about my birth star and the bad luck it carried. Ever since my sister, still an infant, was struck down by polio and lost her ability to walk, it had somehow been my fault — not my parents' for failing to vaccinate her. When my dad had left us for a younger model, again it was my fault — not his or his roving eye. I supposed the lightning, and the fire in its aftermath, had been the straw that broke the camel's back. Two years later, my mum and sister were dead.

I was still lost in the memory when Dhruv suddenly slammed on the brakes, throwing me against the dashboard. Ahead of us was the massive trunk of a tree that had fallen across the road.

'Can't we get past?' Shravan asked.

Dhruv shook his head. 'It's completely blocking the way.'

'It's not much further to the castle,' I said. 'We can walk the rest of the way.'

In the aftermath of the storm, the slope was treacherous, slipping and sliding under our feet. I had to stop several times, holding on to Dhruv. Under my hands, he trembled, and I held on tighter. Somehow, we managed to make our way to the ruined castle.

We filed in through the archway. 'Hello!' Shravan called out. 'Livi, are you there? Nance?'

The smell of chicken soup and baked beans drifted towards us, faint but unmistakable. Someone's stomach rumbled. In the corner was a mound of sand, blown in from the ocean. Beside it was a rusty spade, stuck to the ground at an odd angle, as if it was abandoned in a hurry halfway through digging a hole. To bury what, I wondered. Leading away were fresh footprints, water pooling inside them.

Eyeing them, Dhruv hissed, 'Quiet. There's someone here.'

'What do you mean? Who?' Shravan said. In his haste, he was a few steps ahead.

'Could it be John?'

'He's not here,' Shravan said. His voice sounded strange, faraway like it wasn't really his.

'He might be,' Dhruv said. 'He must be around some-where. The dolls—'

'He's not here,' Shravan said. 'He can't be. Because he's dead,' he said flatly. 'John's been dead for a couple of years.'

CHAPTER FORTY-FOUR

Day Nine: Leela

After the havoc outside, there was a strange stillness inside the castle. It felt like the old walls were mocking the storm, as if to say, *Is that all you've got?* In all its years, it must have faced far worse. This wind, no matter how fierce, wasn't going to bring it down.

Each armed with a torch, we spread out across the courtyard. Our beams sliced through the dark, bouncing off wet stone and glinting against rusted iron fixtures. There was nothing. No movement, no sound except the distant slap of the ocean and the steady drip of water from the eaves.

We were almost about to give up when a muffled sound drifted up from somewhere below. We exchanged glances, then looked at the sleeping bag sprawled in front of us, its zipper down as if abandoned in haste. An open can of beans had toppled over, spilling its contents. It smelt like it had been there a while. We heard it again, this time distinctly more human.

'Hello?' Dhruv called out. His voice echoed back. No response.

'It's coming from down there,' I said, pointing towards the steps leading down to the cellar, the entrance barred by a chained and padlocked gate.

'We can't go there,' Dhruv said. 'The storm's been raging for hours. The rain's relentless. The cellar could be flooded.' That could have been true, but there was barely any water there. Maybe it was because the castle stood high on the hill, or maybe it was the angle of the rain — either way, beyond the dampness under our feet, there was no real water flow inside.

'Come on, Dhruv, there's someone down there,' Shravan said, already moving towards the gate.

'Looks like it's locked,' Dhruv said, sounding relieved. 'Maybe we should wait for the police.'

We heard the sound again. This time it was louder, like a stifled scream.

Shravan darted forward. 'I'm going down.' He pulled at the chain, which came off in his hand.

That was when I noticed the broken rusty lock lying on the ground. Someone had been here.

Dhruv griped my hand. 'Stay. It's not safe.'

I pulled away. 'It could be Livi or Nancy. They might need help.' He was offended and a little worried. I could almost read his mind — if I went, he had to. There was no way he could just stand here and let me go down there. Not without a reason. So, I gave him one. Softening my voice, I said, 'You stay here. You can keep watch.'

He looked grateful.

By the time I reached the steps, Shravan was already half-way down, bent almost double to avoid hitting his head on the low ceiling. Then, he disappeared around a corner, and a moment later I heard him gasp, followed by a crash as he tumbled down the steps and vanished into the dark.

'Leela? Are you okay?' Dhruv called out.

I heard Shravan shuffle, as if he was crawling. God, was he hurt? I was too frightened to call out — who knew what was down there? I stood, hesitating, peering into the darkness below.

Suddenly, Shravan screamed, 'Help! Over here.'

My heart pounded in my ribcage. What should I do? Suddenly dizzy, I leaned against the wall, breathing heavily. A wave of nausea washed over me. Please, God, no. I couldn't faint now.

Then I heard Shravan again. 'Oh, thank God! Livi's here. She's okay.'

CHAPTER FORTY-FIVE

Day Nine: Smitha

I tossed and turned in bed, bewildered by what had come over me earlier. One moment I was fine, chatting about the dead squirrel and my boot. The next, it was as if someone had clamped a hand around my throat, squeezing tight, or had thrown a plastic bag over my head. My lungs burned, I couldn't seem to get enough air. Maybe I was having a heart attack. Maybe I was dying. I let Leela take my hand and tuck me into bed.

Now I felt better — I thought. My face was numb, and I avoided looking in the mirror. The horror on Jay's face told me that it wouldn't be wise. In unguarded moments, when I looked down, I could see my cheeks, and they were huge, like there was a plum underneath the skin. My legs and upper arms still ached from being pressed against the rocks under the driving rain. And my mind buzzed — full of theories, chocolate, and adrenaline.

I thought about men and their capabilities (or lack thereof). All the men in my life had simple minds. They were perfectly capable so long as everything was going according to plan, but at the slightest glitch, the least of life's curveballs, they were left floundering like fish out of water. Take Jay and Aswin, for example. Leela's instructions were perfectly clear — take care of Smitha and call 999. What could be more simple? Yet they seemed utterly lost.

In the end, I dragged myself to the kitchen and made us all strong coffee. It was going to be a long night. At least Aswin had managed to charge the phones.

'I'm not getting a signal,' Aswin called out for the hundredth time.

'Me neither,' Jay said, standing just feet away from Aswin. Could he not at least move a little closer to the window?

'Give it here,' I said, grabbing Jay's phone and striding over to the window. *Emergency calls only.* That would have to do. I dialled 999.

It took ten agonising minutes to get connected, the automated message citing the high volume of calls due to the adverse weather conditions. I was placed on hold for what felt like an eternity. The recorded voice urged me to consider whether my situation was a real emergency. *Oh, for God's sake, just let me speak to a real human being.*

After a few false starts, I finally heard a voice on the other end of a line that crackled ominously. 'What is the emergency?'

I wish I had rehearsed what to say. Should I start with the location or the missing women?

'Hello? Are you there?' The line was so bad it was hard to tell if it was a man or a woman, but at least it was not a robot.

'Ah, yes. I'm here,' I said, flustered. 'We're in Oban.' Would they know that? 'The Williams manor house.' I waited for a response.

'Yes? And what is your emergency?'

Good. 'My two friends are missing — Livi and Nancy.' What did I give their names for? Stupid.

'Did you say friends?'

Why the hell else would I be calling 999? To report missing sheep? 'Yes. Two missing women. Please hurry.'

They transferred me to the police. After a frustrating fifteen minutes during which *adult women*, *in the last twenty-four hours*, *fallen tree*, *storm*, and *low visibility* were frequently cited, I admitted defeat and hung up. Help wasn't coming anytime soon. And according to them, we shouldn't be looking for them either. 'Stay put and let the storm pass' was their advice to me. Thank God I was not the listening type.

CHAPTER FORTY-SIX

Day Nine: Livi

My mouth was dry, and I'd been sitting in the same position for so long that my legs were numb. My ankles were bound together, and the rope around my wrists was beginning to chafe, each tiny movement scraping skin. The duct tape across my mouth tasted metallic, bitter — something like blood or rust. It made my stomach churn. I kept thinking, *If I vomit, I might choke.* The thin fabric of my peacock-green saree offered little protection against the cold stone of the castle floor. My jacket lay discarded a few feet to my left, tantalisingly close. I'd stared at it for hours, willing it closer, imagining the warmth of it. But I couldn't reach it. Not with my hands pinned behind me, wrapped around the back of the stone column like an offering to some forgotten god. I had barely enough space to tilt my head, let alone manoeuvre.

I was fast losing all hope of anyone coming to my rescue. At first, I'd thought Smitha might follow me here and find me, but if that was the case, she would have come by now. I wondered what had happened to her and Nancy. Did they meet the same fate? Could they be here too, and I just hadn't heard them? There was no sound but the distant rumble of thunder. Inside the castle, the outside world was muted.

My screams for help were muffled by the tape, and the effort was exhausting. Besides, who would hear me? The castle was miles from anywhere, its stone walls thick and covered in ivy. I wondered how long it would be before the ivy crept under the stones and brought the whole castle down. By then, I would be long gone, nothing but a heap of bones buried beneath the rubble.

I mustn't think like this, I told myself. It wasn't like me to lose hope. Someone was sure to rescue me before long, weren't they? Shravan would have realised I was missing. If only I hadn't suggested coming here in the first place . . .

Wait! Wasn't that the sound of footsteps? I kept still, in case it was my captor, coming back to finally kill me. But no, that was Shravan's voice, unmistakable, the voice that used to whisper sweet nothings into my ear. Now he sounded scared. I struggled to call out, only managing to produce a pitiful squeak. He was arguing with someone, but I couldn't tell who, or what they were saying. *I'm here!* I wanted to scream. But I knew it would come out wrong — muffled, unintelligible, drowned beneath their rising voices.

I waited, every muscle in my body taut, until, finally, silence descended. I tried again, 'Mmmmm!'

Then I heard Dhruv calling out, 'Hello?'

'It's coming from down there,' said someone — Leela.

Now I caught fragments of what they were saying. I heard the words 'locked' and 'police'.

No, no, no! Please don't go back. Panic surged through me. I mustered the last remnants of my failing strength, and thank God, it came out as a scream that resounded against the stone walls.

'I'm going down,' Shravan said, louder this time. I'd never heard such sweet words.

'Stay. It's not safe.' It was Dhruv. *Don't you dare!* I wanted to scream again, but I didn't have the strength.

Then Leela said, 'It could be Livi or Nancy. They might need help.' Yes. Yes, please, a little help would be great.

At last, the sound of footsteps. They were moving slowly, testing the ground. Then I saw him — Shravan. His eyes on me, and he fell the last few steps.

'Leela? Are you okay?' Dhruv called from above, his voice trembling. I wondered what had happened to Smitha.

Shravan said to someone behind him, 'Oh, thank God! Livi's here. She's okay.' Now he was kneeling beside me, tugging ineffectually at the ropes around my ankles. I gave a muffled yelp, which seemed to remind him of the tape around my mouth. When he pulled at it, it felt as if my mouth was coming off with it. I shook my head. *Please, stop.*

CHAPTER FORTY-SEVEN

Day Nine: Leela

My torch beam travelled around the stone walls of the cellar before it alighted on the figure of Livi, who was lying sprawled on the stone floor. Shravan was kneeling beside her, desperately struggling with the ropes that bound her. 'I can't undo them,' he whimpered.

The ropes were nylon and sturdy, and with all the straining the knots had tightened. There were at least four layers of tape covering her mouth — ripping it off would take her skin with it. Shravan's frantic pulling was only making things worse.

I told him so. 'We need a plan,' I said, scanning the room for something to cut the ropes with. A jagged rock. I thought of the shovel upstairs. But maybe not.

'Mmm . . . Mmm.' Livi's eyes were on her jacket, lying on the ground a few feet away.

'Are you cold?' I asked, removing my own jacket. Hers was soaked through.

'Nmmm . . . Nmmm.' She shook her head and jerked it towards her jacket again.

I went over and picked it up, checking the pockets while she nodded vigorously. Sure enough, there was something hard in the inside pocket — a pair of scissors.

She groaned as I snipped through the rope binding her legs, and then her arms. She attempted to stand, but her legs buckled beneath her, and she folded like a collapsible deck-chair. I caught her before she hit the ground. She was heavier than I expected, given her slender frame.

'For God's sake, Shravan — a little help, please,' I said.

'Hello? Is everything okay down there?' Dhruv called from above. I felt a surge of annoyance. Surely he couldn't still be too scared to come down. For all he knew, our throats could be slashed by now, and he would be standing guard not for us, but the killer.

'You might want to come down and give us a hand,' I said sarcastically. 'Don't worry, you'll be quite safe.'

It took Livi a while to regain her strength. Finally, she could stand, and limped towards the corner, where several metal cans were lined up, smelling strongly of diesel.

'It's all right, the power's back,' I told her, but she ignored me. When she reached the cans, she opened one and tipped it forward, splashing her fingers. Then, she applied the liquid to the edges of the tape at her mouth. It peeled off surprisingly easily.

'Are you okay?' Shravan asked.

'Shaken, cold, but I'll survive. What about Smitha and Nancy?'

I wished I'd brought some water with me. She looked parched.

We looked at each other. 'Smitha is fine,' I said, starting with the good news. 'She's back at the house.'

'And Nancy?' Livi asked. 'Did you find her?'

I shook my head. There was no point lying to her.

'What do you mean?'

'I mean she hasn't come back,' I said. 'She's . . . still out there. It's almost impossible to find anyone in this storm.'

'All on her own,' Livi said. We all knew what that meant. Nancy didn't have much time.

'What happened?' Dhruv had finally mustered the courage to come down. He gestured to the ropes and the scattered duct tape.

'I don't know,' Livi said, and picked up the torch Shravan had dropped when he fell down the steps. 'When we ran out of diesel, I started to panic. Who knew when the power would come back? Then I remembered what the shop assistant had said about the stash here,' she said, glancing at me. I nodded. 'I wanted to come up here and grab a few cans. Nancy wouldn't let me go alone. Smitha stayed at the bottom of the hill. She was afraid she might fall.' Livi's eyes swept the floor, as if searching for something lost. 'Nancy and I came on up together. Suddenly, she started shouting at me. "You did it!" she said. "You spoiled my only chance at happiness." So then I told her that she never had a chance.' Livi burst into tears. This must have been the screaming Smitha heard.

I placed my arm around her shoulders.

'And then?' Dhruv prompted, and I glared at him.

She sniffed. 'Then she went quiet. She said I was right, and she was sorry for shouting at me like that. By then, the storm was getting stronger, the wind really starting to blow. I wanted us to grab the diesel and head back. So, I asked her to wait for me while I fetched it, and I came down here.'

'We found the lock broken,' I said.

Livi smiled. 'That was me. I smashed it with a rock.'

'How come you had the scissors with you?' I asked.

'Oh, just in case. I thought the cans might have been tied up to stop them falling over or getting stolen.'

I was asking these questions because they might give us an idea of where to start looking. 'So, you came down by yourself. And?'

She looked up as if to gather her thoughts. 'I was down here, looking for the cans, when all of a sudden I was hit from behind.' She touched the back of her head — the same spot where Smitha was struck. Her hand came back dry. At least she wasn't bleeding.

'With the torch?' Shravan asked.

'No. What made you say that?' Livi asked.

At least he had the sense not to mention Smitha. The last thing we needed was to worry Livi. He shrugged, moving closer to her. 'Just a random thought. Go on.'

'It was so hard I thought it might have fractured my skull,' Livi said, touching her head gingerly. 'I remember a clang — like whoever it was had dropped some metal object. Like really hard.' As she spoke, she was still shining the torch beam across the floor. 'Ah! That must be it.' She bent down to pick up a length of metal pipe. It was hollow but sturdy, all rusted and mouldy. I winced at the thought of it against Livi's head.

'Stop!' I shouted. 'Don't touch it. There might be finger-prints on it.'

Livi contented herself with shining the torchlight along its length. 'Hang on. What's this?'

A little way off from the rod, something glittered in the light from the torch. It was a ring in the shape of an 'M', encrusted with diamonds. Before I could stop her, Livi was holding it in her palm. 'It can't be. How did it get here?'

It was dented like someone hit it against something hard. I had a strong feeling that the shape of the dent would fit perfectly over the metal rod.

CHAPTER FORTY-EIGHT

Day Nine: Livi

'Wait, I don't get it,' Smitha said, her face twisted in confusion. 'You found it where?'

The ring now rested on the kitchen table, the seven of us huddled around it as if it were some precious ancient relic. The diamond stones scattered the light, casting tiny rainbow-hued versions of themselves across the ceiling. Leela had sensibly forbidden anyone from touching it. My hand was in Shravan's. He hadn't let go since he found me, as if, should he loosen his grip, I could slip away again — this time for good.

'It doesn't make sense,' Smitha insisted when I told her where we found it.

This wasn't the first item on the list of things that defied reason. In fact, most of what had happened in the last nine days made no sense at all.

Smitha scratched her chin. 'What if Maya lost it? Dropped it or left it behind?'

Leela shook her head. 'And how did it find its way into the castle? We didn't even go near it during the picnic. Not to mention that people don't go around losing their diamond rings without making a fuss about it. If she did drop it in a hurry, she would have called. But she's been gone four days now.'

I wondered if it was the same ring. The one John took and Maya later reclaimed.

'I agree,' I said. 'Besides, like Leela said, if she lost it here in the house, how did it end up in the castle?'

'We should call Maya,' declared Smitha.

'And ask her what? *Did you tie up Livi? Kidnap Nancy?* Do you even hear yourself?' Shravan's voice was shrill. He was frustrated, angry, everything that a boyfriend should be when their girlfriend has been hurt, but it was unfair to take it out on Smitha. I put a hand on his shoulder, but he shrugged it off.

He was right though, in a way. Smitha hadn't thought it through.

'Maybe we can just ask her if she's lost a ring,' I said, 'and don't tell her anything else.'

Smitha looked up, and raised an enquiring eyebrow at Shravan.

'What?' he muttered. 'At this hour? It's almost midnight.'

'Well, we can't wait till tomorrow,' Leela said. 'Has everyone forgotten that Nancy is still missing?'

We looked at each other. Was Nancy really lost? She couldn't be, the castle was only a short distance from the main road. Besides, someone had tied me up, and if it wasn't Nancy, then who was it?

'I'm going to call,' Dhruv said, picking up his phone. We listened to it ring.

He was just about to end the call, muttering, 'See?' when the phone crackled and Maya's voice boomed out. 'Dhruv, hi. How's it going? I hear you have it worse up there. How bad is it really?' She chuckled. 'Looks like we left at the right time.'

Dhruv exchanged a glance with Leela, and I caught her stifling a giggle. 'We're okay. Hey, listen. That ring of yours, the diamond one shaped in an "M".' He covered the mouthpiece and muttered, 'She has too many rings—'

'Sssh!' said Leela.

'Oh, that one. I left it at the house. Nancy found it, and she's going to bring it back. She didn't lose it, did she? I told her to wear it—'

'No, no. The ring is right here. Don't worry. And, er, Maya, where are you exactly?'

'Where do you think? I'm at home, silly. Why do you ask?'

Dhruv ended the call abruptly. 'Do you believe her?' he asked.

Shravan picked up the ring and ran his finger over the dent, scratching it back and forth, as if rubbing it could summon a genie — one that would call him master and grant his wishes. 'I can't see any reason not to,' he said. There was something guarded in his expression, the way he was trying not to meet any of our eyes. It made me wonder what he was hiding. 'If . . .' He paused, rolling the ring between his fingers. 'And it's a big if. But if she is here — where could she be staying?'

Dhruv frowned. 'The sleeping bag, the one in the castle?'

Shravan shook his head. 'What? Maya? On a cold castle floor in a sleeping bag? I don't think so.'

This time I believed him. From what I'd seen of Maya — how she avoided having to sit on the cabin floor, even on a mat, and complained about the mud on our picnic — I thought Shravan was right. There was no way she would spend even one night in a sleeping bag.

'And besides—'

'Besides what?' Shravan barked at Dhruv.

Slightly taken aback by Shravan's tone, Dhruv said, 'Well, those cans of beans. Maya really likes beans. It's the one thing she's not too posh to push.'

That much was true. It was just the once, but I did see Maya eat beans straight from the can. She shook me off when I'd suggested that she at least use a plate.

'That's ridiculous. There's a storm raging outside, in case you haven't noticed,' Shravan said.

'And she does have a bone to pick with Nancy,' Jay added.

'Don't we all?' Shravan muttered.

We all fell silent. Shravan was too jittery, too quick to dismiss the idea of Maya being here, too slow to offer any real alternative. His fingers still toyed with the ring, but his eyes avoided us all. It was like he was hiding something.

Finally, Smitha said, 'If it's not Maya, then who was it? From what I hear, Shravan, the knots were so tight that you couldn't get them off. Livi certainly didn't tie herself up.'

Shravan took both my hands and kissed the bruises on my wrists where the rope chafed them, his eyes glistening with unshed tears. 'I don't know. But we'll find out, I promise.'

CHAPTER FORTY-NINE

Day Ten: Smitha

It was the middle of the night and the storm had passed, but I was unable to sleep. Leela had insisted that we try, saying we'd need our strength for the coming day. Jay and I had moved up to the second floor, to Maya's room, so that we'd be closer to the others — another of Leela's little nuggets of wisdom. 'It's better to stay on the same floor. That way, if something happens, the others are around,' she'd said. And Jay — bless him — nodded like one of those bulls in a village procession, right before it charged through the crowd. The 'something' she was referring to, of course, was an armed psychopath, loose in the house, presumably hunting for their next unsuspecting victim. Very comforting.

As a result, Aswin was now in our room, sleeping on a duvet and snoring away in harmony with Jay. So much for my night's rest. I glanced at Jay, blissfully unconscious. That torch should've landed on his head, not mine. Even when he was fast asleep, he still got under my skin.

As I shuffled around in search of my earplugs, I heard Leela and Dhruv talking in the room next to mine. Curious,

I pressed my ear to the wall, trying to catch what they were saying.

'. . . you say that?' Dhruv was saying, as I strained to make out the words.

Leela said something I couldn't make out, followed by, 'Because I didn't. It was dark, and I only had one of the small torches. All I saw was the sleeping bag and the cans.' Dunollie Castle. She must've been talking about when she went back there, after dumping me with Dhruv.

'But you were there for ages . . .' That was Dhruv again. 'It was hard work dragging Smitha through those woods. She was heavy. Didn't even attempt to walk, my shoulders are still sore. Nothing wrong with her legs, she was just putting it on.' This made me want to bang on the wall and shout at him. *Putting it on?* Next time I'd happily thump *his* head with a torch and check how well *his* legs worked.

Their voices fell silent. I heard the rustle of bedclothes, then a soft kiss. 'I'm sorry. How can I make it up to you?' Leela said softly. A few more kisses followed, and I started to feel embarrassed. I was about to move away when Dhruv said, 'Save that one for later.' He chuckled. 'Anyway, you haven't answered my question. Where did you go? I walked to the house and back . . .'

I was grateful to them for finding me. Veena was far too young to be left without a mother. But Dhruv had been trying to be a hero. He'd urged Leela not to go into that castle alone, insisted he would join her. It was Leela who'd told him to take me to the house. But Dhruv was right — Leela had been gone a long time. He left me in the house and went back for Leela. Found her outside the castle. She'd been there all the time but somehow hadn't found Livi, who was down in the cellar?

'I told you,' Leela was saying. 'The slope was slippery. I had to keep stopping, and I kept hearing someone moving around.'

'Do you have any idea how dangerous that was?' Dhruv said. 'There's a madman — or woman — loose. You could have walked straight into their hands.'

An image flashed into my mind, of Maya, a mad glint in her eyes, stalking the castle corridors with an iron rod in her hand. Shoplifting was one thing, but murder? That was quite a leap.

'That's exactly why I was so careful. I waited to make sure there was no one nearby,' Leela said.

'That still doesn't mean you did the right thing,' Dhruv said.

'Let me make it up to you then.' More rustling of sheets, some heavy breathing.

Oh, come on now. Did they have to? I stood upright. I really didn't need to listen to this. But Leela was speaking again.

'Okay, what do you want to know?'

'Let me get this right. So, you wait for the footsteps to die down. Finally, they're gone. No longer hearing the sounds, you carry on up the slope to the castle. Are you saying you never went down to the cellar? You stayed in the castle the whole time? But what I don't get is how did you not hear anything? Livi was right beneath you.'

'I saw the sleeping bag and the cans, and I panicked. I was too scared to call out. There. Happy?'

I knew just what she would do next — turn her back to Dhruv. I used to do the same whenever I was annoyed with Jay. Back when we were young and newly married, this would be enough to get him to surrender, and he'd cover my back with kisses. Ah, those were the days! Studies to keep up, no money, and living with four others in a cramped little house . . . But we were happy then. Now? If I turned away from Jay, he wouldn't even notice. On the off chance he did, he'd just be relieved.

'Hey, hey. Come here,' Dhruv said, which made me smile. I knew it. 'You were much braver than me. When we went back for Livi, you insisted on going down.'

He must have tickled her, because she giggled. 'Stop it,' she said, laughing.

'It was this hand, wasn't it?' He planted a kiss. 'The one that took the torch from me and declared, *They might need help. You stay here.*'

She giggled, saying, 'Stop,' in that way that suggested she didn't mean it.

Naturally, he didn't listen. 'It was this leg, wasn't it?' More kisses. More giggles. 'The one that marched heroically into the dark basement.'

Right. I'd heard enough. Now, where were those earplugs?

Dhruv was obviously more imaginative than Jay, I'll give him that. But when he got to, 'It was these hips, wasn't it?' and I was halfway through jamming the foam into my ears, I couldn't help wondering what exactly did those brave hips *do*? Lead a rebellion? Negotiate peace?

CHAPTER FIFTY

Day Ten: Livi

The wind had dropped, the only sound that of the frogs croaking in some distant stretch of water. I stood by the window, looking out towards an invisible horizon. I didn't need to see the ocean, I could feel its comforting presence. Always had.

Something my mum used to say sprang to mind. 'In a world that aims for the sky, aim to be the ocean.' I'd always taken it to mean that the ocean was deeper than the sky was high, which is obviously not the case. Then she'd explained it to me, standing at this very window on a night much like this one. 'The sky can rage for days, doing its best to stir up the ocean, but it always grows tired. Whereas the ocean is stoic. It submits, ignores the tantrums of the sky and in the end has the last laugh. Be the ocean, darling.'

From then on, I had stood at this window many times, watching the storm heave its last breath, and applauded the ocean for its hard-won victory.

At that moment, I missed Mum so badly. I longed for the touch of her hand, her presence, the way she'd brush that stubborn knot in my hair. I would give anything to have her back. One last time. To know what she thought.

I touched my cheeks and realised I'd been crying. I couldn't remember the last time I'd cried, certainly not when I was lying on the cold stone floor, bound hand and foot.

A draught seeped in through the window, blowing cold air across my midriff. I pulled my robe tighter and knotted it firmly. Something about tying that knot brought a quiet resolve. I couldn't afford to fall apart — not now, not when the end was so close. We would find Nancy, and we would leave this place, I vowed. But what if . . . what if it was too late?

I must have sobbed out loud, because there was a rustle of sheets in the room behind me. 'Livi?' Shravan croaked, barely awake.

I held my breath, hoping Shravan would drift back to sleep. But the thud of his feet hitting the floor made me wince. Damn.

He laid a hand on my shoulder. 'Can't you sleep?'

I wanted to laugh. Sleep? How could anyone sleep when there was a woman out there, probably injured and in pain. She was supposed to be his best friend, for God's sake. I shrugged. 'No.'

'You must be really tired,' he said, taking my hand and running a finger over the bruise. My wince had nothing to do with the pain.

Instead of answering, I said, 'Can I ask you a question? What did Smitha say?'

'About?'

'The person who hit her. All I know is that she was found at the bottom of the hill, having been hit with the torch.'

'She didn't see him — or her,' he said. Her? I turned to look at him, and for some reason he took a step back. 'The ring.'

'Maya's? But she's miles away,' I said. 'You said yourself that there was no way she'd sleep on a castle floor.'

Shravan grimaced. And there it was again, a shadow of something he wasn't telling me. 'But what if Nancy had it?'

'That proves nothing. Nancy was there, we all know that. Maybe she dropped it. That's not exactly a crime.'

I turned back towards the window, rigid with discomfort. Shravan was much too close to me. As if he sensed it, he too shifted away, moving to the other side of the window frame. He leaned there, his face turned towards me. The phrase 'an ocean between us' floated into my mind.

'I suppose she could have dropped it, but what about the dent?' Shravan said.

'It could be an old one,' I said. I didn't sound convincing.

I could feel his gaze boring into me. 'But what if it's not?'

I said nothing. I knew exactly what he meant. That it was Nancy who'd hit us, me and Smitha. Hit us and left us to die. But there was still so much that didn't make sense. Even if Nancy had been jealous of Shravan and me, what did Smitha have to do with it? If it was indeed Nancy, then where was she now?

'She accused you of ruining her life,' he said. 'That's what you said, wasn't it?' He wanted me to say the words, hear me implicate her. Now I did turn to look at him. We glared at each other. Then he threw up his arms in surrender. 'Just consider it, will you? Nancy didn't go into the cellar with you. So, how did the ring get there?'

My head began to spin.

CHAPTER FIFTY-ONE

Day Ten: Leela

The day looked promising, the sky a cornflower blue, as if last night's storm had been nothing but a bad dream. Except for the devastation it had left in its wake — felled trees, branches strewn across the ground. Rubbish scattered like the pawns of a chess game abandoned by a child in a temper. Resilient birds were picking up twigs from the mess to rebuild their nests. Now and then, they were distracted when they found a shiny piece of glass from a broken vase or brass trinket.

Neither Dhruv nor I had managed to get much sleep. We spent most of the night lying side by side on our backs, occasionally voicing a muttered question. We racked our brains for clues, hints of where Nancy could be. I could see it in his eyes, he'd lost hope. Yet he indulged me.

But there was really only one question — where was she? And was she a victim, or was she the aggressor? Damned, or damning? Either way, she couldn't have gone very far, her car was still in the car park. Public transport was out of the question, given last night's storm. All the trains and buses had been cancelled.

I quietly slipped out of the room and tried the police again. It took a while to convince them, but in the end, the blood did the trick — of course, I omitted to mention that it came from an injured squirrel. They would be on their way by now, and soon I would need to wake Dhruv so that he could meet them by the fallen tree and guide them here. First, however, it was time for a chamomile tea and digestive biscuits, and a plan.

* * *

The police finally arrived an hour later. I was not sure what I expected — probably not a search team with sniffer dogs and a helicopter, but at least more than the two who turned up. Neither was wearing a uniform. One was a young woman, the other an older man. They looked so ordinary, they could have been father and daughter out for a stroll.

'I'm DI Alisha Reid, and this is my partner, DC Owen. Which one of you is Lee-law?'

I raised my hand like an eager schoolchild. 'That's me. I called you.'

'Right. May we sit?' the DI asked. Without waiting for an answer, they strolled into the house.

'Come into the kitchen,' Livi said. 'There's tea and biscuits.'

'Sold,' DI Reid replied with a smile that didn't quite reach her eyes.

Once we were seated with our mugs, DC Owen asked, 'I believe you mentioned a missing woman?' He sounded bored. He'd probably much rather be spending his Saturday at home with the kids, or more likely his grandkids, given the lines around his eyes. But instead, here he was, staring at six anxious faces, probably realising his weekend had just been wrecked.

'Yes. Our friend Nancy. She's been missing since last night,' Dhruv said.

DC Owen looked at him as if to say, *And who are you?*

'An adult woman?' said DI Reid. There it was — their favourite phrase. 'It hasn't even been twenty-four hours. I don't quite see why you've called us out.'

'We've called you out because she left in the middle of the storm, on foot. Her car is still here. As you can see, there are fallen trees everywhere. Who in their right mind would walk out under such dreadful conditions?' I was already angry with these two idiots.

DC Owen raised an eyebrow. 'Oh, you'd be surprised what people choose to do. We see odd behaviour all the time.'

'I believe you said you found some blood,' DI Reid said. 'Can we see it?'

'It's in the cabin. Maybe we should go there,' I said.

'How far is it?'

'Oh, not far. A few hundred metres,' Dhruv said, and they exchanged glances.

'First, let's get the story straight, shall we? How many of you are staying here?' She opened a notepad and patted her pockets in search of a pen. When she found it, she flicked the cap off with her thumb. It landed on the table with a thud.

By the time we'd finished giving her a rundown of events, including the dolls and the secrets they revealed, the two officers were looking utterly bemused, and the tea had gone cold. Livi got up to make a fresh pot.

'Now, where were we?' DC Owen said. So far, he'd seemed more interested in the light fittings than our actual story.

'The power went out,' I said.

'It did indeed.' DC Owen laughed. 'For you and half of Oban. It was the worst storm in sixty years.'

DI Reid shot him a look, and I continued. 'We ran out of diesel for the generator. Candles too. The torches were going out.'

'Did you not stock up?' DC Owen said, earning himself another look from his DI. 'Thought you said you were out shopping last night?' He glanced between me and Livi. So he *had* been listening after all.

'Yes. But we didn't expect the power outage to be so long. This is an old house. Takes a lot to keep it warm,' Livi said.

'So, what *did* you buy?' he asked.

'Milk, eggs, toilet paper—'

'Toilet paper?' DC Owen chuckled. 'What did we even learn from the pandemic, eh?'

DI Reid ignored him. 'Then?' she asked, tapping the table — sharp, rhythmic. Her patience was thinning.

'Nothing. We came back.' Livi sounded shaky, probably still feeling the effects of her hours of imprisonment in that cellar.

DI Reid appeared to notice. She glanced sharply at Livi before turning back to me. 'Okay. And then?'

'We went to the cabin — me, Dhruv, Shravan, Livi, and Aswin. To prepare for the last night of Navaratri. I asked everyone to be there by six thirty. We went early. Is this all really relevant?' I asked. Surely they should be out looking for Nancy.

'Everything is relevant,' DI Reid said. 'So, you were in the cabin. And the other three were in the house?'

For a moment, I hesitated. I could've mentioned Shravan — how he'd vanished for hours without a word — but I didn't. Not yet. I nodded. 'Yes. That's when Aswin found a can of diesel stashed in the store cupboard of the cabin. It was half empty. But fuel is fuel, right? By then, the torches we had were dying.' I was rambling. The next part was harder. The blood. The butchered doll. I wasn't ready to say it. Not just yet.

'And you didn't know it was there?' DC Owen asked, looking at Livi as if to say, *How could you not know since it's your house?* He had begun to pace up and down the kitchen. It was deeply unsettling.

'It looked like it had been there a while,' I said.

'And you know that because . . . ?' He looked irritated at my intrusion.

'It had a thick coat of grease and dust over it.'

I didn't like this. These two detectives seemed to be accusing us instead of helping us. I let out a sigh. 'Dhruv and Aswin went out to start the generator, and Livi returned to the house to fetch the others. They didn't have torches or umbrellas. Though umbrellas wouldn't have been much use in that storm.' God, I was rambling again. Anyway, why was I the one doing all the talking when there were three other perfectly capable adults here? Keen to pass the baton, I said to Livi, 'Is that when you found the dead squirrel?'

Livi merely said, 'Yes.' I waited for her to elaborate, but she remained silent.

Great. I gave them a brief version of the events that followed — the lightning, the blood, the dolls, the spluttering lights, and the thudding footsteps. Everything I saw and heard before I hit the floor (I left that part out, I didn't see how my fainting was relevant) — the moment I realised there had been a murder.

DI Reid was immediately on the alert. 'A murder?' Then she smiled, as if all this was one big joke to her. 'Whatever made you think that?'

Biting my lips to hide my anger, I said, 'It was the dolls. One of them was broken, stabbed by Maa Durga.' The detectives looked puzzled. 'That's the goddess doll. And all the blood . . .'

'Didn't it occur to you that it might have been a joke?' DC Owen said. 'Clearly, someone has been playing games. What's her name, the missing girl?'

'Nancy,' DI Reid said. They were both smiling now. I didn't see anything amusing in what I'd told them.

'Ah yes, Nancy,' DC Owen said. 'Didn't it occur to you that it was her? And now she's hiding somewhere—' he gestured towards the garden — 'watching to see how it all ends.'

Suddenly, I wasn't so sure. Could he be right? Was this all just some twisted game? The grand finale that she had planned right from the start. I thought of her scoffing at the traditions, the quiet fury in her eyes every time she looked at Livi. Surely she wouldn't go this far. Would she?

'She has done something like this before,' Dhruv added unhelpfully, a statue brought to life. 'She sent each of us anonymous photos and videos. It was when we were in uni, but we only found out now, from the dolls.'

'See?' DC Owen sounded almost jubilant. If he said, *I told you so*, I swore I'd hit him. 'She'll be back as soon as we've gone.'

A chill crept down my spine. Could she really be out there, watching us? Laughing at us? But it still didn't add up. 'Do you really mean to say, officers, that tying up Livi and leaving her in the castle, and bashing Smitha's head in, were all part of some prank?' The two detectives shared an uncomfortable glance. 'That sounds like one hell of a prank to me.'

DI Reid looked down. 'And a very sick one.'

CHAPTER FIFTY-TWO

Day Ten: Smitha

It was the thudding that woke me. At first I thought it was the storm, pounding the doors and windows. Then I realised it was the sound of people coming and going, their footsteps on the hardwood floor. Both Jay and Aswin were gone. Shit, what time was it? Frantically, I reached for my phone.

In my defence, I had barely slept last night, and when I did, it was filled with nightmares — fuzzy now, but my heart still pounded. All I recalled from them was the rhythmic splashing of water, and the feeling that I was rocking, as if I was in a swaying boat. For a moment on waking, I didn't know where I was. Then it all came back, and I almost wished I was still in the nightmare.

The door opened, and Jay poked his head in. 'Ah, you're up,' he said cheerily. 'The police are here. They'd like to speak with you.' He might as well have been saying, 'Good morning' or 'How are you?' *Oh, by the way, the police are here and my friend's missing, possibly dead. What a lovely day.*

'The police? Have they found Nancy?' I hauled myself up, groaning as my old bones protested. I ached in places I would rather not name.

'No. That's why they're here. They'll find her,' he said, avoiding my eyes.

'What do they want to speak with me for?' I asked, getting up to splash water on my face.

Jay remained standing in the doorway, watching me.

I was sore in too many places to count. I could barely move my neck, it was so stiff. I glanced at my reflection in the small oval mirror above the sink. One eye was bloodshot, and the same side of my face was swollen, the bruise from where I hit the rocks when I fell a deep, ugly purple. By tomorrow, I'd be sporting that charming green-yellow tinge, like a rotting mango. I thought of Veena — would she be scared to see me like this? At least Jay's mum would be happy. I flexed my fingers, which felt like those of an old arthritic woman. I was surprised they didn't crack. I seemed to have aged twenty years overnight.

Jay watched me hobble to the door. He was smirking. He should try lying on a rock for who knows how long in the middle of a storm. It would be good for his soul.

By the time I made it downstairs, the others were already gathered around the kitchen island, along with two strangers. They looked nothing like police. One, a balding white man who looked like he was approaching retirement, was dressed in a black hoodie. The other, a much younger woman, practically a schoolkid, was in a grey jumper and tracksuit pants. Leela rushed forward to help me to a chair.

Someone had made tea, and there was a plate of biscuits on the table. My stomach rumbled loudly. I realised I hadn't eaten anything since lunch yesterday.

Handling me like a fragile parcel, Leela sat me down opposite the two plainclothes officers and plonked herself down beside me, her face scrunched up in concern. I must have looked even worse than I felt, and that was saying something. I could already hear Jay's voice in my head: *It's all superficial wounds, you'll be fine in no time.* Right. For the rest of his life, he'd regret saying that.

Livi was at the counter, wiping its already sparkling surface. The men were huddled at one end of the island, murmuring among themselves like it was an emergency meeting of the Poor Men's Union.

'Smee-ta?' the girl asked. 'How are you feeling?' She stood up and extended her hand. 'I'm DI Reid.'

I waved a languid hand. 'It's Smitha.'

'You know, you really should see a doctor,' she said.

I touched the bruise and winced. 'It's not as bad as it looks.' The last thing I needed was to spend another day in Oban, rotting in some musty waiting room while a GP with cold hands told me to rest and drink fluids like I'd stubbed a toe instead of almost being murdered.

'Oh, and this is DC Owen,' she added. The DC looked bored, glancing at his watch and raising his eyes to the ceiling. He stopped just short of actually yawning.

'So, I believe you were attacked. That right?'

I sure didn't do this to myself. I started to nod, but a sharp pain shot up the back of my neck. So much for trying to be respectful. 'Yes. With a torch,' I said, and felt the urge to add, 'It was a really hard blow too, knocked me off my feet.' Because, of course, I had to pre-empt the inevitable eye-roll. Get it out there before they launched into their high-pitched mockery: *It was only a torch. Come on, Smitha.*

She nodded sympathetically. 'And when the attack occurred, you had gone with Livi and the missing girl, Nancy, to Dunollie Castle. Is that right?'

I gave them a rundown of everything I remembered — from finding Livi with the dead squirrel to our decision to walk to Dunollie Castle in the middle of the storm. Even as I spoke, I realised how ridiculous it must have sounded. Who in their right mind would walk through a raging storm to get a can of diesel that might or might not be there? It had seemed like a good idea at the time. Now, in the light of day, it sounded utterly deranged.

When I got to the part about hearing Nancy shouting to Livi that she'd ruined her life, DI Reid's eyebrows shot up. 'Were those her exact words?'

'Yes. She sounded like she'd completely lost it. It was hard for her, seeing Livi with Shravan, you know? Right from the start, we could see she was struggling. You see, they were once together—'

'No, we weren't. That's not true,' Shravan said. 'She was just a . . . um, friend.' At that, Livi, who'd been silently wiping like she was trying to erase the whole scene, looked up sharply.

Suddenly, DC Owen sprang to life. '*Was*, Mr Shravan? Interesting use of past tense!'

As Shravan opened his mouth to speak, DI Reid raised a hand, with an icy look at the DC. 'Never mind about that. Now, where were we? Ah yes, you heard them arguing. Did you hear them say anything else?'

I glanced at Livi, who'd resumed furiously scrubbing at a non-existent mark on the kitchen counter. 'It was mostly Nancy's voice I heard. She was ranting on about Livi having ruined her life, and things like that. Livi was trying to calm her down.'

Livi had paused her scrubbing and was watching me from the counter.

'So, you heard her clearly, from several hundred metres away in the middle of a storm?' DI Reid said. 'You must have very good hearing.'

Shit, she was right. Did I really hear it, or was I just remembering what Livi told me? In any case, it was too late to backtrack now. I'd look like a fool, or, worse, they might suspect me. So I plunged ahead.

'Yes, my hearing's always been good,' I said, forcing myself to hold DI Reid's gaze. In fact, it was so good I distinctly heard Jay snigger. That man was so dead!

Apparently, DI Reid caught it too. She asked the others to wait outside, while she and the DC spoke to me alone.

Looking relieved, the men made a beeline for the door, while the women hesitated, casting backward glances in my direction as they left.

Shifting the cushion behind my back, I sank deeper into my seat. Truth be told, I was starting to enjoy this — it wasn't often I got to be the centre of attention. These two were lapping up every word I said.

'So, what happened next? After the argument?' DI Reid prompted.

'I heard a loud scream.'

'And?'

'Well, everything went quiet.' That moment of silence following the scream had been more terrifying than anything else that happened. 'I thought about going up to check, but then I heard footsteps behind me.' I realised I was gripping the edge of the table.

'Is that when you were attacked?' DI Reid asked.

'Yes.'

'And you only regained consciousness when the others found you? Do you have any idea how long you were out of it?'

'No . . . Oh, wait. Nearly two hours. We left the house at just after six — I looked at the living room clock when I went to pick up Livi's shoes. Leela said it was a quarter to eight when they found me.'

DI Reid nodded. 'And you're sure you don't remember anything in between those times?'

'No,' I said, louder than I'd intended. What was she implying? That I hadn't really passed out? That I faked it? And I thought, *Ooh yes, I love nothing more than lying face down on a rock with a storm lashing my spine.*

She patted my hand. 'It's all right. It's just that sometimes we pass in and out of consciousness without being aware of it, and we register things that we later forget. Anyway, if anything comes back to you, will you please let us know?'

The two detectives were on their way to the door when it hit me — the rhythmic splashing like an oar in water. A scuffle. Nancy's muffled voice, saying, 'Where are you taking me?' But did it even happen, or was it last night's nightmare? I didn't want to say anything until I was sure, or I would really look a fool. Right now, I was enjoying my role as star witness. They almost caught me in a lie, once. I couldn't afford one more slip.

Long after the police officers had gone, I remained seated at the table, my tea untouched. What should I say, if anything? And to whom?

CHAPTER FIFTY-THREE

Day Ten: Livi

Finally, the detectives had stopped finding the situation amusing. There was nothing funny about any of it. If it were only a case of the dolls being moved and our secrets revealed, fair enough — they could have put it down to someone's warped sense of humour. But the blood, the attack on Smitha, me being tied up — these were no pranks. They were deadly serious.

For a moment, I wanted to believe them. I really did. The idea that it was all Nancy — that she was hiding somewhere, waiting for the police to leave, to make her dramatic reappearance — almost made sense. But then, her voice came back to me. Her wails, sharp and full of panic, echoing in my mind. Desperate. Lost.

Whatever Smitha said to the detectives seemed to have done the trick. When they finally emerged from the kitchen, they were no longer smirking. They asked to see the cabin, and I volunteered to take them while the others stayed behind.

The ground was still sodden after yesterday's storm, the smell of wet grass mingling with that of the rubbish scattered

259

around. Our feet sank into the mud, while plastic bags soared into the air like so many tattered balloons.

One of these landed squarely on the shoulders of the DI, and she swore. Served her right for being so patronising.

'Hold on!' DC Owen called from behind. 'What's this?'

Half hidden under a pile of leaves and plastic bags was one of the traps, my boot wedged in its teeth. The bins were all lying on their sides, their contents spewed across the ground. I stepped on a used tampon. It squelched and promptly buried itself underground.

'Oh, it's a trap for badgers,' I said. 'They're real pests, they come for the rubbish.'

DC Owen nodded. 'Do you mind if I take a few snaps?'

I waved my hand. 'Feel free.' All traces of the squirrel or its blood had long been washed away.

DC Owen snapped a few pictures with his mobile, much good would it do him.

We squelched on in silence, and by the time we reached the cabin, we were splattered with mud. The cabin, of course, was locked — it would be, wouldn't it? The key must be with Leela, back at the house. Even amid the chaos of last night, she'd managed to lock it. I was still not used to this. When my family and I were here, we always left it open. It was perfectly safe out here — I mean, who's going to drive miles just to steal a few old mats?

I tried the door, just in case. 'Don't you have the key?' DI Reid asked.

I shook my head, considering my options. Then I remembered the back door.

'Well, what are we waiting for?' DC Owen asked.

At first glance, you wouldn't even know there was a door at all. It fitted in seamlessly with the rest of the wooden panels, with the latch in the gap between the ones on either side. When I pressed it, the panels folded inward, and we stepped through the opening.

'Oh, cool,' DC Owen said, gazing up at the stuffed deer head and the gun cabinet beneath it. For the first time, his eyes registered something other than boredom. Unusually for a gun cabinet, this one was not glass-fronted; the firearms were concealed behind solid oak doors.

'It used to be a hunting cabin,' I said. 'But now it's just — well, I don't know what it is. A kind of shed, I suppose.'

'That's a shame,' he said. 'May I?' He tried the door of the gun cabinet.

'It's locked,' I said. 'And, unfortunately, there's no back door.'

He looked as disappointed as a child who'd been promised lollipops that were held just out of reach.

'There's just a couple of .416 Rigbys — the type with the original square bridge and bolt action—'

'And hand-filled quarter rib.' He looked positively starry-eyed. 'You have a treasure there, young lady.' It was the first sign of life he'd given all morning.

'Ahem.' DI Reid cleared her throat. 'Can we just get on with our job?' She was looking at the dolls.

I gasped. Leela had told me what to expect — she'd described the stabbed doll, the blood and splatter. But in the light of day, it looked so much worse. The figures were crusty with blood that was beginning to flake, the spear in the goddess's hand was plunged deep into her victim. Her tongue was out, as though she was relishing the kill, thirsting for more blood. Now I understood Leela's fear. She'd been convinced that someone was dead, and no wonder. I stepped back instinctively, colliding with DC Owen.

He barely seemed to register it. His mouth agape, he appeared unable to tear his eyes from the scene.

DI Reid, on the other hand, was totally unfazed, her expression one of mild curiosity. 'Quite a display, eh?'

DC Owen broke out of his stunned silence to ask, 'What does this mean?' He pointed at the showstopper — the Maa Durga.

'That's Maa Durga,' I said. 'She's the Goddess of the Festival. And that—' I gestured towards the victim beneath her feet — 'means Nancy is no longer missing—'

'What?' they exclaimed in unison.

'You mean you know where Nancy is?' DI Reid said.

Shaking my head, I said, 'No.' The word tasted like rust, sharp at the back of my throat. I swallowed hard, fear forming a lump in my throat. The detectives exchanged a glance — confused, maybe even concerned. To them, I must have looked unhinged, another shaken witness unravelling at the seams. But I steadied myself, bracing for the truth I could no longer hold in. 'Nancy is not missing.' I wrapped my arms around myself, the only shield I had against the cold. Against what I was about to say.

'She's dead.'

CHAPTER FIFTY-FOUR

Day Ten: Leela

The police had left, promising to organise a search party. As expected, they'd said it would be hard to find Nancy amid all the destruction the storm had caused. They would need hundreds of people if they were to search the forest. Combing it inch by inch could take days, weeks even, and we had already searched all the more likely places.

Dhruv said we would just have to leave it to them, we'd only get in the way. The holiday was over. Before they left, I asked the police if it was okay for me to take down the dolls and wrap them up. Today was victory day, the day when they could lay down their tools and celebrate their hard-earned victory over evil. It didn't feel like much of a celebration, more like a defeat. At least putting them away would give me something to do, the familiar ritual providing some solace in the midst of sadness. The police said it was fine, it was not a crime scene. I had a feeling they still believed it was all just a prank. Despite the promised search party — if it ever materialised — they didn't seem to be taking it very seriously.

Livi believed me when I said Nancy was dead. I could see it in her eyes. I didn't think Shravan or Dhruv were convinced, although they hadn't said anything one way or the other. Smitha remained silent, while Jay and Aswin behaved as though nothing was wrong. Fine. I didn't need them to believe me. The matter was now with the police, they would get there eventually. Meanwhile, I was keeping my thoughts to myself. 'You can't rush the ripening,' as my mum used to say, 'Fruit ripens when it's ready, and there's nothing you could do, not without spoiling the taste'. But, I was secretly looking forward to being proved right.

Smitha, Livi, and I headed over to the cabin to start packing up the dolls. I opened the door to an overpowering smell of musty rot. I swallowed, blinking back tears. It wasn't that long ago since we set it all up — me, Smitha, and Nancy — chatting, laughing, guessing which doll was who. If only we'd known. I wondered if I could have done something, stopped this somehow. My eyes fell on one of the dancers at Maa Durga's feet — stabbed, crumpled. The same doll that was peering through the window three days ago. Now we knew who it was meant to be. How had it come to this?

Smitha placed a hand on my shoulder. 'Hey, are you okay?'

I glanced at the women on either side of me — beaten and bruised, the real warriors in this fight. They were probably worried that I might faint again. I felt a stab of shame. This wasn't about me. It never was.

Each one of us was worried about the others. 'Are you sure you wouldn't like to rest?' I'd said to Smitha, back at the house. 'Me and Livi can sort this out.'

'What, and listen to Jay moan?' Smitha had said. 'No chance.' Now, she asked Livi how her head was.

'As long as I don't make any sudden movements, it's as good as new,' Livi said. She turned to me. 'You saved my life, and I'll never forget it.'

Her words made me blush. I didn't know quite how to respond. I turned my attention to Smitha. The bruise on her face was now an interesting mix of colours, and she was limping. Nevertheless, neither of them seemed to be suffering any lasting effects from their experiences. The attack on Smitha appeared to have mainly affected her nerves. She jumped at the slightest sound. Livi was perfectly calm and unshaken. The only sign of what she'd been through was the raw skin around her mouth from the duct tape.

The sooner we left here the better. I couldn't wait to put all this behind me. I wasn't sure if any of us would ever truly forget. Maybe, in time, the memories would fade with the bruises, only to resurface in nightmares.

Usually, packing the dolls away was a satisfying ritual, a moment of reflection as I wrapped their colourful faces and laid them to rest for another year. Not this time. This time I was relieved to see the last of them.

I approached the dolls almost fearfully. I dreaded having to touch the blood, lay my hands on the vengeful goddess. Perceptive Livi already had a wet wipe in her hand. 'Here, let me clean it,' she said, picking up the goddess and wiping her carefully.

Grateful for her thoughtfulness, I dragged the wheelie box from the corner closet, ready to pack the dolls away. The smell of blood was fading, replaced by that of burning sage. Livi had thought to bring some and had lit it as soon as we entered. I didn't tell her that some things could not be cleansed.

'What do we do with the broken one?' she asked, referring to Maa Durga's victim — Nancy.

I had no use for broken dolls, it couldn't go back on the steps again. 'Bin it,' I said, wanting it out of sight.

But Livi, her expression thoughtful, set it aside. Our eyes met briefly, and in hers, I saw a quiet defiance — as if to say that as long as the broken doll stayed, Nancy would be found. I wished she was right. She handed me each doll after it had been cleaned, and I wrapped them in their layers of old clothes and bubble wrap, placing them gently in the box. There was comfort in the familiarity of the act of putting them away, along with relief at knowing that there'd be no more cruel displays.

'I'll clear the top shelf,' Smitha said. For a while, we worked in silence, cleaning, wrapping, layering, and laying the dolls to rest. We were all weary, not that it was a particularly demanding task, but from the weight of the lies and secrets we still carried, the words that remained unspoken.

Deep down, they all knew that Nancy must be dead, yet none of them had said it out loud. As if doing so would make it real, and they weren't ready for that yet. She couldn't be far away, but the thought brought no comfort.

And all the while, the important unvoiced question loomed like a dark cloud over our heads. Who killed her?

It could be any one of us. Even Maya. Who was to say she was not lurking around somewhere? Or she could have enlisted Bala — plied him with drink and egged him on. The story of the missing ring, with Nancy as the sole witness, felt a little too convenient. If she was the killer, Maya would know Nancy wouldn't make it back alive, that her secret was safe. Bhoo, being a doctor, would know exactly how to go about it. She had her own score to settle. One push of a needle and the body dumped into the ocean. The current would take care of the rest. They said that John was dead, but was that true? None of us had seen his body. For all we knew, he could have risen again, a spectre hovering among us.

Shravan had the clearest motive. Nancy had threatened him in that note. I might not know the words, but the knife it was attached to was clearly there for a reason. I remembered his reaction when Livi said she wanted to read it, the way he wrenched it from her grasp. I couldn't see Jay or Smitha as potential suspects, they had no reason to want Nancy dead, but what did I know? There were so many secrets among these people.

Lost in my thoughts, I hadn't noticed Smitha. She was standing, frozen, the doll in her hand grasped so tightly I worried it might shatter and cut her.

'Smitha, are you okay?' I extended my hand for the doll, but she didn't seem to see it. She was staring into the distance.

I didn't want to take hold of her or shake her, she was in too fragile a state.

Finally, Livi clapped her hands, bringing Smitha out of her trance.

Smitha opened her hand and gazed at the miniature boat, clammy from her grip, as if she was wondering how it got there.

Livi and I waited for Smitha to say something. Finally, she said, 'I heard the splash of water. Last night, after I was knocked out.'

'It must have been the storm,' I said. 'You could hear the sea from where we were.' Indeed, it sounded terrifyingly close to the castle, as if at any moment it could breach the walls and swallow us up.

But Smitha was shaking her head. 'No, that's not it.' She moved to the chest of drawers, setting the boat down, and stood looking at it.

'Smitha?' I asked. 'Are you sure you're all right?'

She made an impatient gesture. 'Listen. I thought I was unconscious the whole time after I was hit, and only came to when you found me. But later I started to remember things.' She winced. Poor Smitha, it was clear she was in a lot of pain, yet she refused to see a doctor, dosing herself with Nurofen and a handful of strong painkillers from Shravan's medical kit.

'You should sit down,' Livi said.

Ignoring the suggestion, her eyes on the little boat, Smitha continued. 'Mostly it was just the rain and the noise of the wind. But there was this one moment — I remember it clearly. It went very quiet.'

I knew the moment she was talking about. It was when Dhruv and I found Livi's boot.

'Even the waves seemed to stop moving, the wind was still. I thought I'd died.' She swallowed. 'That's when I heard it — Nancy's voice, off in the distance, as if she was moving away. She was saying, "Where are you taking me?" I remember that clearly.'

'Go on,' Livi said. 'What happened next? Who was she talking to?'

In the silence that followed I heard my own heartbeat. We could be close to finding out what happened. But Smitha shook her head. 'That was it, I didn't hear anything else. But a little while later, I heard splashes, like an oar in water.' She turned to look at us. 'What does it mean?' I sensed the tangle of emotions in her, it mirrored my own. She was caught between wanting answers and wanting to run — one foot planted, the other preparing to bolt.

'I don't know,' Livi said, 'but we need to find out.'

'Did you tell the police this?' I asked.

'No,' she said. 'I wasn't sure I'd really heard it. I thought it might have been a dream.'

'Only it's not,' Livi said. 'You see, I heard it too.'

CHAPTER FIFTY-FIVE

Day Ten: Smitha

I hated making decisions — I always festered afterwards, gnawing over every possibility until I'd convinced myself I'd picked the absolute worst option. So, should I go back to the house, or join Livi and Leela on what was most probably a wild goose chase? I had no idea what they expected to find, but there was no point trying to dissuade them. Leela believed the police wouldn't take my story seriously — after all, I could be concussed, and even I wasn't sure if I was or not. Nancy could have just decided to leave, and was perfectly safe somewhere. Maybe this was a delayed meltdown after her big secret had got out. If so, fine. Good riddance. This whole doll business, along with Leela's insistence that Nancy was dead — I just couldn't buy it.

Livi's case was different. Ever since I mentioned the splash of oars, she'd acted like a foxhound who's picked up a scent. Nothing we said could dissuade her from setting off on the hunt.

So, what could I do? In the end, I agreed to go with them, mainly because I didn't want to walk back alone. They didn't seem particularly pleased. I thought they'd rather not have to cope with me in the state I was in.

I suppose I could have waited there for the men to return. They had gone to the police station to file a missing person's report, which should have been done before the police came here, but they'd made an exception because of the storm. They'd been gone a while ago now, so they were due back soon.

I didn't really want to do any of those things. If it was up to me, I'd go straight home to Veena, wipe the candy from her mouth, and hold her sticky little hands in mine.

I'd been told that both Shravan's and Jay's cars had been crushed by a fallen tree. When I saw it, the damage was far worse than I'd imagined. A massive oak tree, torn up by the roots, had squashed the front of Shravan's car like a tin can. Ours just had broken windows. The men took Dhruv's car. The only other functional vehicle was Nancy's, and luckily, Livi had the key.

We drove in a tense silence, not because we were being respectful, but because none of us had the faintest clue what we were doing. The fallen tree that had blocked the road yesterday had been cleared, its limbs still crumpled at the roadside like a dead giant. Livi drove to a spot midway between the castle and the ocean, and parked up.

'This is the nearest we can get by car,' Livi said. 'We'll have to go on foot from here.' She set off, pushing through the undergrowth of brambles and dead bracken, until we were within sight of a clearing where two upturned dinghies were lying on the wet sand. 'People leave their boats here.'

By now, I'd used up most of my energy. Besides, there was no way I was getting into a boat, not after what happened last time. 'I'll wait here,' I said, looking around for somewhere to sit. I spotted a bench almost hidden in the bushes. I'd be able to see the ocean from there. Thinking that I could always scurry back to the car if it got too cold, I asked, 'So, where are you heading?'

Livi took a breath. 'Maiden Island.'

CHAPTER FIFTY-SIX

Day Ten: Livi

The dinghies' tubes glistened in the weak sunlight, still wet from last night's storm. Even from here, I could tell which one had been used last night — the green one. It was wet all over, whereas the yellow boat was dry in patches, shaded in parts under the cover of a bush it had never left. Someone had tried to tug the green one back into place, just enough to make it look undisturbed. But not fully. Not quite.

I went down and dragged the green boat out. Water streamed from the edges as I turned it over, soaking Leela's canvas shoes in the process.

Bending down to wipe the mud off them, she cried out, 'Look! What's that doing here?'

I followed her pointing finger, and gasped. No. It couldn't be. Just to the side of the boat was a tan leather glove. I told myself that any number of people wore leather gloves, that it could belong to anyone. But deep down, I knew just whose it was.

Any hope I had that my fear was misplaced was dispelled when I saw the chain with the letter 'S' on it. It was one of the gloves I gave to Shravan for his birthday.

'Shravan must've dropped it,' I muttered, my voice weak, almost foreign to my ears. I didn't fully understand what I was saying. I couldn't bring myself to look at Leela, too afraid of what her expression might reveal — surprise? Disgust? I stooped to pick it up. There must be some explanation for this. All I had to do was give the glove back to Shravan. No harm done.

'Don't touch it,' Leela barked. 'Leave it where it is.'

She took my arm and dragged me away.

* * *

The ocean churned, its waves matching the turmoil in my mind, pulling me deeper into fear. I glanced at Leela, hoping for some kind of answer, some sign that she knew how this would end. Her face was unreadable, her stony expression told me she didn't want to speak, and maybe neither did I. We rowed the short stretch to Maiden Island in silence. I'd made this journey countless times, and it had never felt so long as it did today.

Out on the turtle-shaped neck of the island, the familiar smell of seaweed and the screech of gulls greeted us. In the same way they'd done the countless times before. Yet somehow today they sounded ominous. Tides in this part of the country were unpredictable. I'd been stranded here before, my boat lost to the ocean. Remembering that, I pulled the boat right up the shore and fastened it to a rock.

We climbed up to a ledge on the cliff face, and that was when we saw her. Leela screamed. It sounded muted, like I was hearing it in a dream. For a long time, all we could do was stare, unable to take it in.

I didn't know for how long I stood there, lost to the world. Leela grabbed me by the shoulders and shook me like a rag doll. Then she slapped me. The shock of it jolted me back to reality, and I wailed — a low, guttural cry that rose from deep inside, followed by a loud, piercing scream that must have echoed for miles. The seagulls that had been waddling nearby scattered and took flight. *Do they eat human flesh?* I thought, the idea strange and horrifying, and I shuddered.

'She might be alive,' I whispered, although I knew that was impossible. Nancy was kneeling, her head bowed over the knife plunged into her heart. Just like Mhairi, she seemed to have her hair tied to a rock. There was a faint mark, not quite a bruise, on the back of her neck just behind her ear.

'We must call the police,' said Leela. She reached into her pocket and pulled out her mobile, her hand trembling so that the phone nearly slipped from her grasp. She dialled 999, and then stared disbelievingly at the screen. 'There's no signal.'

I took mine out — the message on the screen read *EMERGENCY CALLS ONLY*. It should still work, then. I dialled 999, but when it finally went through, there was nothing but static. 'There's a dead person on Maiden Island!' I screamed. In response, I heard a series of screeches and beeps, like morse code. I shook my head at her. 'Nothing. The line's too bad. We should go. Call the police from the mainland.'

But Leela shook her head. She was crying now. 'We can't just leave her alone like that.'

I understood how she felt, but we had to tell the police.

'You go,' Leela said. 'I'll stay here with her.'

I hesitated, unwilling to leave Leela on her own, although there was nothing I wanted more than to get away. 'Go,' she said firmly, and began to climb down to where Nancy was. I watched her for a while, irresolute, and then made my way back to the boat, grateful once again for her clarity.

Instead of heading straight to the mainland, I decided to go to Kerrera instead. It was closer, and there should be a signal there. I could also keep an eye on Leela from there; I wouldn't be able to see her from the mainland.

CHAPTER FIFTY-SEVEN

Day Ten: Smitha

It was beginning to get chilly. I always felt the cold more than most, and now — bruised, battered, and generally falling apart — I felt like a pensioner caught without her thermals. The most sensible thing to do would be to go back to the car. The trouble was, I wasn't sure where Livi parked it. I hadn't been paying attention, following the others blindly, my eyes on the boats and my thoughts elsewhere. Home was just a few hours away. Soon I'd be back and when I was, I'd pull Veena into the tightest hug she'd tolerate and never let go.

That was when I heard it — a rustling sound, the snap of breaking twigs. Then footsteps. Someone was approaching me from behind. *So what?* I thought. *This isn't private property.* I couldn't go about my life like that, always in fear. Determined, I turned, and to my astonishment saw the familiar shape of Maya. Perfectly poised, perfectly wrong. I was about to call out and wave to her, but something stopped me. What was she doing here? She'd left for London days ago.

I moved back into the bushes. Not scared. Not yet. Just confused. Suspicious. And, okay, maybe a little scared.

Maya stood looking out to sea, eyes fixed on the boat, watching the shrinking outlines of Leela and Livi as they faded into the mist. My feeling of suspicion only grew stronger. She was up to no good. Maybe I should warn the others. I considered shouting a warning, but quickly thought better of it. No way was I letting Maya hear me. Instead, I fumbled with my phone and sent Leela a WhatsApp: *Beware Maya. She's back.* The message sat there, undelivered. Brilliant. Of course, I didn't put Livi's number into my contacts, because why would I ever do something as practical as that?

While I stood there stewing in my own uselessness, Maya turned and moved towards the remaining boat. There she stopped, and turned back to face the road, as if she was expecting someone. And I had a sickening feeling that whoever it was, they weren't coming for a picnic.

I must have inhaled too sharply, because her head snapped around, eyes sweeping the area. For a second, I was sure I'd been spotted. Flattening myself against the freezing bench, I tucked my legs up. My heart pounded so loudly I was convinced she could hear it. Right in front of my nose, a crumpled wrapper lay half stuck to the wood, smeared with something brown. I prayed it was chocolate. I blew at it, gently, desperately, but of course, it only rustled in the most conspicuous way possible, clinging on like it had a vendetta. My nose started itching. Any moment now I would sneeze. And I wasn't known for quiet sneezes, I'd never understood people who hardly grimaced and still said, "excuse me". Perfect. This was how it ended. Survived two murder attempts, only for a snack wrapper to give me away. Thankfully, it passed.

Just as her eyes were about to land on me, there was a noise. A second person, their face hidden beneath a hoodie, stepped out of the bushes and approached her. From where I was, I couldn't make out their features — just the tense energy between them. They seemed to be arguing. Sharp, clipped gestures. Heads craning forward. Then it escalated — Maya shoved the hooded figure hard in the chest. They stumbled back, caught off-guard.

I wondered whether Maya ever actually left. But why would she lie? And if she was back, what was this — blackmail? Revenge? Damage control? The questions outnumbered the answers and none of them made sense.

Still mid-argument, the pair slipped out of sight, swallowed by the undergrowth. I froze. Seconds later, the unmistakable sounds of a struggle — a scuffle, branches breaking, muffled grunts. Then, silence. Only the wind and the soft lapping of water. And then the hooded figure reappeared. Alone. They went back to the boat, turned it up and began to drag it towards the sea. Maya was nowhere to be seen.

I watched the hooded figure push the boat out, jump in, and begin to row.

Whatever was going on here, I needed to act. I couldn't just sit here. Suddenly, I longed to be home. I wanted Veena's tiny arms around my neck, her breath warm against my cheek as she demanded the same bedtime story, word for word, again. I wanted to do better — be better — for her. Be the mother she needed. Kiss the freckles on her nose, and love her like she deserved to be loved. And I needed to be the mother who deserved a child like her.

I took my phone from my pocket and dialled 999.

CHAPTER FIFTY-EIGHT

Day Ten: Leela

'Hi, Shravan,' I said without turning round. I'd known it would be him ever since I first spotted the ribbon tied to the knife now plunged deep into Nancy's chest. Poor Nancy, little did she know she was handing her murderer the weapon that would eventually kill her. I remembered the rage in Shravan's eyes as he snatched Nancy's note from Livi.

Maybe I knew it long before then — ever since the dolls were first moved. That there would be a murder. A victim to be claimed. The goddess always demanded an eye for an eye, blood for blood. The only question was whose. Now I knew the answer.

Still kneeling beside Nancy's body, I heard his footsteps draw near. His shadow fell across me. What would he do? Kill me?

Then I heard a sharp intake of breath, a sob. Surely he wasn't sorry for what he'd done? I couldn't see Nancy's face. If I could, what would it show? Surprise? Fear? Did she plead for her life?

I looked up at Shravan. He was barely recognisable, his face gaunt, his cheeks hollow. I didn't understand why he was crying. It was as if he was putting on an act, a desperate attempt to play the grieving friend. Did he think he could still get away with it? Pretend that he didn't do it? Despite the knife. Despite the glove. Good luck with that alibi. He had been gone a long time. Or maybe the tears weren't for Nancy, but for himself. Maiden Island being uninhabited, it didn't get visitors often and the way Nancy was positioned behind the ledge would have kept her hidden from any passing boats. With some luck — and help from the gulls — the ocean current would have carried her away forever. On cue, the seagulls cried, and I shuddered.

To my utter surprise, he said, 'How?'

'How do you think?' I said. 'Where were you last night?'

'What?'

'When Dhruv and Aswin were trying to get the generator going. You were nowhere in sight. You were gone for over three hours. You came back looking as if you'd been in a fight or something.'

No response.

'Shravan?'

'What's that got to do with anything?' he said. 'Anyway, I wasn't here.'

'Oh really?'

'What's your point? I don't see what you're trying to get at with all this.'

Good question. Was I trying to get him to admit to Nancy's murder? I was no detective, and I was defenceless; stranded on an uninhabited island with a man who could very well be a killer. I should have felt scared, but I wasn't. Instead, I was angry.

I got to my feet. 'You couldn't have gone far. The storm was at its height. Anyone with the slightest bit of sense wouldn't have even stepped out of the house. So, where were you?' I gestured towards Nancy. 'Given the circumstances, it's a fair question to ask, don't you think?'

'If you must know, I went for a run. I needed some space. Things had got too much, and I wanted to clear my head.'

'In the storm?'

He shrugged. 'Well, yes.'

'And where did you run?'

'Around.'

'Around where?' I asked. 'There's only one road out. And you didn't know about the fallen tree. You weren't near the cabin, Livi or Smitha would have seen you.' I tilted my head to get a better look at him. 'Where exactly were you, Shravan?'

'In the car park,' he said.

'What? All that time?'

'Yes.'

'Why?'

'Look, we should call the police,' he said. The tears were gone now, replaced by mild annoyance. No anger yet, but it would come.

'It's already been taken care of. They'll be here soon,' I said. 'But before they arrive, you might want to get your story straight.'

He took a very long time to reply. Then, in a subdued voice, he said, 'I was meeting someone.'

'Who? Not Nancy?' I asked.

He didn't answer. His eyes darted, calculating how much to reveal. My phone buzzed. A message from Smitha — *Beware Maya*. I typed back quickly: *Call police*.

When I looked up, Shravan was staring at me. Hiding my phone behind my back, I asked, 'Maya?'

'Yes.' He appeared to be surprised but stopped short of asking how I knew. 'We'd arranged to meet in the car park at half past six.'

My head started to swim. Did she leave? Or had she been here the whole time? I pictured the sleeping bag and the open can of beans. Would Maya have gone so far as to attack Smitha and then Livi? Drag Nancy all the way to the island to kill her? Physically, it didn't make sense. Yet, for some reason I believed that he was telling the truth. 'She never left?'

'Oh, she did,' he said, 'but she came back yesterday.'

'Why?'

279

'Because I asked her to,' he said quietly.

'Because you asked her to?' I repeated stupidly.

Shravan took a deep breath. 'The note — Nancy's note to me, the one tied to the knife. Do you remember it?'

How could I forget? It was all I'd been thinking about since last night. The thought that it was at the root of everything that had happened, including Nancy's death, was so strong that it had grown, flowered, and seeded overnight. 'Go on.'

'To understand the note, you need to know what happened.' Shravan gazed into the distance. 'It must be two years ago now. Maya somehow figured out that it was all Nancy — that she was the stalker, and not John at all. She lost it. She . . . tried to kill Nancy. She couldn't seem to accept that she was no longer in control. She went crazy, and wouldn't calm down. You know how she gets.'

I wondered how this related to the note, but I stayed quiet.

'She had a knife. She was determined to stab Nancy. It nicked her wrist. In the end I had to use scopolamine to calm her down. You know what that is, don't you? They call it Devil's Breath. It's . . . well, it's a mind control drug.' He looked embarrassed.

'Is that allowed?' I asked.

He shook his head. 'I could have lost my licence. But I didn't know what else to do. Once I had her controlled, I was able to hypnotise her. Make her forget that whole thing. In the space created in her memory, I planted a deep hatred for John.' He stopped and hung his head as if he were ashamed. Well, it was a bit late for that, wasn't it?

Maybe that was why Maya wrote the letter — the one blaming John. I'd always thought the timing felt off. If the stalking happened seven years ago, why did John take his life only two years back? Now it made sense. The letter happened.

When he didn't say anything, I asked, 'Then?'

'In that note, Nancy threatened to report me. Basically, she used it to blackmail me into . . . loving her. She said it was the only way.' He spat the last two words out. 'After all these years. After everything I did for her.'

'So you killed her,' I said.

'Me? God, no. What makes you say that?'

'It's obvious, isn't it? You had the motive. She was going to expose you, cause you to lose your licence. You said yourself that she threatened you.'

Shravan shrugged. 'True.'

'So, like I said — you killed her.'

'No. I sent a message to Maya, asking her to come. I thought that if I confessed to her first — told her the truth about Nancy being the stalker — then Nancy wouldn't have anything over me anymore. It would be between Maya and Nancy after that, wouldn't it? Maya could handle her. I thought maybe she could even convince Nancy to overlook the whole thing, and stop trying to blackmail me. She was always good at making a deal.'

Or, maybe Maya went and killed Nancy. Finished what she started two years ago. I'd never liked Shravan — I'd always thought he was selfish. But this? This was something else. This was cold. Calculated. Evil.

Still, it didn't make sense. Maya couldn't have dragged Nancy all the way here from the castle on her own. No way. Unless . . . unless she had help. Shravan's help. He and Maya could be in this together. That would explain how Nancy ended up here, all the way from the castle. The only thing I could think of was to keep him talking, so that he wouldn't harm me. 'So, you met Maya in the car park. What happened then?'

'She never turned up.'

Of course — the fallen tree. She couldn't have made it to the car park. She could have gotten here, though. The road to the jetty where the boats were was clear, and Maiden Island was just a short boat trip from there. But that still doesn't explain how she managed to convince Nancy to come with her.

'Why did Maya leave, Shravan?'

'Huh?'

'When Maya left, Dhruv was very surprised. He kept saying it was so uncharacteristic of her. She's a fighter, he said, not a runner. Why did she even go in the first place?'

He gulped. 'That day when the dolls returned the earrings. Do you remember?' How could I forget? I nodded. 'Maya got hysterical. She couldn't stop ranting about John being back for revenge, that she was somehow his target. She wrote that bloody letter. Oh, what a mess.'

I wanted to say, *It's your mess. You planted the hate, forced her to write the letter.* But I stayed quiet. I had to keep him talking.

'In the end, I had to tell her that John was dead,' he continued. 'Then she got worse. She was convinced it was his ghost, and he was out for blood.' He stopped to stare at me like it was all my fault, as if none of this would have happened if I hadn't talked about the ill omens. Yeah, well — close your eyes all you want, but the world doesn't go dark. 'There was no use trying to talk sense. She was beyond that — kept saying she could stay and fight if it was human. But how could she fight a ghost? A devil.'

Suddenly, a thought struck me. 'This Devil's Breath. How is it applied?'

'What?' Shravan asked, puzzled by this sudden change of tack. 'Either a tablet, or—'

'A patch?'

He looked confused. 'Yes, that's right.'

I knelt down beside Nancy, looking up at Shravan. 'Like this?' I asked, pointing to the marks behind Nancy's ear. There, in the soft spot behind her ears, were three grey patches, arranged in a triangle.

He closed his eyes briefly. 'Oh, God.'

'Let me guess,' I said. From the corner of my eye, I caught a glimpse of something moving through the waves. Boats, and they were moving too fast to be rowing boats. Help was at hand. 'If we check your medical kit, there'll be three missing patches of Devil's Breath.'

He didn't reply. There'd be no point in his denying it. The evidence was there for all to see.

'You almost had me convinced,' I said. 'You would have, but for the smell.'

'Smell?'

'Think for a minute,' I said.

He frowned, shook his head. 'I don't get what you mean.'

'Why do you think Smitha had a panic attack last night, just after you came near her?'

He shrugged. 'The blow to her head . . . Concussion . . .'

'She was perfectly fine until then. Until you went over and put your hand on her shoulder. Wasn't she?'

Shravan's eyes narrowed. There was a dangerous glint to them. 'What are you saying?'

'Lemon and mint?'

'I still don't understand.'

My next words could have landed me in a whole lot of trouble. He could have . . . I dismissed the thought. 'The smell of your aftershave, Shravan. It's quite distinctive. You were there at the castle, weren't you? Subconsciously, Smitha had registered it. And then when you came near her, it triggered a panic attack.'

He laughed uneasily. 'You're mad.'

'Your glove, the one you lost, we found it by the boat. Patches from your bag are missing, and there are patches on Nancy's neck that weren't there yesterday. And the knife that killed her belongs to you. It can't be Maya. By your own account, you didn't even meet her. Maybe she's in Oban. Maybe she isn't. But that doesn't change anything, does it? Because you killed Nancy. It wasn't her. From where I'm standing, you're the one that's mad, not me.'

The boats could be heard now — distant at first, then louder, closer. They would be here any moment. Alerted by the sound, Shravan started to move towards me, backing me up against the rocks at the edge of the cliff.

A few small pebbles rolled from under my feet into the water below. 'You don't frighten me,' I said, my heart in my throat. Surely the police must be here by now. Oh, why didn't they hurry?

283

'Oh, don't I?' he sneered, with no attempt to hide his contempt. 'Well, maybe you should be a little frightened. You're so determined to take me down for one murder, so why not two?'

He lunged, grabbing me by the throat. His fingers were cold, vice-like. I gasped, struggled, but the grip tightened. My vision swam with black spots, my legs gave way. There was no air. No time. I became dizzy. As darkness finally engulfed me, I heard a shout. 'Police! Freeze!'

EPILOGUE

One year and two months later: Leela

The plane is at the end of the runway, preparing to taxi. I wipe the window with my sleeve and peer out into the gloom. Around us, as we go through all the tedious procedures for leaving, Gatwick Airport is doing its best to be festive — trees decorated with tinsel and hung with baubles, wreaths of plastic holly. All the paraphernalia of an English Christmas.

None of it has rubbed off on Dhruv. He's sitting low in his seat, staring into the distance. Dhruv is a pale reflection of the man I married. It's astonishing how much just ten days can change a person. Gone is the brash joker who liked to put me down. Now, he's afraid of his own shadow. He's lost weight too, eaten up by nerves. Dhruv is headed for a breakdown unless I do something. Which is why I'm dragging him away on another holiday — a proper one this time.

Part of him died with Nancy — and he's adrift without his friends. Eight people were lost to him that day, even though only one actually died. Without their support, he has become the man he is today — weak, timid. Whereas I have gained a friend. I meet Livi every week. We never speak of it,

285

but we share an unbreakable bond, forged through grief and karma. She understands me in a way no one else can, and I know the feeling is mutual. We take pleasure in each other's company, sitting side by side on a weathered bench facing out across the Thames, happily munching on waffles or chips.

She often visits Shravan in prison. The only thing I disagree with her about is her insistence that he's innocent. It flies in the face of all the evidence, and I can't understand why she persists in this illusion. She's his only lifeline to the world — his parents and the rest of his family are in India, and he's shunned by his English friends and colleagues. She tells me he's doing well. Good luck to him. For all I care, he can rot in hell. I want to tell her to give up and move on, but I can see it would do no good. She'll have to get there on her own.

In a way, she feels responsible. The first time I met her, she was inconsolable. 'It's my fault he's in prison,' she said.

'He brought it upon himself,' I told her. 'You had nothing to do with it. He didn't have to go so far.'

She shook her head. 'It was all me. Maybe it wouldn't have happened if I hadn't insisted on that holiday.' Her voice caught. This wouldn't be the first time she'd cry.

'Karma will always find a way. You were merely a tool,' I said, with the patience of a mother asking her child for the hundredth time to please put on their shoes.

She grunted. 'Some tool.'

I took hold of her shoulders and shook her gently. 'Remember your brother. He's the only victim here, the only truly innocent one.'

She didn't respond. Her eyes had returned to the Thames, tracing the patterns of the ripples' jumps and leaps.

I couldn't quite recall when I truly came to know. In a way, I always had. But it had been only when I saw Livi in Dunollie Castle, on the day Nancy had been killed that it sank in, the extent of it. Livi had been lying all bloody and sprawled like the dead. Other times I'd wonder if I had always known. Why else would I have told Dhruv to take Smitha to the house and gone up to the castle all by myself if I didn't know at some level?

'I killed Nancy,' she'd wailed then.

I hadn't asked why. It hadn't taken me long to piece together the puzzle — the 'JD' on the door frame, the name of the manor house — Williams. Even though Olivia's surname was Johnstone, the obituary of John D. Williams had told me what I should have known all along. It had been there, plain as day, yet I had been blind. John Dexter Williams — 'our' John — was Livi's half-brother, left by Nancy to take the rap for a crime he didn't commit.

Later during one of our chats, Livi asked, all wide-eyed innocence, 'Do you think I went too far?'

'With what? Which part of it?' I asked.

'All of it — the dolls . . .' she said. 'Especially the dolls.'

I took a deep breath. 'The dolls served a purpose. They had to be moved to bring the rest of it about.' The dolls were her soldiers in the battle for truth — the truth about her brother. 'There's a saying in Tamil, which translates roughly as, "When the soul of truth is consumed by deception, truth will always triumph in the end." Like I said, you were only a tool.'

She heaved a sigh.

'One thing that still puzzles me is the blood,' I said. 'You couldn't possibly have planned to find that squirrel.'

'Ah. I was going to use paint — you know, there was a tin in the cabin. But then I found that little guy, and I didn't want his death to go to waste.' Another soldier in this war. A swan drifted close to where we were sitting, obviously hoping for food. Livi threw him a piece of waffle, which was gone in an instant. It turned one bright eye on her for a moment, and then emitted a harsh squawk. How strange nature is. That something so elegant could sound so, well, ugly.

'When did you decide that Nancy deserved to die?' I asked. Had she planned it long before she even met Shravan?

'It was that day we went to the farmers' market. Remember? You told me that karma sometimes needs a little help. That was when I decided.'

No, that wouldn't do. She wasn't going to pin this on me. 'That's not true.'

'What do you mean?' she asked, without surprise.

An entire flock of birds had now gathered around us — ducks, swans, pigeons — having seen Livi feed the swan. She opened her backpack and pulled out a loaf of bread. Livi was nothing if not organised. She always planned several steps ahead.

'You decided long before then. Is that why you befriended Shravan? Is that why you made him fall in love with you? Was it all fake?' That part never made sense — the way Livi looked at him, the way they were together in the first few days. How they slept together.

'Oh God, no,' she said. There were tears in her eyes. 'That would be going too far, even for me.'

I believed her. 'Then why?'

'I simply wanted to know the truth. When Dex died—' she paused, suddenly overcome with emotion — 'he didn't leave a note. No thoughts left behind to comfort us, tell us he's in a better place, explain why he did it. I was lost.' She took a breath, her fingers trembling as she pulled another piece of bread apart for the birds. 'Then I found the letter, in the cabin.'

It made sense now. Was that why she insisted the dolls were displayed there, in the cabin? Just like how she insisted that Nancy stayed in the room her brother died in? I didn't interrupt, waiting for her to continue.

'At first, I thought it was one of those mails from the bank or an invoice. But then, on the envelope, he'd scrawled, *I can't do it anymore.* Inside was the letter Maya wrote, and the earrings. That's when I knew. But even then, all I knew was that Maya wrote that letter, and Nancy was behind all of it.'

I must have scrunched my eyebrows or something. So, she explained, 'It's obvious, isn't it? The trophies were found in their house. Only two people lived there. If it wasn't Dex, it had to be Nancy.'

Yes, a little unimaginative. I nodded but stayed quiet.

'Trust me. I had no idea about Shravan's involvement, not until the day before.'

'How?'

'He confessed!'

I felt sorry for her. For her losses, yes, but more for what she'd had to do. Not to Nancy, but to Shravan. There was no love lost between me and my dad — never was — so it wasn't hard to sow the pearls and reap the results like a proud farmer. But Livi's case was different. There had been love once, even if it had faded. I could see the conflict flicker in her unguarded moments. The constant doubts — wondering if any of it had ever been real, or worse, if she'd done the right thing. That must have been exhausting. The baggy eyes and faraway looks said as much.

'Are you saying you really didn't plan ahead?'

'No.' There was no conviction there.

Then, the question I had been holding back, the one lurking in the back of my mind: 'When Smitha fell off the raft. Was that really an accident?'

She didn't try to deny it, rush in with excuses or explanations. Instead, she looked away, her face crumpling slightly, and in that moment, I saw it — the truth. The pain in her eyes told me what I had known all along — it was never an accident. Smitha falling, though? Yes. It wasn't meant to be her but Nancy. I replayed it in my mind again — how I had been chatting with Smitha, distracted, until Nancy stood up. Even as I was thinking that was stupid of her, a gloved hand reached towards her ankle — Livi's. But then, I'd thought Livi was trying to help her, to steady her, pull her back down.

But there was no point labouring it now. 'What was your intention when you suggested the holiday?' I asked.

'I wanted to get them together, and make them see Nancy for what she was — a stalker. I did it to clear my brother's name.'

'Is that it? That would have been enough?'

She tore off a piece of bread and threw it to the birds. The entire flock descended, and a green drake emerged victorious. His mate looked less than impressed. He would not get any action soon.

'I hoped so.' She didn't sound very convinced. 'You never asked me how I did it.'

I gave no response. I could picture it in my head — how Nancy's screams would have triggered Livi. How she'd hit her on the head with the torch, and then sneaked down to deal with Smitha, her gloved hand liberally sprayed with Shravan's aftershave. That final touch had sealed it for Shravan. At first, Smitha didn't make the connection, but by the time she took the witness stand she had constructed, with a little help, a fully-fledged conversation wherein Shravan had threatened her and her husband, and even the child.

Maya's testimony was brief, but it landed hard. She showed the court the text from Shravan: *Maya, please come back. Nancy's gone crazy. She's threatening me. Us. Come, before I do something stupid.*

It wasn't much on its own, but given everything else, it made the case for premeditation. She said they'd planned to meet at the car park at six, just like Shravan had told us. But she couldn't get there because of the fallen tree across the road, so she'd turned back. She didn't think much of it until the call about the diamond ring.

Then came the part that changed everything. She saw Shravan sneak off the next day, trying to follow me and Livi to Maiden Island. She stopped him, asked where he was going and where Nancy was. He told her Nancy was missing. That's when she knew something wasn't right, that Shravan had something to do with it. They argued. He pushed her. Then he took the boat and left. She was furious, even deliberated going to the police, but in the end decided against it after Bala convinced her that she was overreacting and anyone would be angry if accused of murder. He said it was the best for her to leave Oban, and according to Maya, she listened.

I wondered if Maya knew how lucky she was — how close she had come to going down for premeditated murder. At first, I didn't realise, not until I caught Livi staring at Maya, and every time she did, I saw her shiver — just a little, but enough. Livi's eyes kept darting between Maya's ring and her face. That was when I realised — the ring, it wasn't a coincidence. Livi had planted it in the castle cellar, possibly days earlier, before the storm. If Shravan hadn't confessed, Livi would have still blamed Maya for the letter that killed her brother. If the other things — possibly planted later — hadn't been found, the police would have grilled Maya more. It would have been her sitting in a prison cell, paying for John's life with her freedom. Karma has its own strange ways.

When I saw Livi on that castle floor, she wasn't wearing her saree. When I asked her about it, she said, 'I changed into suitable clothes. I brought a spare set — jeans and a top.' She patted her backpack.

It's what she was wearing when I found her that night — bloodstained jeans and a T-shirt. She'd rolled up her saree and left it in a corner, torn and wet but otherwise unmarked. I helped her change, draped her in a saree, helped her bury her bloodstained clothes along with the bag. Hitting her on the head had been hard. I hadn't wanted to do it, but Livi insisted. For consistency with Smitha's attack she'd claimed. But I suspected that was her way of punishing herself. Then I tied her to a pillar, hands behind to prove she couldn't have done it herself and plastered her mouth for good measure. It took so long that Dhruv came back, looking for me. I had to make up the story about the footsteps and showed him the sleeping bag and the can of beans. Luckily, he bought it.

Once I asked Livi, how she'd managed to convince Nancy to go with her to the Maiden Island. It couldn't have been easy.

She said, 'A dose of Devil's Breath ensured that Nancy was compliant. I led her down the slope to the dinghy.'

I nodded. 'You set out in a storm in a dinghy?'

'I've done it a thousand times. Besides, what's the worst that could have happened? The boat capsizes, and both of us drown?' She laughed, sending a chill down my spine. She had been prepared to die. Avenging her brother was one thing, but to die in the attempt? The pain must have run very deep indeed that she was willing to die for it.

'Taking her to Maiden Island was a nice touch,' I said. 'Arranging her just like Mhairi.'

'I had to.' Livi hung her head. When they saw that no more bread was forthcoming, the birds flew off. She looked up at me again, fresh tears glistening in her eyes. 'As I was about to plunge the knife in, she came to her senses and screamed out, "Why?" So I told her, "John is my brother." Actually step-brother, but I never thought of him that way. She knew how sensitive he was, yet that didn't stop her.'

'She deserved it,' I said. 'It's good that she realised why she had to die. Otherwise it would have seemed pointless.'

Livi gave me a weak smile. 'I owe it to you. It's your words that gave me strength.'

I waved a hand dismissively. One burden was enough for me, I had my own pearls to carry. I touched my neck, where the string of pearls had left their mark. This was Livi's cross to bear. 'But why Shravan?'

'He was complicit. He knew the truth about what Nancy had done, but kept quiet. He let her get away with ruining my brother's life, knowing that what everyone thought he had done would break him. Then he hypnotised Maya into writing the letter that signed John's death warrant.'

I nodded. I would have done the same in her place. 'But why didn't you come out and accuse him of killing her? You could have said you saw him drag Nancy into the boat and set off for the island. That would have made it easier for the police to find him guilty.'

She shook her head. 'Then Shravan would have been sus-picious of me. If I had made up some half-baked story about him being there, he would have known. And if he knew, he would have found a way to prove it. He's clever. As it is, he thinks I'm the only person who believes in him. Also . . .'

'Also?'

'He wouldn't have let me visit him in prison.'

'Why do you visit him?' I asked.

'To see him suffer. I want to make sure he never forgets. Day and night, he should regret having ever met Nancy. For the rest of his life, he should know no peace.' Her eyes gleamed.

That was enough for me. We never spoke of it again. Occasionally, when we meet, she'll do a tarot reading for me. She reckons I'll soon be having a baby. Who knows, she might be right, and we'll make one when we're away. I hope it's a girl. I can't wait to be a mother — the kind of mother mine never was. A mother who would kill for her daughter, not die and leave her alone.

I reach across the armrest and take Dhruv's hand. He gives me a weak smile. I tell him it's okay, he needn't put up a brave front for me. He can just be himself — a warm, sensitive man, unafraid to show vulnerability. Those ten days made him into the kind of man I always wanted. I'm so lucky to have found Dhruv. I lay my head on his shoulder, and he sighs happily. At last, Dhruv is smiling.

Idly, he plays with the string of pearls around my neck. As we soar into the sky, I think of Livi. You might not have a string of pearls, but you've done well, my girl.

THE END

ACKNOWLEDGEMENTS

Navaratri is all about family and friends, and there I'm blessed with the best. To my dear husband, MJ, who has never read a book (that I have seen) but still found his own way to cheer me on. To my dearest son, Aarudh, for your honest views (and for mostly staying out of the way), and to my darling daughter, Dhiya, for being my sounding board and expert plot-hole checker — thank you. This book is for you, my crew.

When I typed the final sentence of this book, the deadline for the Joffe Books Prize was already very close. I wasn't even sure I'd manage to submit it, let alone win. But somehow, I did both, and I'm still counting my lucky stars.

Thank you to Joffe Books and Audible for this incredible opportunity, and for your deep commitment to supporting underrepresented writers. I'm grateful — and honestly still a bit in shock.

To the judges — A. A. Chaudhuri, Gyamfia Osei, Emma Grundy Haigh, Jasmine Callaghan, Jasper Joffe, and Kate Lyall Grant — thank you for seeing the spark in my story, even in its rough, uncut form.

Kate Lyall Grant, thank you for being an editor extraordinaire and making this book better in every way. Thank you as well to the brilliant editorial team — Anne Durges and Jon Appleton — for your sharp feedback and razor-sharp attention to detail.

To my amazing agent, Saskia Leach: thank you for being my loudest cheerleader, kindest critic and voice of reason when I needed it the most.

Huge thanks to my brilliant alpha readers, Angela Nurse and Silvia Domuta. You read early drafts — sometimes even before they were written down — gave honest feedback, and kept me going when doubts crept in. You were my lifelines, and possibly part-time therapists.

To Debi Alper and my amazing Jericho self-edit writer cohort — Gill, Lucia, Kate, Paula, Katie, Julie, Anja, Richard and Gillian — thank you for all the brainstorming, support, and laughs. Writing this book would have been a lot harder (and much less fun) without you. I only wish Anja Boersma was still here to celebrate this moment. Wherever she is, I'm sure she'll raise a toast with us.

Finally, to Navaratri and the incredible childhood memories it gave me — thank you. To my parents and sister, who made those memories so rich: I couldn't have written this without you. To my mother-in-law, who believed in me more than I did, and my dearly missed father-in-law, who would have been proud.

And to everyone who cheered me on — you made this possible. Thank you.

THE JOFFE BOOKS STORY

We began in 2014 when Jasper agreed to publish his mum's much-rejected romance novel and it became a bestseller.

Since then we've grown into the largest independent publisher in the UK. We're extremely proud to publish some of the very best writers in the world, including Joy Ellis, Faith Martin, Caro Ramsay, Helen Forrester, Simon Brett and Robert Goddard. Everyone at Joffe Books loves reading and we never forget that it all begins with the magic of an author telling a story.

We are proud to publish talented first-time authors, as well as established writers whose books we love introducing to a new generation of readers.

We won Trade Publisher of the Year at the Independent Publishing Awards in 2023 and Best Publisher Award in 2024 at the People's Book Prize. We have been shortlisted for Independent Publisher of the Year at the British Book Awards for the last five years, and were shortlisted for the Diversity and Inclusivity Award at the 2022 Independent Publishing Awards. In 2023 we were shortlisted for Publisher of the Year at the RNA Industry Awards, and in 2024 we were shortlisted at the CWA Daggers for the Best Crime and Mystery Publisher.

We built this company with your help, and we love to hear from you, so please email us about absolutely anything bookish at feedback@joffebooks.com.

If you want to receive free books every Friday and hear about all our new releases, join our mailing list here: www.joffebooks.com/freebooks.

And when you tell your friends about us, just remember: it's pronounced Joffe as in coffee or toffee!